STRANGERS OF THE NIGHT

Touched by Passion

Passion in Disguise

Unexpected Passion

Dear Reader,

Strangers in the night exchanging...bullets, not glances. In this collection of novellas, you'll discover—or return to, if you've been here before—the world of The Crew, a group of people with the desire to research, protect or capture paranormal...things.

Three young people with a shared tragic past that left them burdened as well as blessed with individually extraordinary talents find themselves each the target of forces determined to harm them. Each of them end up on the run, helped by strangers equally as invested in protecting them.

Thanks for reading my sexy paranormal stories about passion and pleasure that goes bump in the night!

Xoxo,

Megan Hart

STRANGERS
OF THE NIGHT

—

MEGAN HART

ISBN-13: 978-0-373-13989-7

Strangers of the Night

Copyright © 2017 by Harlequin Books S.A.

The publisher acknowledges the copyright holder of the individual works as follows:

Touched by Passion
Copyright © 2017 by Megan Hart

Passion in Disguise
Copyright © 2017 by Megan Hart

Unexpected Passion
Copyright © 2017 by Megan Hart

Recycling programs for this product may not exist in your area.

This edition published by arrangement with Harlequin Books S.A.

For questions and comments about the quality of this book, please contact us at CustomerService@Harlequin.com.

Printed in U.S.A.

HARLEQUIN®
™ www.Harlequin.com

CONTENTS

Megan Hart is the award-winning and *New York Times* bestselling author of more than thirty novels, novellas and short stories. Her work has been published in almost every genre, including contemporary women's fiction, historical romance, romantic suspense and erotica. Megan lives in the deep, dark woods of Pennsylvania with her husband and children. Visit her on the web at meganhart.com.

Books by Megan Hart

Harlequin Nocturne

Bound by the Night
Strangers of the Night

Visit the Author Profile page at Harlequin.com for more titles

This collection is dedicated to Jeffe Kennedy, who was there for me every time I struggled with the words.

TOUCHED BY PASSION

Prologue

Jed doesn't like the sound of the babies crying. He can hear them even from the other building, wailing inside his head. He's too big to be one of them anymore. No more diapers. No more crib. No more giant room that always smells faintly of milk and poo. Now he has his own big bed in the dorm with the other kids, and although he misses his mothers, he knows better than to give in to tears. If you cry here in the dorm, you get a beating.

Instead, he clenches his fists tight at his sides and stares up at the ceiling. His cot is hard and lumpy. The blanket scratches his chin if he pulls it up too high, so he tucks it around his belly. The other kids are sleeping, but Jed can't seem to manage. There's too much noise, too much going on. If he gets up now, he could go to the monitor, who will give him some medicine to sleep, but it makes his head feel fuzzy and his belly hurt. He tries to fall asleep on his own.

Tomorrow is dedication day.

The fathers have been watching them all since they were babies in the nursery. They already know which ones are special. Who will be dedicated, who will be sent away.

This is Jed's first dedication time, but he's heard the other kids talking even when they're not supposed to. Everyone's scared about what happens when you're sent away. The rumor is that you get put into the big fireplace in the barn and made into smoke, and Jed believes it. He's been able to "feel" everyone at the farm for as long as he can remember. The kids who get taken away after each dedication, well…he doesn't feel them anymore.

Before he's even had time to sleep, the lights overhead come on. The other kids shift and squeal, crying out in excitement and fear when the doors to the dorm boom open and the fathers are there in their black robes, their white masks. It's supposed to make them all equal, but it doesn't matter to Jed that they all look the same. They all *feel* different.

The kids are up and in a line, marching into the hallway. One by one, they go into the meeting room. None of them come out. They won't know until later who's still left, though of course, Jed will know before everyone else. That's what he tells the fathers waiting for him in the meeting room when they ask him. He tells them who he can still feel. Who he cannot. They stare at him from behind their white masks, nodding when he points to each and names them.

They feel happy, and that makes Jed feel happy, too. He won't be burned up into smoke. He gets the special pudding for dessert that makes the world spin around in many colors. He gets to go back to the dorm and his lumpy bed, where he can only lie on his back, laughing and laughing at the funny way everything grows and shrinks.

He's still laughing when the doors bang open again. More men in black. No white masks. Guns. They kick over the beds, the monitor's desk. They shout. Most of them feel angry, though one or two feel more scared than anything else, and none of them feel nice.

They take all of the children.

Jed never sees Collins Creek again.

Chapter 1

Samantha Janecek had never liked hospitals in general, but she loathed this hospital in particular.

It wasn't the smells of chemicals and despair, though those clung to her like some stinking perfume she could never quite scrub away. And it wasn't the bright, unrelenting lights that forced everyone inside to adjust to some artificial internal clock, although they messed with her sleep so much that she hadn't been able to get more than four hours at a time since she'd started here. More than anything else, it was this uniform.

No scrubs for the nursing staff here at Wyrmwood. Nope, the women had to wear white, starched dresses with Peter Pan collars and a weird belt thing that hit her too high on the ribs to be comfortable. Thick white support stockings, crepe-soled granny shoes. Worst of all, the mesh cap she had to pin into the thickness of her blond hair, which refused to ever stay neatly in the required bun. The uniform was straight out of the late sixties—fitting, she supposed, since the rest of Wyrmwood seemed to have been arrested in that same era. Including the fact there were no male nurses here, only orderlies. They also wore all white, but at least they got to wear pants.

"Morning, miss," said Nathan through the glass as she showed him her ID card and pressed her fingertip to the panel at the side of the door.

When the green light clicked on, she pushed through the heavy door that slid behind her with a hushed whirr. "Hi, Nathan. How's it going?"

"Same old, same old." Nathan shrugged. "Quiet tonight."

Of course it was quiet. Not only were all the patients on the fourth floor secured in their individual rooms behind soundproof walls, but most of them barely spoke aloud. Some by choice, an elective muteness. Some because they'd lost the capability for speech somewhere along the way. It might've been different on other floors, but as she'd never worked on any of them, Samantha couldn't say.

"Have a good one," Samantha said as she signed in using the electronic keypad at Nathan's station.

She paused for the automatic snapshot that would be added to her file, another level of proof that she was who she said she was. That she was here when she ought to be. She'd often considered pulling a funny face during the picture taking, but had never quite dared. Humor was not encouraged here.

She didn't speak to the armed guards posted at the elevator entrance to the floor. One or both of them might be on her team, but she never knew. Never would know, not unless it was necessary. Vadim made sure of that.

Samantha had been working at the Wyrmwood job for the past eighteen months. She'd never asked what strings had been pulled to make sure she was assigned to the fourth floor. She simply followed the rules she'd agreed to when she took the job. The money from the Crew kept coming in, deposited into an account in no way connected to the one she used for her Wyrmwood salary, and which she checked only once a month, using an encrypted burner phone she then tossed immediately. Money she couldn't spend until she was no longer needed here.

The question was, when would she decide that *she* was finished with this assignment? How much longer could she stand it here before she lost more than a little bit of her own mind? Working in near silence all day long, taking the vitals of men and women who were often little more than chilly mannequins. Forcing her body into an artificial day/night cycle that fucked up her social life, not just her mental state. She was not the first person Vadim had ever assigned to this task. Sooner or later, all of those who'd come before her had ended up leaving, some of their own accord and others because they'd stopped toeing the Wyrmwood line. She'd never found out how many of them had ended up as patients themselves. Stopping for a moment in front of a closed door with nothing more than a small viewport in it, she allowed herself the briefest second to touch the cold metal. A little longer, she told herself. Surely she could last a little longer.

At the desk, positioned between the two corridors of the L-shaped building, she managed some banal chitchat with the nurse leaving her shift. Patty was nice enough. She did yoga. Had a bland husband, several unremarkable children and a couple of dogs she referred to as "fur babies" in a way that made Samantha supremely uncomfortable. She and Patty would never be friends—Wyrmwood employees were discouraged from socializing outside of work, anyway, even if they'd had anything in common beyond the job. Samantha knew, though, that no matter how normal Patty seemed, the fact she worked here at Wyrmwood meant she had the highest security clearance possible. It meant that, like Samantha, Patty was capable of killing you with a ballpoint pen or her bare hands. Not only capable, but willing.

"Quiet tonight," Patty said in an echo of Nathan's earlier statement. "You shouldn't have any trouble."

"Never do," Samantha said with the bright, sterile smile she'd cultivated over the years as part of her armor against the "normal" world. It had worked well for this stint in Wyrmwood, that was for sure. That smile, she was convinced, was what had finally earned her the job. "Have a good night. Give the pups a squeeze from me."

"Will do!" Patty gathered her things and signed out of the computer, pausing for another of those snapshots, and left.

Alone at the desk, Samantha released a pent-up sigh and allowed her face to fall into an expression that didn't even come close to a smile. She was still being watched, of course. She knew that. But she didn't have to pretend she was here for a party. If anything, the two performance reviews she'd had since taking the assignment had made note of her "professional demeanor" and "consistent attitude."

Signing in, adding another profile picture to the files, she settled into her seat to scroll through the notes left behind by the last shift. Patty preferred crossword puzzles to extensive note taking, which was fine with Samantha, since there was rarely anything important to note. Fourth floor had twenty patients who required varying levels of care, and all of them were her responsibility.

But she was there, really, to take care of only one.

Chapter 2

If there was something about warm, smooth skin and bristly beard stubble that wasn't meant to send a girl straight to heaven, Persephone Collins didn't want to hear about it. The man in the bed beside her had muscles in all the most important places, eyes as dark as midnight, hair like the sweetest Australian black licorice and, more important, a mouth made for kissing that he hardly ever used to talk. Silence was one of a man's best qualities, according to Persephone.

Well, silence and a nice cock.

It didn't have to be huge, she thought as she rolled over to let her hand trail down his firm, hairless pecs to the bit of fur on his belly. Just proportional. A little lower, and her fingers brushed soft flesh. He stirred, thickening under her stroking touch. His groan made her smile.

He put a hand over hers. "Again?"

"Again," she whispered and lowered her mouth to taste

him. Warm, sweet skin. Tangy. She closed her eyes to savor his unique flavor.

"Please," he said. "I don't think I can."

She looked at him. "Oh, I think you can."

"We've done it five times, babe." His voice dipped low, almost into a growl that became a drawn-out groan when she again dipped her head to take him between her lips.

She ran her hands over her body, knowing exactly what he would see. High, huge breasts tipped with cherry nipples. Flat belly. Wide, curving hips. And also...

"You don't want this sweetness?" She let her fingertips travel over the thatch of soft strawberry hair between her thighs. The hair was really hers.

Not much else was.

The guy on the bed—damn, what was his name, exactly? It began with an *M*. Mark? Marcus? Marcellus? Whoever he was said, "Of course I do, darlin', but you've about wore me out."

Her fingers curved around his shaft again. Stroking gently. Up over the head and around, until he arched. Cock stiff. The sound of his moan rippled through her.

Oh, how she loved fucking.

Especially men built like working out was their job. Oh, right, she thought as he continued to respond to her touch. It *was* his job. She'd met him at the gym. He was a personal trainer.

It surprised her when he sat up to put one big hand on the back of her neck to pull her close for a kiss. She managed to turn her face at the last second so their lips slid against each other quickly, barely connecting. She urged his mouth along the line of her jaw and down her throat. Lower, to her breasts. He licked and sucked at one nipple, then the other, and although this body that he was worshipping was mostly illusory, it still felt good. More than good. Fantastic.

Desire rose within her, trickling through her veins. Filling her. It swept away everything except the urge for mindless ecstasy.

"Come up here." Strong hands urged her upward to straddle his face.

His tongue slid against her, effortlessly finding her clit. His hands kneaded her ass cheeks—plumper than her own. Softer. Her real body was tight, lean, hard with muscles she's built at the gym where they'd met. The gym where he'd never paid a second of attention to her before today, when her rising need had made her focus on him.

Persephone shook away these thoughts. She needed to come, to lose herself in exploding pleasure. To be swept away by fantasy, not reality. She looked down at his face, his eyes closed as his mouth worked on her.

"There," she murmured, rocking against him. Letting the sensations swirl inside her from deep in her belly. "Oh, yeah. Right there. Right there."

She'd intended to ride his cock one more time before using his shower, helping herself to whatever was in his fridge, perhaps lifting the contents of his wallet before leaving him sleeping in the tangled, sweaty sheets left behind after their marathon fuck session. However, she wasn't going to turn down the delight of his lips and tongue against her. It was better, in fact. Taking this pleasure from him without having to focus on his.

He muttered something against her. The vibrations sent another surge of pleasure, up, up, twisting tight and coiling. She cried out as her thighs trembled. Her cunt clenched, throbbing. His tongue swirled on her clit, sending her over the edge at last.

She rode it, shaking and crying out. The climax eased. She rolled off him and limply fell back on the bed.

Silence.

A low chuckle turned her toward him. Persephone pushed herself up on her elbow to look into his face. "Thanks."

Marcus or Marco or whoever he was smiled. Yawned. "You're welcome."

She glanced down at his cock, no longer hard. "You sure you don't want…?"

"Oh, I want." He rolled to face her and put a hand on her hip. "Just can't right now. Surprised I was able to so many times already, girl. Something about you…"

Well, yeah. There was that. She smiled and touched his face. For the briefest moment she thought about letting the pretense drop. Instead, she let her fingers press the spot between his eyes. Gently. Softly.

His eyes closed. He began to snore. She studied him a moment longer, thinking how much nicer he'd been than she expected. Of course, she wasn't going to be around in the morning to find out if she was wrong about him. And the next time she saw him, he wasn't going to recognize her, so it wasn't as though she'd even have to worry about either an awkward conversation or getting the blow-off.

"Good night," Persephone whispered into his ear.

He didn't stir. She got off the bed. Long slim legs and big boobs wavered and shifted. When she looked in the full-length mirror, her real, true image stared back at her. Five foot two. A-cup breasts. Thick, muscled thighs and biceps. Her body was strong and fit, and never let her down, no matter if she was running from the cops, breaking and entering or letting some rando with a hard cock have his way with her. This body, she thought as she cupped her breasts and flicked her nipples erect, was no wonderland. It was the real deal.

Without a glance behind her, she got dressed. She did raid the fridge, snagging a piece of cold pizza and a soda, along with a couple bananas from the counter for later. She did not, however, take his wallet. Didn't even sneak a couple twenties from it. He'd been a good lay but more than that, seemed like a pretty decent guy...

Clearly, she was slipping.

Pushing that thought from her head, Persephone kept her head down once she reached the street and headed for home. Light was tingeing the sky when she got back to her place. Maybe she'd be able to sleep now.

The sound of feet scuffling behind her as she stopped to pull her mail from the box didn't make her turn. She knew who it was without looking. She said nothing as Kane Dennis moved beside her to check his own mail.

"Morning."

She pursed her lips. "Mmm."

He laughed, the sound of it low and rich and rippling through her in a way she hated because of how much she liked it. She pulled out a sheaf of junk mail, the only kind she ever got. Pretended it was something important, like she was a real person who paid bills or got postcards from friends. She shot a sideways glance at him.

Six feet of lean, long legs. Broad shoulders. Taut stomach. Faded jeans, form-fitting Henley under a plaid shirt, unbuttoned but rolled up to his elbows to expose his finely muscled forearms. She was such a sucker for forearms, and his completely slayed her.

"Still having a problem with the hot water," Kane said conversationally. "Not trying to be a pain in the ass about it, but if you could take a look?"

"Now?" Persephone tucked the mail into her bag.

"It would be great if I could grab a hot shower before bed," he told her.

She tucked the inside of her cheek against her teeth at the thought of Kane beneath a spray of hot water, sluicing over the perfect body... She shook it off. "Sure. I can come up now."

"Great," Kane said with a smile that tried to get its way inside her, despite her every effort not to let it. "See you in a few?"

"Yeah, sure," Persephone said without returning the smile. "See you in a few."

Chapter 3

There were twenty patients on the fourth floor of Wyrmwood, ten in each wing. Samantha had never been told
she had to take care of them in any certain order, but
she almost always started at the far end of A wing and
worked her way down toward the end of B wing. Dispensing meds. Taking vitals. Her role as a nurse was
very limited, which was a good thing, since she'd never
had any kind of actual medical training. Her degrees had
been fabricated the same as the rest of her history. Still,
none of her required tasks were difficult, and she'd been
trained to call on other staff if anything did get out of
control. It made her wonder, more than once, what the
Wyrmwood powers above truly intended her function,
and that of the other nurses, to be.

Glorified babysitters, she thought as she loaded the
tray with necessary pills and vials of liquids for each
room and pocketed her stethoscope and thermometer. Or

more likely, part of the experiment, whatever it was. The cameras everywhere, the security. The out-of-date uniforms and strict rules that controlled after-hours behavior. The deathly quiet working atmosphere, no cell phones allowed. No outside reading material. It all seemed designed to drive the staff to madness right along with the patients, that was for sure.

She paused outside A1 to look through the porthole. The patient inside, sixty-year-old Helena, liked to draw elaborate spirals but had been denied the use of a pen or pencil since she'd stabbed an orderly with the point. She'd been allowed soft chalk, though, and routinely covered the walls and floor of her room with intricate designs every day, only to wipe them all away and start over when she'd finished. She never gave Samantha any trouble and was amenable to halting her work long enough to take the drug cocktail she'd been prescribed. She didn't make eye contact with Samantha. She answered when spoken to, but nothing beyond that.

"Do you need anything?" Samantha asked the standard question that was rarely answered by any of the fourth floor's patients.

Helena shook her head, already reaching for the thick block of blue chalk. She turned from Samantha without another word. Outside, Samantha took one last peek into the porthole, but Helena was already back to her drawing.

In a normal job, there'd be patient histories. Records she'd have been able to pull to see why the patient had been put here in the first place. She supposed it didn't matter much. They paid her well enough not to ask those sorts of questions; more important, they paid her enough not to worry about it. Since none of the patients were being blatantly abused and all of them seemed content enough in their captivity, Samantha did her best not to care.

Slowly, she worked her way down the A wing. Whatever fight had been inside these patients in their lives had gone dead a long time ago, Samantha thought as she double-checked the next wing's meds and pushed the cart toward B10. She very carefully didn't think about the man in B1. Not until she got to B5, at least, and then, then...

She smelled lavender.

Closing her eyes as she pretended to fuss with the cart and the meds, Samantha couldn't stop herself from smiling. Jed knew it was her favorite smell. She'd mentioned it once, early on. She'd never told him that she noticed how the scent always wafted around her when she got close to his room. Saying it aloud would mean the ones who watched them would be able to hear. It would be proof that Jed was still capable of manipulating his environment. Proof of a connection between them that she didn't dare let anyone know about.

She drew in another slow breath, though, delighting in the scent. As she stood, the meds for B5 in one hand, the door at the end of the hall opened and Dr. Ransom came through it, flanked as he always was by two guards. He nodded at her, stopping in front of Jed's room.

"Hello, Nurse. I'm here to get Jed for a session."

"He hasn't had his meds yet—" The doctor was already gesturing to one of the guards to step forward and take them from her. With a frown, Samantha pulled the small paper cup from the cart but didn't hand it over. "If you can wait a few minutes, I'll be happy to—"

Again, the doctor cut her off with a dismissive wave. "Not necessary, thank you, Nurse."

The scent of lavender faded, replaced by the chemical, hospital stink that burned the insides of her nose, making her cough. The pills chattered a little in the paper cup, and she forced her hands to stop shaking. "It would really only take—"

Dr. Ransom's head swung around and, for the first time in perhaps the entirety of her working here, he looked Samantha in the face. "Is there some reason you feel it necessary to argue with me?"

"No." With that same bright, plastic smile, Samantha handed over the pills to the guard, who took the paper cup without even blinking. "Of course not."

"Get back to work," Ransom told her, already dismissing her and looking through the portal.

Samantha wasn't dumb enough to say another word. She lingered, though, at the cart, until they brought Jed out. Not in cuffs, although the men on either side of him were clearly ready to handle him if he did anything out of line. He hadn't in the past eighteen months, but she knew he had, a long time ago. Watching Ransom's face, she thought the doctor was sort of hoping Jed would pull something now, so he'd have an excuse to order Jed's restraint.

Was this it? The end of things? Were they finally taking him away? Should she react? There'd been no word from the Crew, and nothing from Wyrmwood, either. No changes in the schedule that would indicate that anything had changed.

Jed didn't look at her when he came out of the room. Not so much as a glance over his shoulder.

She was already planning her attack when the softly drifting scent of lavender returned. She didn't think he even knew she was there. She'd never spoken to Jed about the real reasons she'd come to Wyrmwood, but it wasn't impossible that he knew and understood. Not out of the realm of possibility that he would know before she could, before anyone else could, that his time here was over.

Chapter 4

Jed came back as Samantha was finishing her shift. She heard the doors open and stood up from her place at the desk to look. Ransom hadn't come back with him. The same two guards from before were marching him to his room, a hand beneath each of his elbows to hold him up. He looked exhausted.

"Does he need something? Jed, do you need something?" She came around the desk to face them.

"Doctor said he'll be fine, he just needs to sleep." One of the guards gave her an assessing up-and-down look, and then a surprising grin. "I could use a little something, though."

"Shut up, Clement," said the other guard with a scowl. "Get this door open. Get the guy inside, okay? I want to go the hell home."

Samantha ignored both of them and stepped closer. "Jed?"

He shook his head. "No. Just tired. I'll sleep now. That's all."

He looked terrible, but so did most of the patients when they came back from a session with Ransom. Samantha hesitated, once more wondering if now was the time. She could take out the first guard, no problem, and with great satisfaction, considering how he'd leered at her. The second would be harder to topple, warned and ready, but she had no doubts that she could take care of him, too. Her fingers fairly itched to strike out at both of them, but she didn't show any signs of it.

Vadim, the man in charge of the Crew and the one who'd brought her in on this assignment, had told her there'd be times when she felt ready to act, but that she needed to wait. She'd be told when the time was right. Until then, she was to monitor Jed. To foster a relationship with him, such as she could with limited interactions. She would have to trust the Crew, Vadim had said, and she'd have to get Jed to trust her.

Samantha had never been big on trust, either giving or receiving, but she did believe Vadim and the Crew knew what they were doing. So now, instead of going into battle mode and destroying the two dudes manhandling Jed through the door and into his room, she went back to the desk and gathered her things. She signed out, although until the next nurse showed up to cover her shift, there wasn't much she could do.

"Hey, listen, so maybe me and you..." The first guard had come out of Jed's room and leaned over the desk to give her a wink. "Drinks?"

"You know that's not allowed." Without looking at him, Samantha scanned through the security feeds on the camera, searching for any sign that her replacement was at least in the elevator.

"Hey. I'm talking to you." He went so far as to put his hand over the top of the desk and tried to grab her shoulder.

She pulled away before he could touch her, one hand going up automatically to grip his wrist and break it, before she stopped herself. She did not smile. "I'm not interested in getting fired, Clement."

"Yeah, that pussy isn't worth it, anyway," he said derisively, his mouth twisting. In the next second, he was choking, coughing, doubled over so that she had to stand and look over the edge of the desk to see what the hell was going on. The fit lasted only another few seconds, but when he stood his face was red, eyes streaming tears. He muttered a low curse and backed away from her with a scowl.

A dozen retorts leaped to her lips, but as with almost every other action she ever wanted to take while on this job, Samantha held it back. She gave Clement her patented blank smile and enjoyed the way it made him flinch. The hall door opened, letting in the nurse who'd be taking over, and Samantha pushed past him without so much as a look at his face.

The scent of lavender stayed with her the entire way home.

Chapter 5

It was a rare day when Persephone didn't have anything going on. No repairs to make or schedule for the building. No appointments with the small but consistent stable of men who paid her to be the woman of their dreams... or sometimes, nightmares, depending. She couldn't remember the last time she'd woken feeling semi-rested, without even a tinge of anxiety following her around.

It wouldn't last, she thought as she headed out into the morning, taking the concrete steps at the front of the building two at a time so she could get to the bodega on the corner for a cup of coffee and a candy bar. Caffeine and chocolate in hand, she was already tearing open the plastic when she bumped head-on, literally, into a man as solid as brick. She hit him hard enough to bounce off, stumbling back.

"Watch it," she muttered, preparing to push past him. The guy snagged the sleeve of her sweatshirt, turning her to face him. Persephone was already working, shifting, smoothing the lines and curves of her face to look like someone else. Dark hair instead of bright red-gold. Big tits. Tight top. His eyes went right there, and even if she hadn't masked her face he'd have barely paid attention, so taken was he by the sight of her knockers.

Men, she thought with a sneer. So predictable.

"I'm looking for someone," he said. "You seen her?"

The picture he pulled up on his phone was blurred, but definitely her. Thank god she'd automatically put on the glamour for him. The question was, why did he have a picture of her in the first place?

"Nope. Never," Persephone said. "What'd she do?"

She thought he might say she owed him, or someone he was working for, money. That she was part of a scam. That she'd been caught up in a kinky prostitution ring, and he was part of the sting operation.

"Nothing." Something in his cold, dead eyes left her shivering. "Just looking for her."

Then he backed up and kept walking, leaving her behind. She watched him go, knowing that if he turned to glance back, she would still look like someone else. Uncertain if, in the end, it would matter. If a man like that was on her trail, she might be in trouble sooner rather than later.

He was from Wyrmwood. She felt it. He wasn't one of the soldier guys who'd raided Collins Creek; they were drones that followed orders. This guy was the advance scout, sniffing around to see if he could catch wind of her anywhere.

And if he found out where she really was, Persephone thought, then the other men would come.

Then, they would try to take her away.

Chapter 6

Jed would have liked to really put down that guard who'd been harassing Samantha all the way to the ground, his lungs blowing up, heart bursting from his chest. He'd settled instead for squeezing the asshole from the inside out, just enough to get the guy to back off from Samantha, and even that effort had nearly put Jed onto his hands and knees. There wasn't any blood, though. Whatever damage he'd done to the guard's brain hadn't been bad enough for that.

Ever since he was twelve years old, Jed had discovered the joys of hurting people, especially when the rewards bore merit—video games, chocolate cake, comic books. All he had to do was let Dr. Ransom open the window blinds into the other room and show him the man or the woman in the chair, then he'd have to think really hard and later, not quite as hard and then not hard at all, to make them scream and writhe in agony.

It had taken him only another year to understand that hurting people did not make him feel good. It left him with a sick stomach and an aching head, worse than finishing the puzzles or reading the word cards in the box or any of the other dozens of things they had him do. Hurting people took effort; getting them to behave like his puppet took even more. More than once it left his nose bleeding.

One terrible time, it left him blind.

His sight came back. So did the tests. So did his anger, bigger now than anything else. No more rewards for doing what they wanted. Now he suffered the punishments for refusing. Starvation. Electric shock therapy. When they realized he could no longer be controlled by any of those methods, the drugs began.

At seventeen, he killed a man, but not the one they wanted him to kill. After that, the people at Wyrmwood started to be afraid of him.

Now, at twenty-five, he should still be terrifying them, but he'd spent the last eight years doing his best to convince them that they had nothing to fear.

The testing tonight during his session with Dr. Ransom had been unexpectedly brutal. After years of proving to them he was no longer capable of doing what they wanted, years of taunting them into just disposing of him already, Jed had almost forgotten what it was like when the doctor was convinced he could get a reaction from his patient. Almost, but not quite. His body remembered, anyway, the sting and burn of electricity. The pungent horror of the chemicals they dripped into his veins to make him compliant. There'd been times over the years when it would've taken so little to tip him into death, but they'd pulled him back. So many times he'd have let them—but that had changed when Samantha started working there.

She was not the first person to look him in the eyes, but she was the first to at least try to connect with him as a human being. Small things, nothing that would get either of them in trouble. A gentle squeeze of his shoulder when she took his vitals. A smile. A compassionate laugh at his lame jokes.

He felt it when she left the hospital. If he tried a little harder, he'd be able to feel her wherever she went, but doing that would surely rip something inside his head, so he eased back the small tendrils of thought that had connected him to her in the first place. She'd be back tomorrow, he thought just before he passed out on the hard cot, her face the last coherent thought he had.

Chapter 7

Samantha could not stop thinking about him.

After escaping from the hospital that was a prison, she went home only long enough to change into her work-out gear. She hit the street as dawn pinked the sky, and though her body cried for sleep, the only way she'd get any was to exhaust herself. She set off on a route that would take her through the park, where she could test herself on soft dirt paths and boulders, then along the riverfront and back home before the early-morning-rush traffic started.

Since starting at Wyrmwood, she'd shared perhaps a couple dozen conversations with Jed that weren't related to his medication or treatment. The training and rules had been explicit and strict about having as little contact with the patients as possible. She'd rarely bent the rules and never enough to get any disciplinary action. There was no denying that she felt closer to him than she

did any of the others, but she'd always chalked it up to
the fact she'd been hired to save his life when the time
came. Something like that would naturally lead her to
be more...*affectionate* was not the right word, not even
close. Concerned. Protective. Aware?

She ran harder, leaping a park bench with one foot on
the seat and pushing off with the other on the back, then
hitting the grass with her fingertips digging into the soft
earth before she leaped again. It was ridiculous to think
Jed had done anything to the guard. Though there'd been
plenty of documentation about what he'd been capable of
when he was younger, all the reports Vadim had given
her said that Jed's abilities had begun fading in late adolescence, becoming completely extinct over time.

It had happened with other members of the commune
where he'd been born. Children born with psychokinetic
or telepathic talents had been taken away from the Collins Creek farm under the guise of child protective services, but they'd been sent to places like Wyrmwood,
not foster care. They'd been held, tested. Of those that
had been released in adulthood, none of them had been
reported as maintaining their abilities. Most of the ones
the Crew had been able to track had suffered from the
years of institutionalization. High rates of suicide and
crime had followed. Jed was one of the last of the Collins Creek kids the Crew had been able to find.

She jumped up to grab a low-hanging tree limb and
swung out, arching her back. Landing hard. She no longer
smelled lavender, but the memory of it wouldn't leave her.
There'd been more than a few times when she'd thought
she sensed Jed's presence while she was at the desk, always looking up, expecting to see him there but finding
only empty space. Sometimes, a joke would tickle its
way into her head until she laughed aloud.

Maybe all of that had been Jed. He had come to her defense, not that she'd needed him to, with that moron Clement. Which meant that despite all the information Wyrmwood had been collecting on him, he wasn't telekinetically dead.

But he was going to be physically dead if he didn't reveal that truth to the Wyrmwood team, or if Samantha wasn't able to get him out of there when Vadim gave the go-ahead. It would have to be soon, she thought, thinking of how drained Jed had looked when they'd brought him back to the room.

On the way home, she picked up a burner phone and sent off a text to the number she'd memorized.

How long?

Then she tossed the phone into a Dumpster and continued on home. She didn't worry about how Vadim was going to answer her. He always found a way.

Chapter 8

Persephone had stopped dreaming about Collins Creek a long time ago. If she did think about her childhood, it was only in a series of flashing memories she did her best to shove aside. She and her twin brother, Phoenix, had managed to escape when Wyrmwood attacked and took most of the children away. The two of them had grown up on the streets, running constantly from Wyrmwood's scouts who'd found other survivors and made them disappear. The rumors about what was done to the Collins Creek children had circulated. Phoenix and Persephone had always managed to stay a few steps ahead of them, and in many ways the memories of the things they'd done to survive had been much worse than anything she could truly remember from her first ten years on the farm.

Now, though, she couldn't stop herself from looking over her shoulder everywhere she went. She couldn't prove the guy from this morning had been from Wyrmwood.

Twenty years had passed since the raid. Why would

they suddenly be looking so hard now? Turning over in her bed, she thought of calling Vadim. He'd offered her and Phoenix sanctuary, but her brother had refused, not willing to throw in his lot with a group that, to him, seemed as likely to turn out to be as awful as Wyrmwood. Persephone had not been quite as convinced of that. She had, in fact, done a job or two for Vadim over the years. Never anything serious or long-term. The money was fantastic, but like her brother, she'd never wanted to commit to it.

Vadim would know if there was anything new going on with Wyrmwood, though. Restless, Persephone got out of bed and paced through her apartment, checking as always the exits. One door in, one door out. The only window a single transom on the alley side of the building. She could get through it if she had to, but her real escape was the service elevator, a dumbwaiter, in a closet off the kitchen.

Running through her escape plan calmed her a little, but she was still not going to sleep. She needed something else, and she knew exactly where to find it. She dialed a familiar number.

"Leila? Girl, what are you up to?"

Leila was up to going out and causing trouble, as she almost always was. Persephone didn't hang out with her very often for just that reason—any kind of trouble Leila wanted to get into usually ended up bad. She didn't have the sense of self-preservation that Persephone had, or even Phoenix, who admittedly could be way less worried about keeping his ass out of the fire. Leila's skill was in counting. Her brain was an abnormally brilliant calculator that could figure the most complex equations with little more than a blink or two. She had not yet managed to use this Collins Creek–created skill for much of anything, though. Maybe she never would.

Still, it was good to get out, go dancing. Get a little drunk. Grind on a handsome guy or two or three. Persephone and Leila hit the town, dressed to...well, not to kill, Persephone thought absently as she scanned the crowed for likely prey. She never wanted to kill anyone ever again.

All at once, there he was from across the room. Kane Dennis, the cop who lived in Persephone's building. He was the one with the hot water problem. He was leaning against the back wall, a cup of beer in his hand. Scanning the room, back and forth, as though he were looking for something. Or someone. It didn't look like he'd seen her yet.

She began to layer herself, homing in on his mind. One at a time, that was the only way she could do this. He would have no idea that he was looking at a different woman from the one everyone else could see.

"I'm glamouring for that guy," Persephone said to Leila with a discreet point toward Kane. "You'll be okay here?"

Leila was already tonsils-deep into a make-out session with a guy she'd picked up a few minutes before, and waved Persephone away. Why, exactly, Persephone was doing this when there was a club full of dudes she didn't have to see in front of the mailbox every morning, she could not say. Only that he was there and she was here, and a curling flicker of need was rising inside her that she wanted to sate.

Maybe it was because he was a cop. She would be safe. If someone broke in and tried to take her, she thought, blaming the booze and the smoke and the little white pill of undetermined origin that Leila had slipped her earlier for this ragged train of thought. If someone broke in, Kane would be able to protect her. Wouldn't he?

By the time she got to him, she wore longer legs. Bigger tits as usual, since that's what most men seemed to dig. Soft, round booty. Dusky skin. Dark ringlets. Red lips, dark eyes.

"Hi," she said. "I'm Maria. Thinking about getting out of here, how about you?"

That was all it took. Persephone had not figured Kane for a guy so easily seduced and was in truth a little put off at how simple it had been, but she supposed it didn't matter as long as she got what she needed from him. Hard cock. Big hands. Sweet tongue. They found a cheap room in one of the hotels lining the street this end of town.

He kissed her mouth as soon as they got inside the door, his hands roaming over her. Fingers playing beneath her skirt, he found her already wet. Slick. Hot. He slipped his fingers inside her, fucking in and out, and she opened for him. His thumb pressed her clit, a steady pace that had her ready to go in minutes.

He let her lead him to the bed and strip him down. He watched her do the same. He rolled her over, nudging open her knees. She thought he would go down on her; she hoped he would, but instead Kane pressed a series of kisses to her belly, up to her breasts. Her throat. Her mouth. He'd pulled a condom from his wallet while they undressed and sheathed himself so efficiently that he was inside her in moments.

"Oh," she said. "Okay, then."

Kane fucked her slowly at first, making sure to get her going. When she needed a little extra pressure on her clit, he gave it to her, just right. Persephone rarely had any trouble getting off, but tonight it was taking her longer. Because she knew him, she thought, irritated with herself now that the buzz was fading. She ought to have found a stranger.

She didn't have much more time to think about it then because something in the way he shifted had brought her to the tipping point. They moved together, easily, steadily, and she came in a slow rush of rolling pleasure. He followed with a shudder and buried his face against the side of her neck.

When her phone rang, she was happy to shift out from underneath him so she could grab it. "Hey, girl."

"I didn't go home with that guy," Leila's drunken voice crackled through the phone, a bad connection. "I'm back at my place. You okay?"

"Yes, fine." Persephone glanced at Kane, who'd sat up to look at her. She'd been holding on to her illusion as a matter of habit, a good one, but tightened it now to be sure he had not even a glimpse of her true self. Leila had disconnected.

"I have to go," she said. "Sisters before misters, am I right?"

"Sure. No problem." He yawned and fell back on the bed. "You need a cab or anything?"

"I'm good." She paused as she gathered her clothes to look at him. "Thanks for tonight."

He rolled onto his side to crack open an eye and grin at her. "You're welcome."

It was on the tip of her tongue to offer him her number, which of course would be ridiculously stupid, even if she did use the fake side line she kept for these very occasions. Instead, she dressed quickly and let herself out of the hotel room.

Chapter 9

Jed studied the wooden puzzle in front of him. It was more suitable for a five-year-old than a twenty-five-year-old, but since he'd been given puzzles identical to this one or nearly so since he had been five, he guessed they'd never seen any reason to change. A rectangular wooden base with different sized, shaped and colored holes, meant to hold the brightly colored matching pieces. Unlike a toddler puzzle, this one had more complicated shapes and smaller pieces. The goal: fit the pieces into the slots as fast as possible. He'd been using this same one for so long, the paint had worn down to bare wood in many places. It didn't matter. At this point, the exercise was more of a self-soothing device than anything else.

He shook out the pieces, scattering them across the desk like jacks. He set the base upright and leaned back in his chair, closing his eyes. His hands went to the edges of the table, fingertips touching the worn wooden surface lightly. Through the pads of his fingertips, he could taste the harsh sting of the antibacterial cleanser they used in here every afternoon while he was in session with Dr. Ransom. It was a bad taste, yet somehow comforting. It had been the same for twenty years. Just like the puzzle. Like the lights set on timers to keep him on a regular day/night schedule that had nothing in common with the actual movement of the sun. Like everything else here, over time, the hospital had become...home.

Without opening his eyes, Jed began fitting the pieces into the slots. His fingers moved, stroking over the wooden desk, though now the harsh bite of the chemicals had been replaced by the smoother, older smell of colored paint. Blue star. Yellow circle. Red hexagon.

Faster.

Green cross. Black square. Purple triangle.

Faster.

The wooden pieces fit themselves into place with small, clattering thumps and thuds as they rolled across the desk.

When all the pieces had returned to the base, the vibration in the desk ceased and he opened his eyes. He put his fingertips on the edge of the table again and touched the puzzle with his gaze and nothing more. He'd done this forty-seven times already tonight, and would keep doing it until the lights went off when he was supposed to be sleeping—but of course he didn't sleep. He hardly ever did, never more than an hour or two at a time, anyway.

He closed his eyes.

Faster.

Faster.

He could do this another three times, if he was quick, before it was time for Samantha to bring him his meds. He'd have to be finished before she got here. She had no idea what he was, what he could do. But out of all the people who'd worked here over the years, all the doctors, nurses and orderlies, all the guards, hundreds of people who'd taken care of him—Samantha was the only one who'd made it seem like it mattered. How she saw him. What she thought of him. She was the first person since he'd been sent here to make Jed care about anything.

A scant few seconds before he heard the click of the door lock, Jed had finished his last round of the puzzle and pushed it aside. He was already on his feet, standing behind the red line painted on the floor well away from the door. He smoothed his hair, suddenly self-conscious. He should have quit the puzzle sooner. Brushed his hair, his teeth. Changed his shirt, as if any of the four he owned were not identical.

"Hi, Jed." Samantha's grin urged his own. "How's it going?"

"Good, good. You?" He always sounded such like an idiot when he spoke to her, but she never seemed to notice.

"Oh, I'm dandy." She waited for the door to lock behind her before stepping toward him.

In the past eight years, Jed had never once moved over the red line before that solid click. In eight years, never given anyone reason to fear him. For a brief period of time when he was a teenager, they'd upped his meds to keep him from trying to escape, testing him over and over again to see if he could do with the door lock what he could do with the puzzle, but he'd always failed. It was the type of metal, they said amongst themselves. They had no idea that it wasn't anything to do with that all, but the simple fact that Jed wanted them to stop drugging him.

Not so he could get out. That, he could've done at any

time, despite the drugs and the special metal in the locks.
His memories of what life had been before had never
faded, even through the distortion of childhood. He never
wanted to go back to the life he'd known before coming
here. If that meant spending his life in this room, so be
it. No, he'd simply hated the fuzzy way the meds made
him feel. Slow and thick and stupid.

"Is it getting cold outside?" he asked her suddenly,
regretting the stupid words the moment they flew out
of his mouth.

Samantha frowned and gave him a sideways glance,
then another at the corner of the ceiling where the hidden camera lurked. "You know I'm not allowed to talk
about that, Jed."

"Right, right. I know." Did they really think he didn't
remember there was a world outside these walls? Sometimes, Jed thought, they must. He'd allowed them to think
of him as simple for so long, he must've convinced them
he was also stupid. "I just wondered."

"Can you sit down, please?" She gestured, and when
he had complied, as he always did, always, never diso-
bedient, she made a show of pulling out her stethoscope
but leaned over him as she placed the round part of it
against his chest. "The leaves are changing. The air
smells like snow."

That whisper sent an electric jolt all through him. So
did her touch on his wrist as she counted the too-many
and too-fast beats of his heart. Samantha looked into his
eyes, so close he could see the white specks surrounding
the blackness of her pupil. She gave him a small, secret
smile and waited a moment or so before she officially
took his pulse. Giving him time to relax.

She knew him.

She'd never commented on the embarrassing way his

body reacted to her standard routine. Not when she used gentle fingers to press his neck and throat to check his lymph nodes and his heartbeat again raced, and not when she had him lift his arms to his sides so she could pass her hands along his body and he shifted against the rise in his pants. She noticed it. She had to. There was no way to hide the heat of his skin. But she always managed to be standing at an angle to block it from the camera, and she always took her time to make it possible for him to calm down before she stepped back.

Today (it was really close to midnight, though they wanted him to think it was more like noon) she lingered with the exam. Stood a little closer than usual. She dropped her stylus, a soft-tipped rubber utensil that should not have been able to cause any harm, should he decide to take it from her and shove it into a vulnerable spot. It was a sensible precaution, though he wondered why nobody had ever seemed to consider the fact he'd need no weapon if he really wanted to hurt someone.

And they thought he was the stupid one.

She smelled so fresh, so clean, that all he could do was close his eyes and breathe her in. He wanted to cover himself in her scent, to wash away the stink of this room. Of all the years...

"Jed," she said. Warning. "No touching."

He hadn't meant to. The gentle pressure of his fingers against the inside of her elbow had been involuntary. He didn't move them away. Staring into her eyes, Jed let his fingers trace a small circle on her bare skin.

Her lips parted on a small sigh. She blinked rapidly. At the tiniest hint of her tongue pressed to her upper lip, another rush of electricity jolted through him. He was so hard now there'd be no way she could keep up the pretense of this exam long enough for him to hide it from whoever it was that got their jollies watching.

She should move away from, he thought a little incoherently. She had to know what was happening. He should stop touching her, but he couldn't make himself. Another infinitesimal stroke of his fingertips on her skin had her eyes going wide. Dark.

Her smell changed from fresh air to something his brain told him was flowers, though it had been twenty years since he'd even seen a flower; the taste of her like golden honey, sweet syrup, flooded him through the continuing touch. Every muscle in him tensed, straining, though neither of them so much as moved more than the constant, steady motion of her hands as she made a show of checking his vitals.

Pulse. Temperature. One-handed, not moving so he could keep his fingertips on the inside of her elbow, Samantha kept up a running commentary on what she was doing—for the benefit of the observing camera, maybe. Or for him. For herself, Jed thought irrationally as the steady drone of her voice cracked and dipped for a second before she recovered.

He had never kissed a woman. Never made love. They'd started giving him porn when he hit adolescence—an outlet, they thought, so any pent-up desires could be dissolved. Preventing him from what, from violence? From yearning? It had worked, to a point, he thought now, but you couldn't replace human touch with paper pages or digital images. You couldn't replace making love to a woman with your own hand.

He wanted to kiss Samantha. He wanted to touch her. He wanted to make her shiver and shake, not the way the women in those movies did, but from deep inside her core. For real. He wanted to hear her say his name while her body tightened around him...

Samantha put her hand over his, her eyes closing. Her body tensed. She shook, but so briefly there could be no way anyone but Jed would notice. A small moan slipped out of her, covered up so fast by a cough as she turned her head that again, nobody but he could've possibly heard it.

"You have to stop." Her lips moved, in silence he understood, anyway.

Ashamed, he let her go. Samantha took a step back, almost stumbling before she caught herself. Her eyes opened. Gaze focused. A flush had spread up her throat to paint her cheeks. With her back still to the camera, shielding him, she pulled the small cup of meds from her uniform pocket and made a show of dispensing them.

"Take your vitamins," Samantha said.

They weren't vitamins, but at least they weren't hallucinogens or sedatives. He swallowed them with the bottled water she gave him from the small fridge next to the desk. By the time he had, he'd also managed to will his erection back down.

"Careful, you've spilled," she said calmly without looking away from his eyes, not so much as a glance at the small wet patch on the front of his pants.

Still watching out for him, he thought. Doing what she could. His balls ached, but he didn't dare even to shift in the chair.

They shared a look, lingering as long as they dared. At least he imagined they did, but when she cut her gaze from his, Jed had to admit that perhaps all of this was in his head. Surely Samantha didn't have any romantic feelings for him. How could she? He shouldn't mistake kindness and a sense of duty for anything like affection.

In fact, he should be ashamed of using his talent to inflict his lust on her.

"Do you need anything?" she asked him.

He needed lots of things, none of which she could give him. "No, thanks. Is it almost time for my session with Dr. Ransom?"

"Yes. I…think so." Again, her cheeks colored as she checked her watch. "Wow, yes it is. I lost track of time."

"The exam took longer today," Jed said, watching her.

Again, Samantha snagged his gaze with hers and didn't look away. She smiled. "Yes. A little longer."

Behind her, the green light over the door clicked to red. She didn't turn to look at it, but noticed him staring. She straightened, tucking the empty tin back into her pocket and patting it. She smoothed the fine tendrils of pale hair that had fallen over her forehead and cheeks. She cleared her throat and took another step back.

"Everything's fine, though," she said.

Jed smiled without much humor. "Isn't it always?"

"No," Samantha said even as her mouth formed the word *yes*, adding, "Don't forget to buzz if you need me."

I need you. I always need you. His answer, unspoken, could not possibly have reached her. His talents didn't extend to projecting thoughts.

Still, she nodded as though she'd heard him, but that was his own foolishness. His own desire. Without another word exchanged, Samantha left the room and the door locked behind her, and Jed forced himself to get out of the chair so nobody would think something was wrong.

Chapter 10

Leaving her shift in the light of day meant Samantha would be going home to blackout shades and a white-noise machine—but there'd be no easy sleep for her this morning. Not after that interminable five minutes in Jed's room. Not with the memory of his touch lingering.

A cold shower didn't help. She tried it, of course, running the water as frigid as she could stand it until her teeth chattered and her nipples peaked to near-painful tightness—but getting out, drying off, every stroke of the towel's soft fabric against her had Samantha's nerves tingling. Now she lay naked in her bed, the covers tossed off to expose her to the chilly autumn air, her window open to let in the breeze, because after a night's work in Wyrmwood she couldn't bear to be closed in, not even inside her own apartment.

Stretching, letting her naked skin shift on the sheets, she tried not to touch herself but gave up after a few minutes of halfhearted resistance. She'd been on fire since giving Jed his exam—the same one she gave him every shift. A quick check of his temperature, his pulse, his glands, the clarity of his eyes and little more than that. It was required, but useless, since the likelihood of anything being wrong with him that nobody hadn't already noticed was so slim.

It was not the first time she'd murmured to him about the world outside, completely in defiance of the rules. Nor the first time she'd lingered over the exam, if only because of the way he'd pushed himself into her touch the way a cat would, purring, butting at her hand for the barest scrap of affection. Nobody touched him unless they were examining him. She knew that much, not from anything she'd ever been told as a staff member, but from the reports she'd studied, provided by Vadim and the vast reference and research sources of the Crew.

Nobody touched Jed to comfort him, not since childhood. Certainly never to arouse him, though she'd noticed about six months into her stint there that he'd begun reacting to her in that way. She'd never made a fuss about it, at first because she didn't want to risk them pulling her off duty taking care of him, for fear there was any kind of connection between them. Later, to keep him from being embarrassed. Now, she noticed but never acknowledged it because she couldn't admit to anyone, not even herself, how knowing that the simplest touch of her against him got him hard. How he looked at her, hungrier for that ten minutes they shared than he ever was for the trays of bland food they brought him.

Tonight was the first time, though, she'd ever had a similar reaction.

Her hand slid between her legs to cup herself. Fingers slipping inside. She was still slick. Her clit, still sensitive enough that the slight flick of it from her thumb forced a sigh out of her.

He'd almost made her come while barely touching her.

With a low groan of frustration, she stopped. This was no good. She didn't want to admit that she thought of Jed in that way. Jed, the man she was supposed to protect. Not lust after.

Still, the job with Wyrmwood had made it impossible for her to have much of a social life, which left nothing but the touch of her own hand. It had been about a week since the last time she'd pleasured herself, and she was surprised she'd made it this long without taking the time to get herself off. No wonder he'd been able to bring her so close, Samantha thought with a sigh as she rubbed her clit in a slow, steady circle. She was definitely in need of an orgasm.

The scent of lavender. It teased and tickled her nostrils. Memory, she was sure, but caught up in the eroticism of her own touch, she didn't think much about it beyond that. She let the smells wash over her, urging her toward release.

Sometimes she used toys, but tonight the touch of only her fingers was getting her there. That and the memory of standing next to Jed, her fingertips on his wrist and feeling the suddenly swift throb of his heartbeat. His erection, conspicuously thick in his scrubs. The small wet spot of his precome that had stained it...all that from doing nothing but sitting near her. The thought of it was intoxicating and had her slipping over the edge into a hard, brief orgasm that left her breathless and sated... for now.

She gave herself a few minutes to luxuriate in the afterglow, which was nowhere near as nice as it would've been if she had been with someone else, but it would have to do. She'd already filed her daily report for the Crew, but now she rolled out of bed and slung on a silk kimono to sit at her desk and flip open her laptop. She typed in the web address of the secure reporting site and scrolled back through all the information she had on Wyrmwood. On Jed. Her notes were complete and thorough and said very little because there wasn't very much to say. She went in. She did her job. She came home. She waited for word on when it was time to get him out of there.

And sometimes, she thought with a small pang of guilt, she made herself come when thinking about him.

She wasn't surprised when her computer rang. Surely they monitored when she logged in, and what she looked at. "Vadim."

He smiled at her from the small video chat window on her screen. "Samantha. What's going on?"

She did not want to tell her boss about the sexual encounter today. It was an embarrassing lack of self-control on her part. It might get her pulled from the assignment, and there were so many reasons she didn't want that to happen—some she'd own up to and some she would not.

"Nothing," she said after a second's hesitation. "Can't sleep. Just trying to refresh myself on the case, I guess."

"There's nothing new in there. If there were, I'd have alerted you." Vadim tilted his head to study her. "You haven't heard anything from the hospital, have you?"

"Of course not. Like they'd tell me anything." She snorted soft laughter and shook her head.

Vadim was no longer smiling. "It's going to be soon. Our source says the paperwork's been filed for his transfer."

The transfer from Wyrmwood to an unknown location. They didn't need to know where they were taking him to understand that he'd be killed wherever he ended up. "Why do they bother, Vadim? Why not just overdose him at the hospital? It's not like anyone would know."

The words were truth but tasted bitter, making her sneer.

Vadim shrugged. "Who knows, other than even their most vetted employees could end up with too much information, and they don't want to risk it? Better to 'transfer' the ones they're no longer interested in using to someplace else and simply dispose of them along the way."

Samantha shuddered at the thought of it, of Jed being put into a white van. A gun to his head, maybe, or a simple injection. His body put into an unmarked grave. Vadim gave her a curious look, even as she quickly smoothed her expression.

"You'll be ready?" he asked. "The only time you'll be able to extricate him is in that small window between him leaving Wyrmwood and before he arrives at where it is they plan to take him."

She'd known that when she took the assignment. Breaking him out of the hospital was an impossibility, no matter her level of skill or how much the Crew could help with computer hacking or other measures to get past security. She'd always known she would have to wait until they were transferring him and move at that time. So why, then, did she feel so suddenly desperate not to wait any longer?

"It's been years." She leaned closer to the computer, staring into the camera. "Is it possible they're simply going to leave him alone? There are plenty of residents at Wyrmwood living out their lives without interference."

"Not a single one of the children captured from Collins Creek have been left to live without interference," Vadim said. "The ones that showed no abilities were, of course, put into the foster care system. The others have either been kept, as Jed's been kept, or exterminated."

"There are some others," Samantha said quietly. "The ones who got out."

She'd read about them in the files. A few obscure references, no more than that, these special children almost as much of a myth as Bigfoot. Sometimes spotted in the wild, but never captured, their existence never proven.

"You know as well as I do that nobody's ever been able to connect anyone out there with Collins Creek. It was swept, the residents removed and most of them died during the raid." Vadim paused. "Certainly we've had many cases of men and women with extraordinary psychic talents, but none of them have been connected with the farm or the cult. And even if they were, does it matter? Your assignment is to protect this one man."

"Of course." She nodded, pulling the robe closer around her throat from the sudden chill sweeping over her.

"Samantha, you should know I have no doubts about your ability to handle this assignment. You're very, very good at what you do." Vadim did smile again, though the effect of it was probably less reassuring than he meant it to be.

Samantha saw no point in false modesty. She'd spent her childhood being trained to survive any situation, including the impossible, like an alien invasion or the rise of the undead. She'd joined the Crew after several stints in government organizations so secret even she wasn't sure who ran them—only that the training she'd had as a kid had been nothing compared to what she'd learned there. Those skills and credentials had been what got her approved to work at Wyrmwood. "Yes. It's not that I'm worried about it… I'll be ready. But…"

"Yes?"

Samantha shook her head, knowing she had to own up to it. "It's the subject. He seems to have formed an… attachment."

"Ah. Can you use it?"

Startled, she recoiled with a grimace. "What? No! Why would I?"

"If it was necessary to gain his cooperation, I would expect you to, especially if it was to help protect him." Vadim shrugged, eyeing her.

"I fail to see how encouraging him to have a crush on me could help protect him." The words came out too sharply. She sounded guilty.

Vadim gave her a narrow-eyed look. "The subject has been kept in near isolation since childhood. Before that, he'd been raised in horrific social conditions. Understandably, he could be expected to form an emotional or sexual attachment to an attractive caregiver. The records show you are likely not even the first…"

That made her feel all kinds of irritable. She'd read the reports, of course, about the nurse who'd been removed from duty when her relationship with Jed had become closer than the Wyrmwood executives decided was appropriate. That had been when he was little more than a kid, though. It wasn't like what was between the two of them. It couldn't be. She kept her expression smooth. "We don't talk about it, of course. I do my job. I leave the room. I wait."

"Ah, yes. The waiting. Well, we're all waiting."

"And why?" she demanded suddenly. "Why not just take him out of there now? There has to be a way!"

"If there was, don't you think we'd have gotten him out of there long ago?" Vadim fixed her with a stern look. "Even with inside help, Wyrmwood is impossible to break into or out of."

"Nothing is impossible. I thought that was the Crew's motto or something like that."

Vadim laughed without much humor, although his dark eyes did twinkle. "If we had a motto, I suspect it would be more like 'nothing is improbable.' As it is, you won't have to wait much longer. All the signs are pointing to his imminent transfer. Be prepared to hear more as early as next week."

"If you can tell they're getting ready to transfer him," she began, but stopped at the look on the older man's face. She'd never made Vadim angry with her, and she wasn't about to find out now what might happen to her if she did. As charming and paternal as Vadim could be, there was a darkness in him that Samantha recognized…and didn't want to mess with.

"This connection you believe he's begun. Is it something you reciprocate?"

"Of course not," she said steadily, getting his gaze head-on as best she could through the computer screen. "He doesn't deserve to be put down like a dog that's lived past its use, that's all."

Vadim said nothing for a moment or so, studying her. Not for the first time, Samantha wondered what Vadim's talents were. She wouldn't have doubted that one of them was reading minds.

"Be ready," he said finally.

Chapter 11

"How are we feeling today?" Dr. Ransom pushed his glasses up higher on his nose with one hand, tapping his pen against the desk with the other. "Nurse says you didn't eat your breakfast."

"Her name's Patty," Jed said mildly. Dr. Ransom never knew their names. Jed wouldn't have been surprised if the doctor barely remembered Jed's name. He certainly hardly ever used it.

"Was there something wrong with breakfast?"

"I didn't feel like eating today. That's all." Jed used a small push, a tiny one, undetectable, to still the doctor's tapping pen by making it microcosmically harder to move. Just enough to make the other man feel as though he didn't want to make the effort, but nothing close to him feeling that he was being manipulated.

It had taken Jed a long, long time to refine that skill. Many hours of having to listen to the doctor's relentless fidgeting.

"Not hungry? Not feeling well?"

"I don't like pancakes," Jed said.

Dr. Ransom looked confused. "No? Who doesn't like pancakes?"

"Me. Never liked them." Jed leaned back in the chair, one leg crossed over the other, with a grin. Blank and empty, stretching so wide it felt as though his teeth were the size of dominoes.

"Well. I suppose I can make sure the kitchen never sends you pancakes again."

That wasn't going to happen. If anything, now that he'd made his preference known, he'd be served pancakes three or four times a week, and that was because they liked to mess with him that way. The truth was, Jed preferred pancakes to eggs, but although he knew that lies were the devil speaking with his tongue, he didn't care. He'd stopped caring about that a long, long time ago, about the same time he'd decided to stop playing by their rules. He was simply careful about how he went about it, that was all.

When Jed didn't answer, Dr. Ransom looked concerned. "Nurse said you didn't get out of bed at the usual time, as well."

"Her name is Patty," Jed repeated.

Dr. Ransom put the pen down completely and laced his fingers together. "Patty."

"Samantha is the day nurse. Bryant and Carl are the orderlies. Stephen is the janitor."

"You've never interacted with the custodial staff," Dr. Ransom said.

And the janitor's name was not really Stephen, but the doctor wouldn't know that. Jed shrugged. He thought about using his talent to take up the pen and bury it point-deep into the wood of the desk, but didn't want to give them the satisfaction or deal with the consequences.

"Is there a reason why you overslept today, Jed?"

The fact he'd been unable to sleep last night, tossing and turning after the interlude with Samantha. He wasn't about to admit that to Dr. Ransom, though. As far as the doctor was concerned, Jed barely knew the nurse, and that was how he wanted it to stay.

When he was fourteen or so, there'd been another nurse. Miss Jean. That was how she'd referred to herself, and how Jed still thought of her. Miss Jean had worn the same uniform as all the other nurses, the same as it had been in all the years Jed had been in Wyrmwood. She'd had pale, short hair and wide green eyes and a smile that reminded him of his birth mother's, when Mother had been happy. Miss Jean had never looked at him the way the others had sometimes. Afraid. No matter what he did or how he behaved, Miss Jean always stayed calm, friendly, kind. And because she never gave him reason to misbehave, slowly, slowly, Jed had stopped always trying to cause trouble.

When it had become apparent to the unseen—whoever was in charge, the ones he'd learned watched and judged, but never met with him in person—that Miss Jean's influence was changing Jed from who they wanted him to be into something else, something less violent, well. Miss Jean went off shift one day and never came back.

That was when Jed had started training himself to unlearn all the things they'd taught him.

Eleven years later, and the daily testing had stopped. His sessions with Dr. Ransom had gone from five days a week to twice, each session only lasting thirty or so minutes, since there never seemed to be much to say anymore. It couldn't be much longer, now, Jed thought. Until they either killed him, or let him go.

"Jed?"

"I was tired, I guess. Had a bad headache." That part was true enough, though it wasn't like his head didn't always throb with the effort of holding himself back from giving them what they'd been after since he was five.

"Your medicine should prevent that. Your vitals haven't changed. Your blood pressure is fine."

Jed had learned to control that, too.

"Maybe it's seasonal allergies," Jed said, deadpan.

Dr. Ransom didn't smile. He did, however, lift up the pen again to scratch a few notes on the pad in front of him. "I'm going to prescribe you something new. For anxiety."

"No! I mean," Jed said in a calmer voice, "I'm not anxious about anything."

He was already on some complicated cocktail of pills designed to keep him under control, but it had been years since they'd felt the need to use anything to keep him calm. He wasn't going to go back to being chemically brain-dead again. He couldn't. He would die first.

"Just a little something," Dr. Ransom said in that soothing tone he always employed. He looked at Jed over the rims of his frameless glasses. "It seems to me that you haven't been yourself lately."

Himself? Ransom had no idea who Jed was. Nobody did, including Jed.

"Is it because of the tests?" Jed asked bluntly.

The doctor hesitated, cutting his gaze from Jed's. "Of course not. You know we've always made it clear that our concern is for your well-being. Never any test results."

It was what they said, but never what they'd meant.

Jed frowned. "New meds won't make it any easier for me to do what they ask."

For the first time since Jed had entered the room, Dr. Ransom smiled. The effect of it was chilling—a stretching of the older man's lips that in no way resulted in any humor reaching his eyes. Ransom tap-tapped his pen rapidly against the desktop.

"We only want what's best for you, Jed. We're your family."

"The only one I have," Jed replied, sincerely if not gratefully.

Ransom's smile stretched wider, showing his yellowed teeth. "You've been at Wyrmwood a long time. We've worked together for a long time, too. I'd like you to know how…fond…of you I've grown over the years."

Jed shifted in his chair, wondering if the doctor expected a matching response. He couldn't make himself lie, so he stayed quiet. After a moment, the doctor's smile faded. He tapped his pen once or twice more, then closed the folder.

"You can go back to your room now. Our session is finished. Unless you have something you need to talk about?"

Jed shook his head and stood. "Not really. Will there be a test?"

"Oh, no." Dr. Ransom laughed. "No more tests will be necessary."

Relief and terror in equal parts raced through Jed, who did not react in any visible way. He nodded when Ransom repeated that he'd be sending Jed some new meds, but didn't protest again. As he left the room, a guard on either side of him, he considered striking out. Surprising them.

They'd kill him without a second thought—he knew that—and wouldn't suicide by armed guard be a better way to go than waiting, waiting for them to finally decide to end his life by some other method? Wouldn't it be better to go on his own terms? But of course, he only walked meekly between them without a word and stepped through the door into his cell, where he waited for whatever was going to happen next.

Chapter 12

There was always a way to get whatever you wanted, if you knew how to ask. Unlike her brother, who could simply make you do whatever he desired, Persephone had learned the best ways to ask. A quiet word in the ear of the skater kid on the corner who hooked her up with some weed before passing along the word to someone else, who got the news to the contact Persephone needed. Eventually, a woman pushing a stroller took a seat beside her. The woman bent to offer the toddler in the stroller a lick of her ice cream.

"Word is, they're getting a little desperate. Losing funding. Need something to get their grants back." Suburban mom cooed at her child for a second, then pulled a package of baby wipes out of her purse and started to wipe the kid's face.

"Does that mean they're actively looking for us again?"

"If they get one of you, they could make a case for

keeping the program open. We've had no word that they're doing anything major, but I'd be careful, yes. They have freelancers working on it."

Persephone sat back on the bench. "Bounty hunters?"

She'd dealt with bounty hunters before. The guy from the other day had sure felt like one. Not a very skilled one, she thought with some relief and a little alarm at how close he'd been to her, even if he hadn't known it.

"They don't have the means to put together any kind of teams like the one..." The mother trailed off, looking around, but they seemed to be the only ones there.

Persephone nodded. "I got it. You don't have to say."

"The reality is, the organization has been privately funded for a long time, but they're on the way out. They're swirling the drain. Without a big benefactor or some kind of breakthrough, they're going to have to close completely. Look, I'm on maternity leave right now, and the only reason I agreed to meet you is that this is really low priority. You know they don't have eyes and ears all over the place, they're not monitoring the entire world or anything. Vadim said to tell you that they've assessed the danger to you as minimal, but that doesn't mean you shouldn't be careful."

"I know."

The woman studied Persephone. "He said to remind you that you have a place with us whenever you want it."

"I'm doing all right. Thanks." Persephone stood.

"Even so, he told me to remind you." The woman stood, too, and pressed a small square of paper into Persephone's hand. "Call him on this number when you're ready."

Chapter 13

Waking from a nightmare, she realizes all too quickly that this has not been a dream. The ringing in her ears is still so loud all she can do is clap her hands to the side of her head and rock back and forth until it eases. She's alone. Whoever did this to her has left her for dead, she thinks, and risks running a hand over her body, checking for wounds.

The blood covering her is not hers. The bits of flesh and bone and brain, also not hers. Her fingers clench, remembering the feel of the weapon in her hands, but she can't remember shooting anyone. Unsteadily, she holds her hands out in front of her, inspecting the nails, grimy with filth.

She has killed with these hands.

The question, with the answer she can't remember, is has she killed now? Or perhaps not if, because it feels so obvious that she has, but who? She can't even remem-

ber who she was fighting. Staring at the tufts of fur beneath several of her fingers, stroking along the slices in her clothes and the torn flesh beneath, Samantha thinks maybe she needs to ask not who.

What.

Blinking to clear her vision, she makes sure she can stand upright before she tries to go anywhere. She's in a safe house, not one she remembers, but she recognizes it without too much effort. Bare floors, bare walls, utilitarian furniture. Nothing to show anyone on the outside that there's anything here but an almost empty house waiting for someone to occupy it. Nothing to stand out to anyone who came to the door.

She hopes nobody does that now. The beige walls are spattered with thick dark fluid that smells of dank earth. The furniture, a brown plaid couch and matching armchair, are overturned, the stuffing torn out. It would be so very clear this house was the scene of something awful.

She doesn't call out. The ringing has faded enough that she can, if she strains hard enough, hear more than the buzz. Her feet are steady, planted shoulder-width apart. Her fingers ache; she forces them to relax and open. She doesn't search for her weapon. She already knows it's gone.

Whatever happened here was recent enough that the blood is sticky, but not dry. Her wounds still seep. She could not have been unconscious for more than twenty or thirty minutes. Listening hard, Samantha waits for some clue to tell her what went on, but she hears nothing but the harsh rasp of her own breathing.

In the next room, she finds him. Eyes wide. Mouth open. He stares at the ceiling, the ribbons of maroon on his throat evidence of what killed him. A familiar face.

Her father.

She kneels next to him without bothering to check for a pulse. You can maybe survive a wound that leaves your trachea hanging out of your throat, your bones poking through the skin, but only with immediate medical attention. It's very clear that her father went down alone. He won't get up again.

She tries to cry and can't. Later, she thinks she ought to have tried harder. He raised her, after all, in the absence of a mother. He did the best he could. But she thinks he wouldn't have wanted her to weep, not because it was a sign of weakness, but because he'd passed from this life and into the next. The one he'd always taught her was the better one.

The rest of the house is empty. There are signs, left behind by other safe house users. A code—something like the symbols used by transient hobos in the thirties to distinguish friendly homes from those where a man looking for a meal and a hot shave would instead get a serious thrashing. This house, she reads, is no longer safe.

"No shit." The words leak out of her on a tongue sore from being bitten.

In the kitchen, she finds no signs of struggle. In the fridge, a gallon of milk hasn't turned, and she gulps it greedily although she doesn't like milk. Her stomach bucks a protest, but she keeps it down. She spits a few times into the sink. Pink. Again. Clear this time. She puts the jug on the counter and both hands on the rim of the sink, gripping hard as the floor tips and tilts. When she's once more gathered her balance, she uses the sink to wash her face and rinse her mouth. She watches the water swirl away the blood and bits of fur.

She stands there so long, she realizes the light outside has gone from night to day.

She's lost time again, but this time remembers coming

into the kitchen. Drinking the milk. Going to the sink. She remembers her father is dead, and that someone before her tried to warn them that this house was not safe, but she still can't recall what brought them here.

She remembers she hadn't spoken to him in months, though. Before this. How they'd had a final falling-out— he wanted her to keep moving with him, and she wanted to find a place, settle down, keep a job. Have a life. They'd parted on bad terms.

With a gasp, Samantha shakes herself awake again. The faucet is still running, the water ice-cold. She turns it off. Closes her eyes.

Did she kill her father?

No, no, that can't be. She runs a fingertip over her teeth, careless of the gore still grimed into her skin. She wouldn't have done that. And it doesn't explain the fur.

She will never fully remember what brought her to this house, or what happened inside it. She will find the text on her phone from her father asking her to meet him at this address. Nothing more than that. But she does learn what happened to him, and that is because several days after burning that house to the ground in the hopes she can prevent anyone from finding out it had been a haven for the people her father had believed in, a man named Vadim approaches her in a coffee shop two towns away. He sits at the table outside, where Samantha is turning a lukewarm paper cup of shitty coffee around and around in her hands without being able to drink any of it. He says nothing, not even when she recoils as though she might hit him.

"I know what happened to your father," he says in the calm and steady voice Samantha will come to learn so well. "If you want to know, come with me."

So she does.

* * *

Jed was dreaming.

He knew it, of course, because in the waking world he would not be dancing slowly with Samantha. Her head would not be on his shoulder. His hand would not be on her hip. He surely would not be moving with her to the strains of some classical waltz, both of them keeping perfect time as he led her around the floor.

He would not be kissing her.

But this was a dream, and he had them so rarely that he was not willing to give this one up. Aware of being watched, knowing they would be monitoring him, it didn't matter because the press of her mouth on his was too good. The slide of her tongue along his, too sweet.

He groaned when she aligned her body with his. Softness. Breasts and hips and the curve of her ass under his hands. His cock ached. She rubbed herself against him. She slid a hand between them. Stroking.

"Kiss me," she said.

He did. Then again. She shivered and tipped her head back to give him access to her throat. Her collarbones. She was naked, all smooth skin and warmth. She pulled him down onto a bed—where had a bed come from? He didn't know. Did not care. All the mattered was moving his lips and tongue over every part of her body.

He found the salty heat between her thighs. He parted her. Found the small spot that made her writhe and sink her fingers into the meat of his biceps. He licked her, soft and slow and steady. When he felt her body tense, he moved up and over her to sink inside her.

It's a dream, he thought. *None of this is real.*

He couldn't stop it, though. Pushing his cock inside her heat was better than anything he'd ever imagined possible. He pushed deeper, deeper, pleasure consuming him.

In the way of dreams, some of the details were blurry. Her face, though. Her smile. Her body, welcoming him. All of that was clear as anything.

He moved faster, and she moved with him. Everything around them faded away until it was only the two of them. Naked, skin on skin. Mouth on mouth. Heat and wetness and friction, building up and up until he couldn't hold back anymore.

He woke a second or so before his climax. Fingers clutching the sheets, body tense and straining, he gave up to the rush of pleasure. His cock was so hard it had slipped free of the waistband of his scrubs, and hot fluid spurted onto his belly in a series of forceful jets that left him spent and breathless.

Let them watch, he thought, blinking at the ceiling. Let them get their jollies, if they did. Let them monitor him, make their reports.

He was still alive, and his body was still his, no matter what they did to him. They couldn't take that away. And they could never get inside his head.

Chapter 14

"We've arranged for you to switch shifts with the other nurse," Vadim said via video call. "It seems she and her husband were the lucky winners of a weekend in the Poconos, and they haven't had a real vacation in years. She was quite beside herself with excitement."

Samantha had come in from a run, still sweating, drinking from a tall bottle of fruit water. She tipped her chair back to eye the computer screen. "It's happening? You have confirmation?"

"Bentley cracked the encryption on the transfer orders. It's going down tomorrow."

"And if it doesn't? If it's a decoy?" Samantha didn't like the sound of this. Most of the work the Crew handled dealt with the research and occasional hunting of creatures. Sometimes hauntings. Not double agenting for secret private organizations determined to raise an army of telekinetic soldiers. She was confident in her skills, but it all still depended on accurate information.

"Then we'll arrange for you to switch shifts again."

She laughed at that with a shake of her head and swallowed another gulp of water before capping the bottle and setting it on the desk. She leaned forward, wrists on her knees, to look closer at the laptop screen. She swallowed again, this time against a slightly bitter aftertaste that didn't come from the drink. "Do you know how they plan to do it?"

"As the nurse on duty, you will be asked to give him an additional amount of sedatives in order to keep him calm when they come for him." Vadim looked serious.

"And I'll palm it?"

"No. You'll have to give it to him, of course. He needs to be compliant when they take him out. No chance of him using any of his abilities, should they not have gone latent the way they believe. He'll need to be controllable until you can get him to us, where we can keep him safe."

This didn't sound right to her. "But if he knows I'm there to help him…"

"He killed three men with nothing more than a twitch of his fingers, Samantha."

"Years ago," she countered. "And I'm willing to bet they deserved it."

"We can't risk him getting out of control. You could be hurt or even killed."

"He wouldn't do anything to hurt me," she said, thinking of all these last months, of the scent of lavender, the tickle of fingertips at the back of her neck. Of the guard who'd been harassing her, the one who'd been put down so easily by something unseen.

"You can't be certain of that, and we won't risk it."

Samantha frowned. "I don't like the idea of drugging him, Vadim. It will make it too hard to work with him."

"All you need to do is take care of the guards and get the van to the rendezvous point. We'll be there to help."

She still didn't like it, but there was no point in pushing it. "Fine. So I give him the drugs. Then what?"

"They take him. You follow. Dispatch the guards. Take the van."

"I'm ready," she said quietly. It was what they'd spoken about early on, almost two years ago, when Vadim had first asked her if she'd be able to take on this responsibility. What she would be ready to do in order to save this man's life.

Vadim paused. "Samantha, I don't think I need to impress upon you how much we appreciate your contributions to the Crew. How valuable you are to us."

"It's always nice to be loved," she said with a small smile. "But what are you getting at?"

"We've been aware of the Wyrmwood facilities for a long, long time. This is the first time we've successfully infiltrated. This would be our first successful extrication of one of the original Collins Creek subjects. We're counting on your many skills to get Jed Collins out of there as unharmed as possible…"

"That would be the ultimate goal, yes. To get him out without being harmed, without anyone being harmed. Without bringing any attention to the Crew." She studied him through the computer screen. "But that's not what you're getting at."

"You're important to us, that's what I'm getting at."

"More important than Jed?" Samantha asked quietly.

Vadim nodded, looking serious. "Absolutely. If it comes down to it, Samantha, and you feel you've been at all compromised, no matter where you are in the rescue, you get out. Even if it means leaving him behind."

"Leaving him to die?"

"Yes," Vadim said.

"I'm not going to do that." She shook her head. "No way."

"Samantha, Jed's been kept in a high-security facility for almost the entirety of his life. The studies and tests they did on him before his skills began to deteriorate were some of the most highly controversial results ever to come out of a program like the Collins Creek experiment. The Crew's been aware of him for a long time, but we're not in the business of making soldiers. Nor in rehabilitating them…"

"He's not a soldier." She shook her head again, forcing herself not to raise her voice. "I mean, I've read the reports, too, and yes, there were all those tests, all the things they proved he could do…but he doesn't do them. He can't anymore. He hasn't been able to, not in years. That's why they're going to kill him—he's done being useful."

"Samantha, I think you need to ask yourself something." For a moment, she was sure Vadim was going to question her about the inappropriate sexual attraction she'd been fighting, but the older man simply said, "What's more important to you? Saving his life? Or saving your own?"

Saving Jed's life, or saving her own.

It seemed like a simple choice, didn't it? It wouldn't even be the first time she'd had to face a choice like that, and look, Samantha had her damage. Everyone did. Hers was that she'd been raised by a man who'd taught her how to kill someone with her bare hands before she'd ever learned to drive a car. She'd grown up in bunkers and safe houses, surrounded by weapons and preparing every day for the end of the world. If it came right down to it, she'd always known that if there was a choice between saving her own life and that of another, she was going to look out for number one.

That did not mean she was the sort to cut and run, though. She never would've agreed to take on this job if she hadn't believed with everything inside her that not only could she protect and rescue Jed Collins when the time was right, but also that he was worth making the effort for.

As a child, Jed had not understood what a full belly felt like. In the compound, there were no regular mealtimes. Deprivation was constant. Fasting had been considered a way of praying and starvation a blessing.

He'd rarely been hungry since coming to Wyrmwood, but his stomach grumbled now. He'd been avoiding finishing his meals. The bitter undertaste of the drugs had kept him from it. They were trying to sedate him beyond the pills he was regularly given.

Scarier than that was the fact nobody had said a word about the unfinished trays he sent away after every meal. Two days since his last session with Ransom, and Jed had barely nibbled some dry toast and eaten a handful of nuts. He'd expected to be called down to the doctor's office after the first day of not eating.

It was time, he thought. Or would be, soon. The thought didn't upset him as much as he thought it would.

Still and silent, he closed his eyes. Let his breathing slow and deepen. He was far from sleep, but even if they were still somehow monitoring his brain waves, it wouldn't matter. He didn't have consistent brain waves, nothing that could be called normal, even for himself. It had been one of Ransom's greatest frustrations, that inability to compare and contrast the test results to see if they could re-create what happened when Jed used his abilities.

He sent out some tickling tendrils of thought, creeping like mice along the edges of the room. To the door. Around the frame. Through the cracks. Whispering into the hallway. Inching like a worm in the patterns on the tile, toward the nurse's station.

He stopped, startled enough to open his eyes before forcing himself to close them again, shifting as though he were dreaming. That was silly. He hadn't dreamed in years, though none of the unseen observers would know that.

Samantha was in the chair behind the desk. Playing a game of solitaire with real, physical cards. The edges soft and worn. Her fingers moved quickly, flipping the cards. Matching. Laying them down.

When he sent himself out this way, it had always seemed to Jed as though he were floating. Invisible, even to himself. He could feel himself reach for something, but his body didn't actually move and he didn't see his own hand. Nor his body. If he turned to face a reflective surface, all he saw was whatever was behind him. He could feel, though. The coolness of the tile floor on his bare feet. The hush of the air currents pushing warmth from the vents in the ceiling. He could smell the scent of her soap and the mint gum she chewed.

He'd been "flying" for years. It was the only way he could tolerate being kept in that small room, the only breaks being the walks to the testing rooms or his sessions with Dr. Ransom. When he was younger, he'd gone outside, but it was harder to control himself without walls and a ceiling to keep him anchored in place. When he was a little older, he'd considered letting himself get lost.

Never coming back. His body would eventually die, and he would…what?

He'd never figured that part out.

Now, he watched her. This was not her shift, but a quick nudge of the computer pulled up the schedule to see she'd switched with Patty, who was taking a few days off. He did it so fast, opening and then closing the file to return the monitor to its sleep screen, there should've been no way for her to notice.

Samantha, however, paused in the placing of the card in her hand. She looked up, not at the computer, but out toward where Jed would've been standing, if he were physically there. She tilted her head, a small smile quirking the side of her mouth. Without moving her head, she allowed her gaze to cut toward the computer screen. Then flicked back in front of the desk. She gave a low murmur and shook her head, then bent back to her cards.

I'm here, he wanted to say. *I'm right here, and I need you to see me. Really see me.*

He could've pushed those words into her mind, but again restrained himself from crossing that line. He continued to watch her for a while, thinking of the dream. It was the closest he would ever get to her, he thought, unable to make himself move on. He moved in a slow circle around her, taking in the card game. The opened wrapper of her granola bar. His phantom stomach clenched with hunger. She looked up, though there was no way she could've heard the boing-going of his belly from this far away.

Again, she tilted her head. Listening. She put the cards down, sweeping them into a pile and tapping them to get them in place before setting them aside. She looked at the computer, still asleep.

"Jed?" she whispered.

Swift as a blink, he was back in his room. Sitting up on the bed, blinking, gasping aloud. Both hands clutching his guts, his hunger pressed aside for the moment by a spasm of nausea. He swung his feet over the side, letting his shoulders hunch. Not caring if the unblinking and all-seeing eye of the camera watched him.

A minute or so later, the door opened. He lifted his head without moving from the bed. Samantha stepped through with a tray she set on the table without a word.

"You should eat," she said.

"Not hungry."

"You're hungry," she said. "I…"

Felt it.

Jed did not allow himself to react. He couldn't read minds. He could catch feelings, and because people didn't think in sentences and paragraphs, but in images and scraps of emotion, he could sometimes get a handle on what they were thinking. Or maybe he only imagined he could.

"I don't want to eat," Jed said.

Samantha moved closer. Briskly, she pulled out her stethoscope. "How about I check you out, make sure everything's okay?"

"I'm fine," he said. Too harsh. Too cold. He didn't want her to touch him.

She stopped a few feet from him. "Jed. If you're not feeling well, I can call the doctor."

"I feel fine. I'm not hungry. Just tired. Go away and let me sleep."

She took another step closer to him. He shrugged away from her touch on his shoulder, though he wanted nothing more than to lean into it. To gather her close, to press his forehead against the welcoming softness of her belly. To have her stroke her fingers through his hair…

"You need to let me check you out," she said in a firm, no-nonsense voice that finally made him look at her.

"Or what? You'll call the guards? Have them restrain me?"

Her pale blue eyes flashed for a moment, but the rest of her expression remained neutral. "I don't want to do that. I just want to make sure you're all right. That's all. Your chart says you haven't eaten in the past couple days, and I have some new meds I'm required to give you. On an empty stomach, they could make you sick."

"I'm not an idiot," Jed said. "I've been on some kind of medication or another for the past twenty-some years. And I don't need anything new, so you can take them and shove them up Dr. Ransom's ass."

He said it to shock her, to get a reaction from her. Not pity. That would've pissed him off. But something. An acknowledgment, maybe, that this situation was as fucked up as a life could be. It might be all he'd ever really known, but he still knew that.

"I know you're not an idiot." Now she glanced upward at the camera. Her expression firmed. She looked at him. Lowered her voice. "You should eat to keep up your strength."

"They put stuff in the food," he said, not bothering to keep himself quiet. He also threw a glance toward the camera and its bland, unyielding gaze. "I told Ransom I didn't need anything for anxiety. He's having them put it in the food. I can taste it. I don't need anything else on top of it."

An expression he couldn't name skittered across her face. Her lips pressed together. "Will you let me examine you for the records? Please. I'll just check your vitals. Same as usual."

He stared at her for a long, silent moment before finally nodding sharply. "Fine. But I'm not going to eat anything. I told him, I don't need anything to keep me calm."

"Of course not." She moved closer. Her fingertips pressed beneath his jaw, probing. She pressed the back of her hand to his forehead in a gesture that surprised him, but swiftly took it away so she could use the stethoscope. Listened to his heart. Took his pulse. The grip of her fingers on his wrist sent his heart beating too fast, the way it always did, but he forced himself not to react.

"They'll come for you." She said it so low into his ear that he couldn't be sure he'd heard her. "Soon. When they do, I'm going to get you away from here. But you need to pretend to take these meds for me. Please."

Then she stepped back, out of reach. "I can't make you eat, but we both know I can call the orderly in here and force you to take the medicine. I don't want to do that. I don't think you want me to have to do that, do you?"

Who was going to come for him? He had heard her say it, he knew it. He hadn't imagined it. And he knew she was right, because he'd been waiting for that to happen. The question was, how did Samantha know it?

"No," he said after a moment at her hard stare. "I guess I don't."

She held up a needle and syringe. Usually they gave him pills. For a second or so when she stepped closer, he was sure she still meant to drug him, and he tensed. Pushing. She felt it, he could tell. Her eyes went a little wide.

"It won't hurt," she said in a bright, false voice, her gaze boring into his. "I promise you."

He knew better than to trust her. She worked for them, didn't she? Yet something made him hold out his arm, bare below the short sleeve of his faded gray scrub shirt. He braced himself for the pinch and sting of the needle, but Samantha kept up a low patter of meaningless small talk as she placed the needle against his skin, but not into it. She dispensed the contents into a small cotton ball she then pretended to use to cover up the puncture.

"There," she said. "You're going to be just fine."

Samantha wanted to linger, but that would be the best way to ruin this whole operation. Instead, she looked closely into Jed's eyes, thinking of the reports that had tested his telepathic talents. When he was younger, he'd been able to choose the circle, square, wavy lines, whatever was on the small cards used in the test kit. He'd been tested for other thought reading, too, without any confirmation that he could do that. Somewhere along the way he'd stopped being accurate. The reports had determined he was incapable of anything beyond the most average of guesswork. His abilities to manipulate physical objects in his environment, that had been substantiated, but they'd never been able to prove he could read minds. One of the doctors had postulated that, even worse, Jed's ability to predict and empathize with the emotions of others was far lower than average.

They'd started assuming he was a sociopath.

Samantha had grown up among sociopaths and didn't believe Jed fit that diagnosis. On the subject of telepathy, she wasn't certain, but right now, she was going to try.

She concentrated, not sure what exactly she was even trying to convey, other than a sense of...comfort? Protection? Reassurance, she thought, though watching Jed scowl, she didn't feel like he was very reassured.

As his caregiver for the past eighteen months, she'd done little more than check his vitals and bring him food once in a while. Their conversations had been necessarily limited. Their physical connection even less so. So why, then, did she feel closer to this man than she'd felt to anyone else in her entire life?

"You're going to feel sleepy," she told him quietly as she put the sharp into the small red box in her pocket. Her eyes searched his for any sign he was on board with this, but there was no way to know what would happen.

"I'll be fine," Jed said.

Something sifted through the air between them like a breeze, moving the tendrils of hair that had escaped around her face to tickle her cheeks. She closed her eyes at the embrace—and it *was* an embrace. A caress. As soft and specific as if he'd reached a hand to cup her face.

She hadn't meant to go off plan, but the idea of sedating him had not settled well with her, no matter what Vadim had said. Jed had not lost his talents. She felt it. She wasn't sure how much control he still had over them, but the last thing in the world she wanted was for him to be left unable to defend himself.

They'd tried to make him into a soldier, she thought. When the time came for it, she might need him to be able to fight.

She risked squeezing his shoulder, a definite no-no on the list of rules regarding the Wyrmwood patients, but what were they going to do? Fire her? Beneath her fingers, Jed's muscles bunched and tensed, although he remained stone-faced. Hands in his lap. Something about it broke her heart in a way she wasn't expecting.

"Are you sure I can't call down to the kitchen for you?"

Jed shook his head without answering. She backed up a few steps. Samantha pressed her fingertip to the door lock and stepped through it. At the sight of the two armed guards, neither of whom she recognized, she quickly shook her head and stepped back into the room, locking the door behind her. Hands flat on it. Facing Jed.

Her heart raced, but she didn't let it show. Instantly she'd begun the mental countdown. The list in her head of every escape route she'd planned since starting here. That had been her father's training—always be ready with a way out.

"I didn't write down your vitals," she said brightly, with a clap of her hands. She moved toward him with a pasted-on smile. "I'm going to have to check you again."

Jed narrowed his eyes. "You never…"

"They're coming," she said in a low voice. Not caring so much now if whoever was watching overheard her.

They were beyond that now.

She didn't hear any muffled voices outside the door. Nothing like a warning. She wouldn't have—the doors here were thick, lined with metal. Soundproof.

Jed stood. "You should go. I don't want you to see this."

Surprised, Samantha shot him a look. She wanted to reassure him again, to tell him that she had this covered, that they weren't going to kill him right there. She drew in a long breath, then let it out. They had guns. This was it. It was happening.

When the door opened, she stepped in front of Jed, addressing the guards in a loud, hard voice. "What's going on? I didn't get any updates about this."

"Step aside, ma'am. We're here to take the patient for some routine testing."

"You'll have to show me your paperwork." She put her hands on her hips, playing up the irate nurse. "You should know this patient is not to be removed from this room without the appropriate precautions. This is highly irregular."

The shorter guard stepped forward. They were both armed, but their weapons were not in hand. She was going to assume they both had hidden weapons in addition to the ones she'd already noticed, but for now she had to worry about the guns she could see.

"Just send him forward," the shorter guard said. "We have directions to take him."

Let them take him, Vadim had said. *Then follow.*

The plan didn't feel right.

"I'm not going with you," Jed said matter-of-factly, as though he was commenting on the weather.

The guard on the left smiled. "Sure, kid."

The other one wasn't as nice. "Shut up. You, get out of the way."

He jerked his chin at Samantha. She settled him with a steady, imperious look. Wyrmwood had a lot of rules, but taking shit from a pair of goons was not one of them.

"C'mon, kid," said the nicer guard as he stepped forward. "I don't want to have to get harsh."

Before he could get any closer, he let out a loud, long cough and stumbled. He tried to take another step but looked as though he was struggling against a glass wall. The other guard let out a startled noise, a muttered curse.

"I'm not going with you," Jed repeated. "But keep on coming. Let's see what happens."

That's when everything started going wrong. The guards moved, one toward Jed and the other toward Samantha. She slipped a hairpin from the heavy bun at the base of her neck, pulling the edges open. With the pin between her fingers, she stepped forward. Ducking low before either of the guards could say a word, she swept the taller guard's leg, not expecting to send him down, just push him off balance. It worked. The taller guard took a hopping step away from her. Without stopping, Samantha moved again, jamming the hairpin into the meat of his calf and pulling it free to stab upward into the hand reaching to grab her.

The shorter guard shouted and grabbed her hair. Without the pin to hold the bun in place, he got a handful, but the thick length of it slipped free as she twisted. Then she was up, ramming her head into his chin and sending him back against the wall.

She acted without thinking ahead more than a move or two. Anticipating what would come next, but ready to adjust if she was wrong. Punch, kick, jab for the eyes.

The taller one caught her by the throat, hauling her upright. Neither of them had pulled their weapons—a fact she noticed even with the wind being strangled out of her. They might be there to take Jed away, but they had not been ordered to kill him. Not here, at least. As the red spots began dancing in the edges of her vision, though, she had time to think that they'd have no trouble killing her.

Not that she was going to let them, of course.

She let her body go limp, not fighting, and the sudden weight pushed the guard off balance. In the next second she was up again. His gun was in her hand.

He was on the ground. Then his partner. She'd shot both of them in the legs. The other guard had a hand reaching for his weapon, which she grabbed. Her ears rang from the sound of the shots, but she took the time to aim once more, this time at the camera. When the red light went out, she turned to Jed, who'd stood without moving the entire time.

"I'm a little insulted," he said. "You'd think they'd have hired way more competent guards."

Chapter 15

The woman staring back at him, a gun in each hand, had barely broken a sweat. Her blond hair had come loose from the tight bun she always wore. Her shoulders and chest heaved with her breathing, but her expression was calm. She was still Samantha, but somehow she had become a stranger.

"More will be coming, and they will be more prepared," she told him. "We should get out of here. Now. We don't have much time."

Jed didn't move. "The first attempt on my life came when I was twelve. One of the orderlies had managed to bring in a shiv. He cut me with it before I was able to break all of his fingers. Then his neck. I did it without touching him. There've been two 'rescue' attempts since then. I say *rescue* sarcastically, because I'm guessing wherever they wanted to take me would've been worse even than Wyrmwood."

"They weren't here to rescue you. They were going to take you someplace and kill you."

"I don't know that," he said bluntly, eyeing her.

"You have no reason to trust me," she agreed, which was exactly the right answer to ensure that he did trust her.

Jed looked around the room, then down at the guards, writhing in pain and screaming out curses nobody else could hear. She'd shot the camera while barely aiming. She was good.

"Who sent you?" Jed asked.

Samantha shook her head, that glorious fall of golden hair cascading over her shoulders and down her back. "Nobody. It doesn't matter now. Just know that I'm here to get you out of here, and we have to do it now."

He didn't have to be able to read minds to sense a lie, but she was right. There wouldn't be much time. He'd wondered if there really was someone watching the video feed at all times, and now he was about to find out.

"Don't you want to kill them first?" He pointed at the guards.

Samantha looked surprised. "I'm not usually one to kill for the sake of it. They're neutralized. Isn't that enough?"

The shorter guard started to cry softly. To plead. The other guard muttered a string of threats that Jed ignored.

"You have a soft heart," he said to Samantha.

She laughed, the sound giddy and abrupt and out of place here and now, but welcome for all of that. "That's not what my last boyfriend said. C'mon, before someone else shows up."

He could take care of whoever else might show up. After watching her dispatch the two guards, he figured

Samantha could, too. That didn't mean he was going with her.

"You can't make me go," Jed pointed out, already moving toward her. "They'll kill you for all of this, but they're not going to do anything to me they hadn't already planned to do."

"Why would you want to stay for that?" Samantha asked sharply. She pressed the door lock and opened the door, looking out. Apparently satisfied with what she saw, she looked back at him.

"Because maybe it's my time," Jed said. "Time for this to all end."

She shook her head and grabbed the front of his shirt. "Bullshit. I didn't risk my life so you could stay back like a lab rat, one they're aiming to kill. Let's go."

He followed, if only because she'd yanked him so hard that he would've stumbled if he hadn't moved. Samantha moved to the door, pressing her fingers into the lock. The door didn't open.

She muttered a curse and shot a glance over her shoulder at the cameras. "They know."

Jed moved over the red line, tensing for a few seconds automatically, although he knew nothing would happen to him. Behind him, the guards groaned and writhed, letting out soft shrieks when he sent a wave of agony to keep them from getting up. "Move away."

"But the metal—"

"It doesn't matter." He took a faint joy in surprising her, but didn't waste time explaining. It needed only a small push, an easy twist of the lock's interior tumblers, and the door was buzzing open.

There were more guards out there, faces obscured by masks. Armored vests. Giant guns. Samantha shouted, but her hands went up. Jed, grateful she hadn't tried to fight them, held out a hand with his fingers spread. The three guards in the front went to their knees, backs arching and booted feet drumming at the tile floor.

It hurt.

He didn't stop. Once it had begun, he wasn't sure he could stop. Too many years of suppressing himself. Too much anger, coming out now.

He curled his fingers into fists. Pushed outward. Feeling each of the guards, the ones on the floor and the ones behind them, still standing. Feeling Samantha.

Then he felt nothing much at all.

Samantha didn't know what happened. First there were a half dozen guards in the hallway, all of them in riot gear and armed. In minutes they were on the ground, writhing and screaming. There was blood, lacy spatters on the tile. Her head ached, and instead of the smell of lavender, her nostrils burned with a bitter stink she couldn't identify.

Jed had done this without so much as a single mutter or gasp. Now he staggered, a hand going to his temple. A thin runner of crimson trickled from the inside corner of his left eye.

She didn't wait. She took him by the elbow and herded him toward the stairs, certain the elevator would be shut down. The alarms in Wyrmwood seemed to be as hushed as everything else in the hospital, no sound, but eye-piercing blue-white lights that lined the corridor had begun to throb and flash. The door to the stairwell was locked, of course, her fingerprints doing nothing to open the lock. Jed did that with a weary sigh and shake of his head.

"Are you okay?" She slung his arm over her shoulders, supporting his weight.

"What are we going to do?" His voice was slurred,

but he wasn't sagging against her. He was still moving. "They're going to be everywhere."

"This isn't how it was meant to go." They rounded the landing and kept going.

Incredibly, he chuckled. "So in other words, you have no idea."

They got to the bottom of the stairs, and the door there proved to be no more trouble than anything else. There weren't any guards waiting for them, although the lights were still flashing. Nathan had risen from behind his security station, his eyes wide. His hand went to the gun at his belt.

"Samantha!" His gaze went to Jed, eyes going even wider. "Oh, shit."

"I don't want to hurt him," Jed said.

Samantha didn't want Nathan to get hurt. When he sat back down, she pushed Jed past him, to the front doors. To the parking lot beyond. Then to her car, which she'd parked as usual to the far end of the lot. She slid behind the wheel; Jed was passenger. Her keys were in her purse, which was back on the desk.

It didn't matter. She looked over at Jed and he took care of that, too. The car's engine churned, turning over. Something about it didn't sound right, but when she put it in gear and stepped on the gas, the vehicle shot forward. She drove, fast as she dared, certain that at any moment a fleet of SUVs were going to show up on her tail.

Beside her, Jed's head drooped. Concerned, Samantha poked him. "Put your seat belt on."

He gave her a strange look. "Huh?"

She gestured. "Your seat belt…"

Too late she realized it was entirely possible he had no idea what a seat belt was or how to use one. An eye on the road, she reached, but there was no way she was going to be able to grab the belt. She had to pull over and put it on him, and risk being caught. Or she could keep going and risk killing him if she got into an accident.

"They can't see us." His voice slurred. He drooped forward even more.

Alarmed, Samantha braked slowly to keep from sending him through the windshield. "Jed. Are you okay?"

"They can't. See. Us. Blocking. Feel." With that, he fell forward, hard enough to smack his head on the dashboard with a thud so loud it hurt her head.

Chapter 16

Jed couldn't remember the last time he'd actually slept so hard that when he woke he didn't know where he was. Maybe never in his life. He woke now, disoriented. Dim light, so much darker than the almost constant pale glow he was used to. Pain ripped through his head and he rolled onto this side, thinking he might get sick. He fought the nausea off and sat up.

"Hey." He felt her before he saw her face in the soft glow of a candle she lit. Samantha smiled at him. "How do you feel?"

"Bad." He let his face fall into his hands. "Where are we?"

She cleared her throat. "It's a safe house."

"How safe?" He gave her a sideways look.

"As safe as…it can be. Are you hungry? I have some soup. It's not very hot. But it will settle your stomach." She leaned forward into the circle of golden light. "Jed, I'm going to touch your forehead. Okay?"

She'd asked permission first. He moved his hands away from his face to look at her. "Why?"

"I want to be sure you don't have a fever. You've been sleeping for the past day and a half, and you were burning up. May I?"

"Why are you asking me?" he said in a flat voice.

In the candlelight, Samantha's blue eyes looked very dark. "Because I think you deserve the right to decide who puts their hands on you."

"You're not really a nurse, are you." He'd suspected as much for some time—she'd never "felt" the way the other nurses had.

"No."

He didn't seem feverish, but that wasn't why he hadn't yet given her permission to touch him. He was more afraid of what he might do now that they were away from the hospital, with nobody to stop him from kissing her. His head ached and buzzed in the aftermath of all the pushing he'd done. His self-discipline would be nonexistent.

"What are you?"

Samantha looked surprised. "I'm…just a person."

She was more than that, but he could tell she wasn't being facetious. "Are you a soldier? Who do you work for?"

"I work for an organization called the Crew that specializes in investigating and proving or disproving the existence of paranormal or other umm…" She coughed lightly. "Oddities."

"Like children bred and raised in a cult designed to create extrasensory mental abilities?" He turned to face her. His headache was softening. His mouth, though, had gone dry, his throat scratchy. If he'd been asleep as long as she'd said, he'd missed several doses of meds. This was going to hurt.

"Yes, like that. Are you sure you feel all right?"

He frowned. "Of course I don't feel all right. I just got busted out of a top secret research facility to prevent my murder. Unless you still plan to off me."

"No!" She looked startled and shook her head, moving closer. "No, look. I know you have no reason to trust me…"

"I can feel if you're lying to me," Jed interrupted in a low voice, very conscious of her body heat and the faint smell of her shampoo.

She studied him for a moment with a curious tilt of her head. A faint smile. "Can you?"

"Yes."

"Can you feel anything else about me?"

Jed looked into her eyes. "Yes. I can tell that you want to touch me. I told you, I don't have a fever. But if you need to check, go ahead."

"I don't need to check you for a fever if you're feeling all right. But I do want to touch you. Yes. Can you feel that?"

He could feel something inside her, but it was so much a part of everything that made Samantha who she was that he couldn't untangle it from the rest. She moved closer to him. He tensed, unsure of what she meant to do. At the brief brush of her fingertips across his forehead, he sighed and closed his eyes.

"What do you feel about me?" she asked quietly.

He tried to show her, but although it was easy enough to make things happen around him, making a person *feel* something was completely different. There was more to it than emotion. Desire. Longing. Anxiety. There was also sensation.

The touch of fingertips on the inside of his wrist.

The smell of her shampoo.

The sound of her voice.

He tried his best to give her all of this, everything that made up who she was, to him. Convinced he'd failed, Jed opened his eyes. Samantha's eyes glistened with tears.

She kissed him.

Chapter 17

Even as Samantha slanted her mouth against Jed's, she wondered if he was manipulating her into this. She knew all too well what his talents could do. Yet, there'd never been anything in her life that she wanted to do more in that moment than to kiss him, and she hadn't even tried to resist it.

His lips were soft and warm. They parted instantly when she put her mouth on his. He was surprised, she thought as she cupped the back of his neck. He wasn't trying to get his tongue inside her mouth. She'd startled him. It didn't matter. The kiss deepened in the next minute, and she couldn't tell and didn't care who'd initiated it. There was an ebb and flow to this kiss she could not deny.

Neither of them could.

She did not break the kiss, but she did ease her mouth away. She pressed her cheek to his. Her other hand went to his chest, over his heart. Hers was beating so hard she could feel the throb of it at the base of her throat, and after so many months of checking his vitals, she could tell at once that his was beating much faster than normal, too.

"The other day. When you were giving me the checkup," he said.

She remembered. "Yes."

"I'm sorry. I shouldn't have…it was wrong to do that to you."

He was serious. She sat back, frowning. "What?"

"I shouldn't have touched you like that, without asking. Without you saying it was okay."

"You didn't touch me, Jed."

He furrowed his brow. "I did, and you know it. I don't have to use my hands. You know that, too."

"Did it feel like I didn't want you to?" She sat back, but only a little. She let the hand over his heart slip down his arm to circle his wrist. Then to take his hand, linking their fingers. He wouldn't look at her.

She'd never seen Jed react emotionally to much of anything. She'd long assumed it was the meds they kept him on. The years of isolation and lack of normal social contact. Now, though, he pressed his lips together and swallowed hard, blinking away tears.

"Jed." She turned his face gently to face hers. "Did it ever feel to you like I didn't want you to touch me?"

"I don't know!" he shouted, and pushed away from her to stand and pace.

She'd chosen the small, empty bedroom off the safe house kitchen because of its first-floor access, in case they needed to get out the windows, which had been covered with blackout curtains. It was little more than the size of a walk-in closet, barely big enough for the sagging twin mattress on the floor, so he didn't have much room to move. He spun on his heel when she stood, moving in front of him so he had no choice but to face her.

"You know how I feel. If I had ever once thought or felt like you were manipulating or hurting me in any way, you'd have known it." Samantha wasn't positive if this was true. There'd been hundreds of tests done to research what Jed could do. Nothing about how it affected him emotionally or mentally. "Right?"

Reluctantly, he nodded. "Yes."

"You didn't hurt me. You didn't do anything to me that I didn't…want." It was her turn to swallow hard.

"But why?" he demanded. "Why would you want anything like that from me?"

She shook her head. "I don't know."

"Pity," he said with a sneer that hurt her to see. "Curiosity."

She couldn't deny that at least a little bit of that was true. But not all of it. "Why does anyone ever want something like that from another person? Who knows why two people connect? I've never been able to figure it out. And you know what, I'm not sure I care, to be honest. I haven't been with anyone for a long time. Sex feels good—"

He snort laughed, half choking. "Sex!"

"It feels good," she continued. "Especially with another person, especially with someone you care about. So maybe it wasn't right, what you did. It wasn't right for me to allow it or enjoy it, then. I was your caregiver. It was crossing a line. But it felt good and I didn't stop it. So, who's the one in the wrong?"

"It made you feel good?"

Heat crept up inside her as she lifted her chin. "Yes. Very good."

"It wasn't sex," Jed said. "Not real sex."

He was a virgin, Samantha thought suddenly. All those

years locked up. She wanted to take a step back, but his expression told her he knew what she was thinking. She didn't move. She reached for him instead, snagging his wrist to tug him a step closer to her.

"You didn't do anything to me that I didn't want, even if I didn't know until you did it that I wanted it. And I won't…" She coughed lightly, unsure how to go on without embarrassing them both. *Screw that*, she thought. They were on the run from people who wouldn't hesitate to kill them. She'd gone off plan and had no backup from the organization who'd hired her to protect him. They were in a tiny box of a room with nothing more than a candle and a mattress on the floor. If she couldn't be honest with him about this now, there wasn't going to be any better time. "I won't touch you unless you want me to."

"How could you think I wouldn't want you to?"

Because it was crazy, she thought as Jed moved toward her. Because there wasn't time for this here or now. When he kissed her, there was no more thinking. No more excuses. Jed kissed her as though he'd been waiting a lifetime for the chance to put his mouth on hers, and in a way, maybe he had.

At the stroke of his tongue, Samantha gave a small moan. His hand tightened in her hair while the other found her hip and anchored there. He pulled her against him, and the heat of his erection nudged her through the thin fabric of her nurse's uniform. Somehow they were on the mattress, Samantha straddling Jed's lap as he tugged and tore at the white tights she'd hated since the first day she'd been assigned them. His fingers found her heat beneath; her white cotton panties were about as far from romantic as she could imagine, but he didn't seem to care.

"Oh, my god," Jed whispered into her mouth. "You're so hot, Samantha. So wet."

He'd boldly slid two fingers inside her before she could say a word; all that came out after that was a gasping sigh that spiraled up into a low cry when he began to slide them in and out. Something nudged at her mind, a feeling she remembered from the days in the hospital. Like an inquiry. But this time she knew it was Jed, and she opened herself up to it. Embraced him not only with her body, but her mind.

"Oh…" he said. "Yes. That, there. Now I know."

He might never have touched a woman this way, but it didn't matter. Whatever he was feeling from her showed him exactly what to do. Kissing her harder, he pressed his thumb to her clit, circling as his fingers moved inside her.

Her fingers dug into his shoulder as she pushed herself up a little to slide her hand between them and get at the loose tie of his scrubs. Somehow in seconds after that, he was inside her. She had his face in her hands. Their teeth clashed and she let out a small, surprised laugh that turned into a moan when he sucked her tongue.

Jed's hands slipped under her ass to move her. They rocked together. The sound of their breathing was loud in her ears, harsh in her throat as she gasped with the pleasure filling her.

They should slow down, she thought. Savor this. Make it special…

"It's all right," Jed said. "I don't need candles or rose petals, Samantha, just fuck me."

His words sent shards of icy fire through her. She ground herself against him as her climax rose. Shuddering, she tipped over the edge with her face pressed into the curve of his shoulder. For a moment she couldn't move, she could only let her body take over, clenching on him.

It seemed that was enough. Jed said her name in a low,

hoarse rasp and arched. His fingers tightened on her hard enough to hurt, but only for a second before he eased the grip. They moved together for another few strokes before she looked into his eyes, once again cupping his face.

Jed blinked, gaze hazy. He slid his tongue along his lower lip. She'd seen him smile before, but this was the first time she'd ever seen it fully reach his eyes.

"Thank you," Jed said. "Wow. That was amazing. You were right, sex is great."

He didn't have to be able to feel her to know that whatever he'd said wasn't quite right. Her quickly shuttering expression did that for him. Samantha made to get off him, but he held her hips and waited until she'd looked at him.

"Wait."

"We need to clean up and get some sleep. We need to be out of here when it gets dark," she said matter-of-factly. "I need to get you to a rendezvous point where they can take you to someplace really safe."

"Samantha…didn't you…want to?" Again horrified at the thought that somehow he'd manipulated her into having sex with him, Jed let her go.

She got up, rearranging the clothes they hadn't even taken off. Was that the problem? Should he have undressed her all the way? They should've been naked. Had he misread her?

"I wanted to. Yes. I told you, sex feels good. And you obviously wanted it, too. So we're both good. That's all. I'm going to the bathroom."

He followed her, waiting outside until he heard the water running in the sink before nudging open the door. "You're angry."

"No. Look." She turned. "I was assigned to take care

of you, to protect and watch over you and to get you out of there when it was time. Not to fuck you. This complicates things, that's all."

Jed had watched hours of daytime television, enough to know that what she said could be true. But... "Does it have to be?"

She stepped aside to let him into the bathroom, where he used the toilet unselfconsciously until he noticed she was looking away with a strange expression. He finished and turned to the sink to wash his hands. It hadn't occurred to him to be modest about it—he'd spent his entire life being observed through cameras.

"I'm sure you've watched me pee before," he said.

She shook her head. "That's not... Jed. We can't..."

"Can't what?" He shook his hands as dry as he could and took her by the upper arms. "Samantha, talk to me."

"Can't you just feel what I'm thinking?" she said, sharp and fierce.

Angry? Disappointed. No...something else he couldn't quite name.

"It doesn't really work that way," Jed said. "You should just tell me."

In answer she left the tiny bathroom and headed back to the small bedroom, where she kicked off her shoes and stripped out of the shreds of her tights. She tossed them in the corner, then put her shoes back on. He watched her from the doorway for a few seconds before coming into the room to stand near the mattress.

"You can have it," he said, pointing. "To sleep."

"Don't be ridiculous. We can share it."

"It's not much better than the floor," he pointed out. "And I don't want you to feel like you have to."

She drew in a long, deep breath. "C'mon. Let's just

get some sleep, okay? When it gets dark, we'll get out of here."

Together, they stretched out on the hard mattress. There wasn't much room, but he put his back against the wall to make sure there was space between them, which she seemed to want. Without the candle, the only light came in through cracks around the closed door and the rooms beyond.

He listened to her breathing slow. She was dozing, not fully asleep. Because she was making sure to be ready in case she needed to protect him, he thought.

He didn't want to need protection.

Jed put a hand on Samantha's hip, urging her back against him. She woke, everything about her going tense and alert and aware, but she softened after a second and shifted to let him hold her. He wasn't entirely sure why she'd gone distant from him, but if this was the last chance he ever had to hold her, he was going to take it.

"You're not like anyone else," he said against her shoulder, his voice muffled.

Samantha drew a breath and turned her face a little. "No?"

"No."

"You don't really know anyone else," she said.

Jed closed his eyes, breathing in her scent. "I know you."

"Yes," Samantha said after her heart had thumped four or five times. "You do know me. I'm not entirely sure how, but you do."

"I'm sorry if I upset you."

She didn't say anything for long enough that he'd started to drowse. Her voice was quiet enough not to fully wake him, but he knew it wasn't a dream. "Is it crazy for me to feel like I know you, too?"

Jed nuzzled the back of her neck. "Nobody else ever has."

Her shoulders rose and fell; she gave a hitching half sob that made him open his eyes and frown. He hugged her, marveling in this simple contact that meant so much. Felt so good.

"You're going to have a whole, huge world to learn. New people to meet. This won't be... I will just be the first," she said. "I won't be the only."

He wasn't sure how to answer her. He could feel her confusion and the rest of her tangled emotions, but that didn't mean he understood them—because she didn't. "Do you want to be the...only?"

"That wouldn't be fair." She didn't turn from his embrace, though something in the way she tensed made him feel as though she wanted to.

Jed laughed. "What's fair? I can't think of much of anything in my life that's ever been fair."

Samantha sat, twisting on the mattress to look down at him. "But this should be."

He sat, too. "What are you saying?"

"Never mind. We should rest. Are you feeling okay?"

He wasn't, but it had nothing to do with his efforts during their escape. As she settled back onto the mattress, once more putting a distance between them, Jed tentatively tried to reach toward her with his talents. To figure her out.

But no matter how he tried, he couldn't get inside her.

Chapter 18

The safe house had running water, but it was cold. That turned out to be fine. They didn't have time to linger over anything, and the frigid water slapped some sense into her. Yesterday had been a mistake, there was no question, but it didn't have to be irreversible. In a few hours, they'd reach the pickup spot where Vadim's Crew members would take Jed somewhere safe.

In the kitchen, she found him at the sink. "You shouldn't stand by the window."

He looked at her. "It's fine. I can't feel any of them around here."

"Could you? If they were close enough?"

"Yeah." He shrugged. "I could feel if someone meant harm. Maybe not who it was or where they came from, but yeah."

"We need to get going. It's about a five-hour drive."

"I'm not going," Jed said.

Samantha shook her head. "Yes. You are. Please don't make me—"

"What?" Jed asked calmly. "What can you do to me, Samantha? I know you're trained. You've used weapons. I know you've killed a man."

She tensed, stepping back involuntarily. "It was the job. He—"

"He made you afraid. I know. I can feel that. But do you think you could kill me? I know you felt like you might have to," Jed said. "I know you weren't sure if you could. Do you think you could now, to stop me from getting away?"

She could not, and he had to know it. She shook her head, her eyes meeting his. "Why do you want to get away? I'm trying to help you. The Crew is trying to help."

"I spent almost my entire life locked away while people tried to get inside my head. Do you think, now that I'm out, that I'm going to allow anyone to lock me away again?"

"They won't," she began, but stopped herself. In truth, she had no idea what Vadim planned to do with Jed.

"There came a time when I knew I could get away from Wyrmwood at any time," Jed said. "When there was nothing they could do to keep me. I could've killed them all, Samantha. Or just hurt them. I could have walked out of there at any time without anyone getting hurt at all. I didn't for a long, long time because I had no reason to believe that anything beyond the walls would be any better. Until you came along."

"Let me take you to people who will help you," Samantha said. "You don't have to do this alone."

He shook his head. "I'm not going with you."

"Where will you go?" she demanded. "You don't know

how to drive a car, you have no money, no identification, nothing…"

Jed shrugged. "You know what I can do. I'll make my way. Maybe I'll travel. See everything I only ever watched on television."

"I can't let you go," Samantha said.

She didn't mean only that she could not let him run away from the Crew. She meant more than that. He had to know it, she thought as the scent of lavender came up to surround her. She couldn't let him go, because he'd come to mean too much to her.

He had to feel it, didn't he?

"You don't want to hurt me," she said in a low voice. Time had slowed and the world around her had gone a little blurry.

"I'm not going to hurt you, Samantha."

She woke up on the bare and lumpy mattress. Darkness outside. He had not hurt her, no.

He'd left her.

Chapter 19

Persephone hadn't seen her brother in months, but that didn't mean much. Phoenix had a wanderlust and an inherent distrust of anything resembling settling down. The last she'd heard, he was somewhere in Europe, playing with a minor princess from some small country she didn't remember the name of. So when she opened the door to a knock, seeing him on the other side was a surprise.

She ought to have known better, because a day later, he'd managed to get her to write down all the login information for her bank accounts, all of them, even the hidden and secret one she kept for her shady business deals. Then he'd made her forget she'd done it, so when she woke up and found him missing along with a note of apology, he'd already wiped her out.

He'd left her a gift card to the coffee shop, though. What a prince, she thought as she used it to pick up a coffee and a muffin. What a fucking prince.

"Hi, Persephone."

She turned, already feeling a flush of heat in her throat because she knew that voice. Kane. He smiled at her. She couldn't manage to give him one in return.

He lifted his cup toward her. "This place makes the best coffee, huh?"

"Yes." She couldn't stop herself from thinking about kissing him. She never saw any of the other men she went to bed with, and this was why, she reminded herself. It made her want to kiss him again, and that was too dangerous with anyone, but especially with him.

Somehow they ended up sharing a table and he was making her laugh. Making her forget that Phoenix had screwed her over, or that her life was a long string of bad decisions and shady situations. With Kane, she didn't feel like she had to put on a show...except of course she did, Persephone reminded herself with a shock when she looked at the clock to see that an hour had passed.

They walked out together. On the sidewalk outside, a man wearing jeans and a coat too heavy for the late fall day watched them from the corner. A cigarette in his mouth. Assessing. Keeping her attention seemingly focused on Kane, Persephone created an illusion of a much older woman, heavier and dowdy, for whoever that guy was. When she looked again, he was gone.

It didn't mean he'd been looking for her, she thought. It could've been anyone. Or maybe he wasn't working alone, and even though she'd sent the illusion his way, someone she hadn't even seen might have been able to match her to a picture.

"You okay?" Kane paused at the top of the concrete front steps of their apartment building. "You got quiet."

Persephone shrugged, knowing she seemed distant now and not liking it. But what could she do? Giggle and coo with him? Tell him she'd already seen him naked but he had no idea it was her?

"Fine. Just need to get some things done." She left him and went down into the basement to her own place.

She should pack her shit and go. She had cash hidden away for that very reason, a stash her brother hadn't seen, so hadn't been able to steal from her. It would be enough to get her settled someplace else. Get her away from anyone who might've tracked her here, who was watching.

Or she was being crazy, overreacting, she told herself and forced a breath, then another. She thought again of Kane's touch, his mouth, but now she thought also of the way he'd made her laugh. He was more than good-looking—he was smart and funny, too. And, for whatever reason, he seemed to be into her.

She should go, Persephone thought as she pulled out her laptop and started scrolling through her contacts to see what kind of financial business she could get going for herself, and quick. Run. Leave this behind.

But the lingering flavor of coffee was nothing like the way Kane had tasted, and so even though she knew she was being crazy, she was still going to stay here for a while longer.

Chapter 20

Six months later

It was time to stop looking for him. Jed had vanished as completely as any human being could, and considering the vast extent of the Crew's reach, that said something about how insistent he was on not being found. Samantha had taken jobs that sent her all over the country and none of them had brought her close to finding him.

He was not coming back.

At first, she'd told herself it was because she was worried about him making it out there in the world, but she knew he'd have found a way to be okay. Later, when the search had continued, she had to admit there was more to it than her concern for him. She missed him. She... wanted him.

It hadn't been love, she told herself now, sullen and cranky as she dropped her bag on a chair in the Crew cafeteria. She wanted food first. Then a shower. Then her bed. She'd finished investigating the possibility of a werewolf attack in the middle of Montana, a gig that had meant a lot of long hours in the wilderness. She'd been cold. Hungry. A few times, scared. Whatever creature had been killing hikers, though, she had not confirmed it was a werewolf.

The job had brought up a lot of her past. The final night with her father. The blood, the fur, her lack of memory. She'd return to Montana soon, but Vadim had called her back before the case had been completed, and she didn't know why. Didn't care, so long as the money came in.

Now, all she cared about was getting something in her stomach.

But there he was, standing in front of her. Eyes a little anxious, but a smile on his face. He'd put on some weight and muscle, and a bristly scruff of reddish beard covered his chin. He looked tired.

"Jed!"

He kissed her, and she let him even though she knew she really should pull away. Her arms went around his neck. Their teeth clashed; she laughed. He sighed. His hands buried themselves in her hair. People were staring, but she didn't care. There was this, only this.

"Shhh, shhh," he said against her mouth. "I didn't want to startle you. I was going to wait until you went to your room, but I couldn't. I saw you, and I couldn't wait. Samantha…"

She broke the kiss then, breathing hard. "Where have you been? Never mind. It doesn't matter."

"I'm here now," he said. "I'm sorry it took me so long."

"I'm so damned angry at you," she said.

She kissed him again. Harder. His tongue stroked hers.

She could not get enough. She wasn't crying, not really, but the world had blurred with the force of her emotions.

"You should be. I was wrong to ditch you. I just had to…"

She cut him off with another kiss. Looked into his eyes. "I understand. I get it. You had to."

"I'm here, though," he said. "I didn't want to keep moving on around in the world without you. All the things I saw and did, everything I thought I wanted to do all those years in the hospital, none of them seemed to matter very much without you next to me."

Samantha drew in a slow breath, aware that everyone in the cafeteria was carefully pretending not to eavesdrop. Not caring what they heard. "That's the nicest thing anyone has ever said to me."

"I don't know a lot of things. It's going to take me a long time learn them. But one thing I already know is there's nobody else in the world I want to be with. First, last, only, Samantha. That's what I want."

His expression made it clear he thought she was going to argue with him, and she knew that would've been the wise thing to do. She couldn't make herself do it. Whatever they would have to deal with, the two of them could face it together, she thought as she kissed him again, this time to the slow round of applause from the people around them.

"Yes. All right, then," she said into his mouth. "Me, too. All of that, and anything else that comes along. I'm in."

* * * * *

PASSION IN DISGUISE

Chapter 1

Staying up all night meant sleeping late the next morning, at least for most people. For Persephone Collins, it meant waking up when the light hit the sky even if her eyes were still gritty and her body aching, even if she wanted nothing more than to be lost in dreams for another hour or six. That was the price you paid for a life of crime, she told herself without even trying to stifle the jaw-cracking yawn. She needed coffee.

She needed a lot of things.

Last night's haul had included enough cash to get her through the next few weeks, if she was careful, but Persephone hadn't spent her life being careful. She counted it out carefully, though, separating the bills and tucking away the largest, a rare fifty, inside the hardbound copy of *The Complete Ray Bradbury Collection* that she kept on the top shelf of the basement apartment's built-in bookcase. She'd picked up the book at a yard sale for a quarter, but it now contained easily several thousand dollars' worth of paper money. Any time she found a bill bigger than a twenty, she tucked it inside. It was the only thing she'd be sure to take with her if she ever had to run.

For today, though, she didn't think she'd have to run. Today she was content to start the coffee brewing while she dispensed with the rest of the cash. At the stove, she made herself an egg and put it onto an English muffin before settling at the table with her laptop and a huge mug of steaming black coffee. She had a lot of leads to follow up on, more than a couple scams to continue.

She wasn't expecting a knock just before eight in the morning, but as the superintendent of a building that hadn't exactly been lovingly tended over the past decade, she also wasn't surprised by the rap of knuckles on her door. Mug in hand, she opened the door to find Kane Dennis on the other side.

He grinned and held up two big cups of what smelled like perfect coffee from that place down the street. When she didn't move forward, he held one out to her. "Here."

"I have some," she said with a lift of her mug. "But thanks. Wow. What's it for?"

"For fixing my hot water…again." Kane's grin softened as he sipped, still holding out the insulated cup. He let out a long sigh. "Mmm. Man, I do not know what they do to that coffee there, but it's so, so good. You sure you don't want it?"

Persephone knew that was true without taking a drink. That coffee shop was like magic. Her own mug, which had been filled with perfectly adequate brew, was no longer quite as appealing. She stepped aside to let him in, waving him toward the table even as she was thinking of excuses to get him out of her apartment without seeming too obvious that she was trying to get rid of him. "You didn't have to do this. Fixing your hot water is my job."

"Does that mean I can't show you my appreciation?" Kane set the cup he'd brought her on the table and looked around her apartment, those gray eyes noticing every detail.

Because that was what he did. Paid attention. Put the pieces together to figure out the truth.

Persephone put her mug on the counter to take a sip from the other cup. "God. So good. So fucking good." She glanced up to see him looking at her. "What?"

Kane shook his head with a small smile. "Nothing. Glad you like it. I figured you would."

For a moment, a long, long moment, she considered tossing the coffee into the sink and tossing Kane onto the table to have her wicked way with him. She could start at the bottom and work her way to the top, she thought with a glance at his heavy black work boots, then those long, long denim-clad legs, those muscled thighs… And she stopped herself before she could get herself into trouble. If Kane had seen her looking, he didn't show it, but that small grin of his had widened.

"Well, hey, thanks for the coffee," Persephone said abruptly, guiding him by the elbow back toward the door.

Kane paused in the doorway. His smile faded. He studied her. "Persephone…"

"What?" Irritated and also a little flustered now at his perusal, she sipped. The coffee burned her tongue, and she winced. Scowling, she lifted her chin. "What?"

"Is there something about me that you don't like?"

She paused, choosing her answer cautiously. "What do you mean?"

"Have I done something to make you think I'm a jerk?" Kane shook his head before fixing her with a steely gaze. "Because it seems like no matter what I do, you look at me like I've somehow done you wrong."

Staring at him now, all she could think about was the way his bristly chin had felt against her throat when he was on top of her. Heat rose up her neck to paint her cheeks. She cut her gaze from his, not wanting him to see her blush—although, of course, he would. Kane saw everything about her.

Everything but the fact she'd been fucking him, randomly on and off, for the past six months.

"I don't think you're a jerk," she said when so much silence had lingered that not saying anything had become awkward. "But…"

"But what?" He eyed her over the rim of his cup.

"We aren't friends."

Kane's mouth twisted. Not quite a smile. "Why not?"

Because she got free rent for being this beat-up old building's superintendent, but she paid her bills through a variety of grifting, scams and outright thievery. Kane was a detective who spent his days and nights putting people like Persephone in jail. Because every other week or so, Persephone used the twisted powers of her brain to make him think she was some other woman so she could pick him up at the local dive bar, take him home and have her wild, wicked way with him. Because she didn't want to have to explain to him where she'd been born and raised and what had been done to her to make her into the freak she was.

Without answering him, she took another sip of the coffee he'd brought her and tried to give him a hard stare. It didn't work very well, because doing that meant she lost herself in the soft gray depths of his eyes, and then she was remembering about the last time he'd been on top of her. How he'd felt inside her. How he'd made her come… and again, she forced herself to get her shit together.

At the sound of Kane's sigh, she waved a hand toward him. "I'm pretty sure your life isn't going to suffer much harm if we aren't besties."

Kane's laugh sound a little stung. "What if I think that having you as a friend would make my life better?"

At this, she took a step back with a lifted brow. "Right, and clearly, whatever you think or feel or want takes precedence over what I think or feel or want. Right? Because you're a guy?"

"Hey, that's not what I—" Kane broke off at the sight of her expression. "Fine. Sorry. I'll go. Thanks for fixing the water heater."

"Thank you for the coffee," Persephone said crisply, leaving no more room for conversation.

She waited until he'd let himself out before she flattened herself against the back of the door and closed her eyes. She listened for the sound of him moving away. For a hesitant, heady moment she imagined him on the other side of the wood, listening for her exactly the same way. Waiting for her to open it, to ask him inside. To take him to bed.

Or to be buddies, Persephone thought with a small curl of her lip. Friends. Maybe they could kick back with a couple of beers and catch some type of sports on TV.

There weren't many things Persephone felt guilty about in her life. The scams? If anyone was stupid enough to fall for them, they deserved to be bilked out of the contents of their bank accounts. The stealing? Okay, so maybe she wasn't quite Robin Hood, but she never took more from anyone than they could clearly afford to lose. And as for using men for their bodies to get her off so she could occasionally sleep longer than twenty minutes a night? None of them had ever complained.

She did feel bad about the way she'd treated Kane, though. He was never anything but nice to her, and she did treat him like she thought he was a jerk. The coffee in her hand was far from the first kind gesture he'd made. It shouldn't have mattered, but something about it did.

She tossed it in the trash.

She went to her bed and slipped beneath the sheets naked, knowing already that no matter how much she tried, she was not going to be able to get enough rest. For that she needed to be worn out from fucking, orgasm after orgasm, and that would require leaving her apartment and trying to find a pickup, and while it wasn't impossible, it didn't seem likely to be easy at nine in the morning.

Persephone closed her eyes. Her hands moved over her body, finding all the secret places that brought her pleasure. It wasn't working, not easily. Not the way another person's touch would have worked.

Not the way Kane touched her.

His hands move over her hips, fingers digging a little into the flesh as he pulls her a little closer to the edge of the bed. Her knees skid on the soft hotel sheets. Her fingers, too. She is facedown, ass up, as the saying goes, and her breath comes swift and rasping in her throat as she opens herself to him.

He's a bit too tall to enter her from behind, but when his thick cock slides inside her, it hits at the perfect angle to make her cry out. Her cheek presses the mattress. Her mouth open, lips wet from the tip of her tongue.

Earlier he kissed her hard enough to bring the taste of blood, and it was this roughness that she thinks of now as he fucks into her. His fingers squeeze her harder. One of his hands slips around to stroke her clit in time with every thrust. It's exactly what she needs, exactly where she needs it.

It's even better when he starts to talk. Urging her in that low, growling voice to let him make her feel good. To give her body to him. He demands her pleasure, and this urges her body to respond exactly in the way he's asking her for.

Muscles tense, tight, her thighs shake as her hips buck. He fucks deeper into her, but not faster. Each stroke of his cock inside her heat is echoed by the circling of his fingers on her clit. Ecstasy builds inside her. Higher and higher, until, finally, she explodes.

Quivering in the aftermath of her orgasm, Persephone let out a small moan and buried her face in her pillow. She'd been thinking of the last time she'd seduced Kane. Of all the men she'd slept with in her life, why was it this man was the one her mind turned to when she needed sexual release?

It was dangerous, she thought as her eyes drifted closed. And she was drawn toward danger, always. She strained toward sleep. Kane was dangerous to her, because she liked him.

Chapter 2

Kane Dennis hadn't fallen off the turnip truck yesterday, as the saying went. Not that Kane ever said it, not aloud. It was something his grandfather, the man who'd raised him, would've been likely to say, though, and in situations like these it seemed appropriate.

Persephone from the basement apartment was hiding something. It was in the way she rarely met his gaze, even when he caught her staring. It was something in her posture, how her head went up and back so straight every time she saw him, as though he'd surprised her into a fight-or-flight reaction and she was just barely resisting the urge to either kick him in the junk or run away.

The question was not, however, what she might be hiding, but why on earth he gave a damn. Whatever it was, it didn't affect him in any way. In the beginning when he'd started getting that vibe from her, he'd been on the lookout for any signs of the usual—drug dealing, prostitution, fencing goods. Anything he would have found impossible to look beyond because it was going on literally right under his nose.

There'd been none of that. Only the subtle, persistent feeling that she knew more about him than he could ever discover about her, and that was what had gotten under his skin like a sliver. That's what he told himself, anyway. That it was curiosity. That she seemed interesting, a woman with stories to intrigue him, a woman who might not be repulsed by the ones he had to tell. It had nothing to do with her body, Kane told himself as he avoided the cranky elevator for the stairs, up a flight to his apartment directly above hers. Nothing to do with her soft strawberry blond hair, cut short to emphasize her giant dark brown eyes and the smooth expanse of her pale throat...

Nothing to do with that at all, he told himself grimly as he went inside his own apartment and dumped his now cold coffee down the sink. How had bringing her a cup of coffee made him into an asshole? Or had it been the fact he'd had to ask her why she didn't like him that had made the corners of her mouth turn down the way they had? Worse than that, what the fuck was wrong with him that seeing her clear discomfort and distaste only made him think about her more? *We chase what runs from us,* Grandpa Charles would've said, and Kane had to agree.

Persephone Collins was running from him, and it drove him crazy with desire because he couldn't figure out why.

"I'll give you a hundred." Chuck gave Persephone a glance over the rims of his reading glasses and shrugged at the sight of her disgruntled expression. "It's the best I can do. Look, you know I can't move this shit very fast. Bring me something I can actually sell, I'll pay you more."

Persephone eyed the array of slightly less than brand-new cell phones and flash drives she'd brought him. She'd known it wasn't likely Chuck would cross her palm with much more than a few pieces of silver, but for the past two weeks she'd kept her sticky fingers to herself—unless someone was foolish enough to walk away from their laptop or phone in a hotel lobby or a coffee shop long enough to get a refill.

"They're all wiped," she pointed out. "Unlocked."

He shrugged again. "Yeah, yeah, but look, you can pick up a refurbed phone for pennies on the dollar anymore. In the box. With a charger."

Persephone frowned. "Fine, I'll take the Benjamin."

It was better than nothing. She pocketed the cash and ducked out of the used electronics shop, glancing out of habit from side to side as she headed down the street. Chuck ran a mostly clean place, hadn't been the target of any raids or anything like that, but you never knew. Maybe it was time to get out of the sticky-fingers game, she thought as she grabbed a bottle of water and a candy bar from the small newsstand on the corner—paying for it with cash from her pocket, not stealing it, although there'd been times in the past when she'd lifted food to keep from starving. She was well beyond that now.

Her phone buzzed in her pocket as she tore the wrapper from the candy. Chewing nougat and chocolate, she answered without looking at the name or number on the screen. Only one person was allowed to get through to her directly on this line.

"What," Persephone said. The liquid male chuckle tickled her eardrum through the distance, and she held the phone away from her face for a second before putting it directly against her mouth to amplify the chewing noises.

"You're disgusting," Phoenix said.

Persephone swallowed the bite of candy. "What do you want? Let me guess, you've run out of funds and you don't have a sugar daddy or mama waiting in the wings."

"Cold, sister mine. So cold."

She pressed her lips together to fight off a smile. He was going to try to charm her, but damn it, she was mad. Phoenix had blown through town a few months ago and emptied her bank account by simply reaching into her brain and forcing her to give him the account numbers and passwords he'd then used to legitimately transfer all her funds to him. Sure, she could've taken it to the authorities, but that would've opened up investigations on her, and he'd known that.

"I would've just given you the money, you know," she said as she hopped the four concrete steps to the front door of her apartment building. "Why do you get to wipe me out?"

Her brother's chuckle went a little darker, enough to raise the hairs on the back of Persephone's neck. Like she could ever forget that behind the laughter and jokes, the put-upon front of laziness and congeniality, her twin brother was as fucked-up as she was. Perhaps more, because Persephone liked to tell herself she maintained some level of morality, no matter how gray, and Phoenix had no such pretense.

"Because I knew you'd be fine," he said simply. "You always are."

"You don't get to come back around into my life and make like you didn't totally fuck me over." Her tone was as cold as his. "What do you want?"

"Can't a baby brother check in with his big sister to make sure she's all right?"

Four minutes had passed between her entrance into this world and his. Persephone unlocked her door and went inside, closing it after her. She tossed her bag onto the couch.

"Forgive me for assuming you have an ulterior motive," she said. "I guess I'm just not a fucking idiot."

Phoenix burst into laughter that urged her to join him, although she kept herself from it. "No. I would never say that about you."

"What do you really want?"

His laughter and his voice softened. "I really did want to make sure you're all right. I wanted to make sure they hadn't taken you."

"You would've known that right away, Phoenix. You didn't have to call me." Her voice was softer, too. She couldn't feel the same connection to her brother that he had with her—Persephone's talents affected other people's perceptions, while Phoenix was able to actually manipulate them into action. No matter how far apart they were, he was always able to sense her, even if he couldn't pinpoint her thoughts.

"You felt upset a few times."

She flopped onto the couch and propped her feet on the table. "Everyone feels upset a few times."

"I never do."

"You don't have to brag about it," Persephone said. Phoenix *could* feel. He just didn't do it the same way most people did. Then again, she thought, did anyone ever feel the same way anyone else did?

"Are you okay?"

"Nobody took me," she said in a kinder tone. Maybe

she had only four minutes on him, but that still made him her baby brother.

Phoenix didn't speak for a few seconds. "They took Leila."

"What?" Persephone sat up straight. "No. How do you know?"

"She sent me an email telling me she thought someone had been watching her. Following her. Then nothing, for months. Yesterday she texted me that she was in a safe place. That she was happy there. That I should consider changing my mind."

Persephone fought a wave of guilt. She hadn't talked to Leila in months, not since the last time they'd gone out dancing and drinking and picking up men. That wasn't unusual. Leila could be difficult to be around, because she was constantly screwing up her life.

"So...that's not a bad thing," Persephone said, thinking of the several times she'd felt like she was being watched. Nothing had happened in months. She still had Vadim's number and the knowledge that she had a place with the group he worked for called the Crew. It wasn't unbelievable that Leila might have taken him up on the offer. "She's safe and happy."

Phoenix made a noise low in his throat. "Of course she would say that to throw off any suspicion. They took her, and they've brainwashed her."

"Phoenix..." Persephone sighed. "You can't be sure. Did you text her back?"

"And have them figure out where I am? No way. I'm not giving them the key to the castle. Fuck that."

Persephone thought a text was the least likely way anyone would ever be able to track them, but what did she know? "She said she was safe and happy. Don't you think if they were really trying to lure you in that she'd have asked you for help, tried to trick you into going to her? I'm sure she's okay, Phoenix."

"You think she went willingly? She allowed that guy to just take her in? You think she's really all right with them?"

She shook her head. "I don't know."

"You wish you'd gone with him when he asked you to," Phoenix accused in a flat voice.

"No," she said. "I don't wish that. But I don't worry that they're going to come along and drag me off to lock me up somewhere. I believed him when he said I would have the choice. That you'd have a choice. You even said you didn't feel anything in his head that meant he was lying."

Phoenix made another of those noises. "Not about that. About everything else, though. His whole head was a lie."

She sighed. "You know if you go to work for him it means room, board, salary. You know Leila was never able to get her shit together. If she went somewhere that helped her out, who are we to judge?"

"You want to be someone's pet?"

"Of course not," she told him, even as her thoughts flashed against her will to Kane, which was ridiculous since she didn't want to be kept by any man. Especially not him.

"Something's going on with you. I'm not close enough to know it…"

"I'm fine," she said, her tone harsher. "And I'm still pissed at you."

"Nah, you're not. I knew that before I called." Her brother laughed. "But I have a mind to pay a visit, anyway."

"I don't have room."

Phoenix snorted. "You'd make a place for me."

"On the floor," she told him flatly. "On a set of jacks."

"You love me," Phoenix told her calmly, which was the truth, of course, no matter what he'd done. "And I love you. I'm sorry I cleaned out your bank account. I put it all back, by the way. Plus some."

She wanted to ask him how he'd managed to do that, but he'd disconnected before she could. Shaking her head, Persephone tossed her phone onto the table and got up to head for the kitchen in search of a meal that would fill her belly better than a candy bar. She put a frozen pizza in the oven while she flipped open her laptop at the kitchen table and scrolled through her emails, searching for any from Leila. She found one from months before, updating Persephone about her latest series of misadventures. She hadn't outright asked for money, but the subtext had been there.

Frowning, Persephone did a quick search, but that was indeed the last time she'd heard from the younger woman. She sat back in her seat, thinking hard. No texts had come in from Leila, but she probably didn't have Persephone's direct number. Opening one of the apps she kept for sidelines, Persephone scrolled through requests for pictures of her feet, tribute photos from men who'd already sent in their financial donations without even waiting to hear if she was going to accept them, junk and scam emails.

I decided to go with them, the message said. Tired of struggling. Want to be with people who understand. It's good here. You'd like it. Text me.

With a soft mutter, Persephone checked the date. Late yesterday afternoon, which meant she'd texted Phoenix first. That made sense. Leila had always liked him better. Most women did.

It didn't mean that Leila was in trouble, or that she'd been brainwashed the way Phoenix believed. The only way to find out would be to reply to Leila's message and see what she said. Typing in a swift reply, Persephone hit Send and waited. It came a minute or so later.

He is nothing like we were afraid of.
   You should come.

Chapter 3

"*It would be nothing like Collins Creek.*" The man who calls himself Vadim has a kind voice, although his eyes are a little scary. He smiles, but something in the rest of his face makes him feel dangerous. Or that he could be, anyway. If you pushed him too hard.

"*I don't know why I should go anywhere with you,*" Phoenix says belligerently with a toss of his long hair over his shoulders. He's pushed his way between Vadim and Persephone. It's a sweet gesture, but Persephone doubts it would do much good if Vadim really wanted to bring them harm.

Vadim spreads open his fingers and shrugs. "*I'm offering you a roof over your heads. Food in your stomachs. Safety.*"

"*Your safety sounds a lot like prison to me,*" Phoenix says. "*C'mon, Persephone. Let's get out of here.*"

"*Wait.*" She puts her hand on her brother's wrist. He

shrugs off her touch with a scowl, but she ignores it. She focuses on Vadim. "Why? Why should we trust you? How did you find us?"

"We've been tracking all the children from Collins Creek," Vadim says. *"So many of you have been lost, Persephone. So many of you we can't help. But you and your brother..."*

"Fuck off," Phoenix snarls. *"Come on, Persephone. Let's get out of here."*

But she can't. Not yet. They've been running too long. She's hungry. She's tired.

"Where would we go?" she asks.

Vadim smiles. This time it's a little more believable. "We have facilities all over the world. Where would you like to go?"

"What would we have to do?"

"Work with us. That's all. People with your unique skills are always valued in the Crew."

The Crew. The first time she heard the name, Persephone had laughed, thinking he must be joking. A group of people who investigate the strange and extraordinary has such a plain and unassuming name? It was ridiculous.

"And if we decide we want to leave?"

"It's a contract. Like anything else. You're free to leave according to the terms in the contract. We don't keep anyone against their will. We don't make you do anything you don't want to do. We train you to use your skills, and we give you assignments based on what you're best suited to do. You're compensated for it. Very nicely."

Phoenix fixes her with a long, hard glare. "We've done well enough on our own. There's no reason why we should sign anything with you. And I don't need you to teach me any damned thing."

"You can always learn something new," Vadim says

calmly with barely a glance at her brother. He's got her in his sights. She wonders what he sees.

Persephone thinks that might be what is agitating Phoenix so much—that Vadim is paying more attention to her. And there's not a sexy vibe from it, either. They've dealt with that, living on the streets for the past few years. She's done her share of using sex as currency. Phoenix has done his, too. But she's definitely not getting that feeling from Vadim right now, not for either of them. Whatever he wants from her, it's not her body, and that's why she trusts him but her brother does not.

"What if we still say no?" Phoenix challenges.

Vadim shrugs and gestures at the sparsely furnished motel room where he found them. "You walk out of here."

"And if we change our minds?" Persephone asks.

"Then you contact us."

"We won't change our minds," Phoenix says and grabs her by the hand. "Come on, Persephone. Let's get out of here."

She's the one who looks over her shoulder as they leave. Vadim is staring. He mouths something at her just before the door closes off the sight of him.

"You will be safe."

Chapter 4

The Slaughtered Lamb had been sold and bought several times over the past ten years, each owner adding or taking away something to add their individual touch to the place. The pub had suffered for it. Kane could recall when the dark atmosphere had been kitschy, not merely worn-out, and when the drinks had been cheap and the food good. Now he sat beneath a set of flickering sconces made to look like gaslights and a portrait that from one direction showed a beautiful young woman in a historical gown, but from the other showed a werewolf.

He should call it a night. He hadn't been planning on hooking up with anyone when he got in here, but funny how a beer or two could get a man thinking about it. Especially when faced with a tiny-waisted brunette with curves that wouldn't quit. She'd been eye-fucking him from across the bar since she arrived about twenty minutes ago and slipped into the spot he'd been heading for.

He'd considered sending her a drink, but that would mean he'd have to have a conversation with her, and unless he really wanted to take her home...

Shit. She'd seen him staring and now she was getting up to cross the room. He hadn't meant to make eye contact, and why? Because he was stupidly hung up on someone who clearly thought he was a douchecanoe. Kane looked up at the brunette, who'd tossed the fall of her heavy dark hair over her shoulder and was giving him a slow, easy smile.

"Hey," she said with that subtle twist of her body that emphasized her hips and breasts, that trick women did when they wanted you to not just look but also touch. "I'm Jena."

"Kane," he said. "Hi."

"So look, Kane," she said as she leaned closer so he could hear her without problem over the noise from the rest of the pub, "here's the thing. I'm about ready to head out for the night, but I was wondering if you'd like to come along with me? Or better yet, I could go home with you."

It was not the most blatant offer he'd ever had, but it ranked right up there. The funny part of it was, it was exactly what he needed in this moment. A no-frills, no-effort-needed, straight-up hookup. If she'd played at seduction, he'd have sent her on her way.

Instead, he gave her a thorough up and down perusal, making sure she knew he was checking out every bit of her before he fixed his gaze on hers. Smiled. Stood. "Sure. Let's go."

Persephone had spent longer than usual on what she thought of as "the glamour." It was not truly physical, because her body never actually changed. It was all illusion, a short-range manipulation of whatever parts of the brain controlled vision, smell, touch. Everyone else in this place would see her for what she really was, but Kane, the man upon whom she'd set her ravenous, manipulative sights, would be enthralled so long as she kept up the effort of the illusion.

She'd considered asking him to take her to a hotel, but she knew he didn't have money to toss away on something decent enough not to give her the shudders. Besides, in the morning when she slipped out of his bed, it would take only a few minutes to get back to her place, where she could get between her own sheets and hopefully drift off to sleep with a body worn out from a few rounds of amazing sex. She'd done it before.

When he led her into the building's lobby and toward the elevator that broke down more often than it worked, however, she hesitated. Fucking in an elevator was one thing, especially if it was the kind lined with mirrors so you could watch yourself reflected into infinity. This elevator didn't have any mirrors, it smelled vaguely and constantly of cat pee, and the last thing in the world she wanted was to get trapped inside it with Kane while she wore a fake face. They'd have to wait for hours before someone could get them out, and that person was most likely to be her, and that would quickly become a clusterfuck of epic proportions.

"Um..." she said, holding back. "How about the stairs?"

She jerked at thumb toward the small hallway next to the mailboxes set into the wall. Kane gave her a curious look she couldn't interpret, but nodded. He glanced over his shoulder as he led the way, holding open the heavy steel fire door so she could go first.

"What a gentleman," Persephone, a.k.a. Jena, murmured with an extra swing of her hips as she started up the stairs.

Let him admire the badonk in her donkadonk, she thought with a small smile that faded when she got to the landing and looked over her shoulder, intending to give Kane a sexy, come-hither look.

He was frowning.

"Something wrong?" Persephone hesitated, a hand on the railing, to study him.

"Have we met before?"

She started back up the stairs. "I don't think so."

He followed her through the metal door at the top of the stairs, but she held back to let him lead the way to his apartment. Once inside, she also held back to let him make the first move. Sure, she'd put on this face, this body, this hair, all designed to get Kane's hormones roaring. And sure, she'd gone after him in the bar the way a wolf would take down a deer with a broken leg.

That didn't mean she didn't like to be pursued.

She didn't have to wait long. In a few long strides, Kane had her in his arms. His mouth slanted along her own in a perfect, sensual pleasure that always made her wonder how he knew exactly how to touch her, every single time.

He broke the kiss to brush her lips with the tip of his tongue, his eyes searching hers as she shivered. "What did you say your name was?"

"Maria." Shit. Shit. No, she'd said—

"I thought you said it was Jena."

Persephone straightened her shoulders and gave him a tipped, coy smile and a flutter of her lashes designed to send a man straight to his knees, which was the perfect position for him to get between her thighs with his mouth. Kane didn't kneel, but his gaze did go heavy lidded. Dreamy. His eyes lost their usual sharp, fierce focus.

This was glamour of a different sort.

"Maybe you meet so many girls whose names you don't ask that you got me confused with someone else," she said with a practiced pout. She put herself into his arms, offered her mouth, pushed her hips forward to rub her belly against his hard crotch.

It worked, of course. There was a reason cats butt your hand to get them to pet you. Persephone's pussy knew how to do the same thing.

She knew where his bedroom was. Even if she hadn't been here a dozen times in the past year, it mirrored her own, immediately below. She waited for him to take her there, though, letting him grip her by the upper arms and turn her. Still kissing, they moved across the L-shaped living room and through the small arched alcove between the kitchen and hallway, then a few steps more and into the bedroom.

Persephone breathed in the familiar, strongly male scent of the space where Kane slept and dreamed. She wanted to bury herself in his pillow but settled for letting him push her gently onto the bed, where he climbed up her body and fit himself between her legs. One hand hooked beneath her knee to tug it upward; she hooked her foot behind his calf.

The kisses deepened. His mouth moved over her chin, down her throat, along the sloping curves of her high, big breasts spilling out of the tank top. As always, the strange juxtaposition between the flesh he appeared to be stroking and his touch upon her actual, real body was jarring and arousing and strange and exciting. Sometimes, when she allowed herself to dwell too long on the fact that she only fucked men when she looked like any other woman but herself, it was melancholy.

Not tonight. She wouldn't allow herself to feel anything now but rising desire, slightly violent. Consuming her. Filling her. She needed him to strip her bare and wear her out. She needed him.

She needed him…

Persephone sat up hard, backing out of Kane's embrace before she could stop herself. Her head knocked the painted concrete wall. No headboard. It didn't hurt, but the noise was loud enough that she gave a startled "oh!"

"You okay?" Kane had pushed onto his knees, head tilted as he stared at her.

She arched her back, shaking off the sudden rush of unwanted emotions trying to flood her. "Oh, yeah, baby. Just…eager."

She kicked off one high heel and let her naked toes run up over his belly to press his chest. Men went wild when she did that. She could never figure out why. Something about the push and pull between them dominating her and yet somehow submitting at the same time. Some kind of illusion of power and control. All of this was illusion, she thought as she watched him look over the lithe, curving body she'd presented to him.

For a terrible moment she thought he'd changed his mind about her. There'd been two times with Kane that had ended up with them back here in the morning's wee hours but not engaged in sex. Both times, he'd started off strong and eager, but something had changed his mind and he'd asked her to leave before they fucked. She'd never been able to figure out what had tipped him the other way, but tonight looked as though it might be heading that direction.

No, no, she couldn't let it. It was too late to go out trolling for another hookup, but more than that, Persephone didn't want to. The sex with anyone else, no matter how adequate, could never compare to the nights she spent with Kane, and it had been too long since the last time with him. She needed this right now—for more reasons than she cared to admit.

She pushed outward with the small and curling tendrils of her will to shape herself in his gaze. "Kiss me."

He did, for a second or so. Kane hissed in a gasp when her fingers slid beneath the edge of his shirt and against his bare skin. She put a hand behind his neck, fingers curling, nails digging a little deep. They worked quickly after that, stripping down at the same time until she lay back on the bed with him kneeling over her. He wasn't fully erect yet, but she let her hungry gaze linger on him before she looked up at his eyes. She'd meant to say something sexy, alluring, seductive, but at the sight of his look Persephone's words clipped themselves short against the backs of her teeth.

Again, she wondered with some alarm if he meant to tell her she had to leave. Again, she eased the tickling swirls of her senses to shadow and shape his. It should've been freaky for him to see the long dark lengths of the hair she'd conjured getting shorter, to hit her just above her shoulders, or to see her breasts becoming smaller, her ass more rounded, yet because all of this was hallucination, all Kane would see was her becoming his ideal. He wouldn't even know she didn't look the same as she had earlier in the night. And in the morning, when he woke to an empty spot in the bed beside him, he would have only the vaguest memory of what she had looked like at all.

"Kiss me," Persephone whispered again with a crook of her finger to get him to lean down and take her mouth with his. She meant to say more after that, but the taste of him chased away her words again so that all she found was silence and sighs.

When he ran his hands up her sides to cup her breasts, she arched into the touch. Her knees fell apart of their own accord so her body could open to him. He surprised her again when he slid his mouth down her throat and over her breasts, to her belly, to her hip and then oh, yes, fuck, right there. Right to her core, and he fastened his tongue and lips on her clit and began to lick and suck in a steady but delicate rhythm that had her lifting her hips to meet every stroke within moments.

He'd never gone down on her before. She'd had his cock deep in her throat, and they'd fucked in every position either of them had ever thought to try, but he had never had his mouth on her pussy. Persephone had never asked him for it—she never asked any man for it, though she never turned it down if were offered. She gladly gave herself up to it now, letting pleasure fill her up and wash over her until she was muttering his name from between clenched jaws, unwilling to completely give him everything inside her.

He hummed, sounding delighted. The thrum of it sent another slow, rolling wave of desire coursing through her. Her clit pulsed on his tongue. His hands slipped beneath her ass to lift her closer to his kisses. He murmured again, wordless noises of approval and desire that pushed her closer and closer to the edge.

He blew a soft gust of breath across her as he replaced his tongue for a moment with his fingers. A different pressure, but the same pace. She wasn't going to hold out much longer and didn't want to. The idea of asking him to hold off so she could come with him inside her crossed her mind, but greedily, Persephone didn't manage to keep herself from taking just…a little…more.

As always, her orgasm teased her for what felt like forever before finally she could no longer crest. She had to fall. Plummeting, she writhed and shook and shuddered.

Again, she cried out his name. She also looked down at him to find him looking up at her.

She expected an arrogant smile, pride in the way he'd just gotten her off, but confusion blurred his gaze. His mouth was open and wet, and the sight of it continued to arouse her. At least until he blinked rapidly and pushed himself up onto his knees to look down at her.

Before Persephone had learned the extent of her talents in manipulating the way others perceived her, she'd often stuttered in holding on to the glamour. There'd been times when she'd altered her appearance based on whatever she sensed the other person desired, but she hadn't lost the ability to hold on to the illusion. Not in years.

Now, panicked, she reached to touch the soft, red-gold feathers of hair above her ears that had been dark brown and to her shoulders moments ago. Her breasts had shrunk yet again, filling her palms with a familiar weight. How long had she been looking more like herself than an image? It took her only seconds to return to the projection, and by the way Kane was frowning she was relieved to see that her change could've been no longer than that. Long enough for him to notice and be shocked, but not long enough for him to have truly seen her.

Not her real self, not Persephone. Never that. It would be her downfall.

"I thought… I must be drunker than I thought." He shook his head and wiped his mouth with the back of his hand. His cock, despite his consternation, had gone thick and hard. Ready for her.

"Not too drunk to fuck, baby," Persephone purred, putting on her persona even as her heart thumped unsteadily and she had to take a few seconds to center herself. "Come here."

Kane shook his head. "Listen, you're sexy as fuck, and any other time I would be already deep inside you, but..."

She sat, closing her legs self-consciously. Her pussy still throbbed with aftershocks, and when she shifted, she could feel slickness on the insides of her thighs. With a shiver, she covered her breasts with her arms.

"But you want me to get out?" she asked.

Kane ran a hand over his dark hair, rumpling it. "I think it would be best. I can call a car for you, or..."

"No. It's all good." Persephone got out of the bed and began to search for her clothes. Very aware of Kane's eyes on her ass as she bent over, she considered putting a little shimmy in it to tempt him, but didn't. It was awkward enough that he was kicking her out. The last thing she wanted was to try to seduce him only to be utterly rejected.

He walked her to the door and kissed her there, but on the corner of the mouth. Almost the cheek. Bemused, Persephone patted his arm and kept her mouth shut. She wasn't going to offer to see him again, for sure, but she did wonder what on earth had changed his mind about fucking her. She glanced over her shoulder as she headed for the stairs to find him watching her with a narrowed, focused gaze.

Oh, shit.

Chapter 5

Kane had gone for a run before work. Using his muscles, pushing his endurance. He'd spent the rest of the day on paperwork and following leads. Funny how television and the movies showed detectives almost always in the street chasing down the bad guys. They never showed all the work it took to find them first.

Now he was at home with a takeout carton of Chinese and a six-pack of beer, his laptop open on the kitchen table in front of him. He had more work to do. He'd already done a search for his hookup from the other night, but nobody matching the name she'd given him or the description had popped up. There was no reason for him to think she was any kind of criminal or anything, but something about her had set off an alarm bell in his head.

Going down on her had been incredible. She'd tasted like the sweetest honey. Her body had softened and bloomed under his tongue and lips. When she came, he'd been able to feel every tremor, every flutter. Kane loved cunnilingus, but he rarely opened with it—that wasn't something for a first encounter, and he hadn't had more than a first encounter with anyone in close to two years. He wasn't sure what had prompted him to get his mouth between her legs, only that everything about the evening had been a little off, a little strange...a little extraordinary.

It hadn't been the booze, he knew that. But something screwy had been going on when he sat up to look at her and it seemed for half a second that there was an entirely different woman in his bed. Just for a blink he'd seen Persephone writhing beneath him, her body arched and shaking from the orgasm he'd given her. Only for a blink, and Jena or Maria or whatever she claimed her name was had been back again, and he'd gone all wiggy and sent her home. So what the hell, he thought, was up with that?

He'd done a search on Persephone before but had also found nothing. No criminal record at all. Not even a parking ticket, which wasn't so odd considering that as far as he could tell, she didn't own a car.

Swigging beer, Kane tapped his computer to wake it up, then let his fingers rest on the keyboard. If he kept digging, he was going to find out who she was and where she came from. The question was, did he really want to know? What would happen when she was no longer a mystery? And what would he do, he thought, if he found out something he'd feel compelled to take action on?

So many questions, and he wasn't usually the sort of guy to dwell on this kind of thing. Damn, the woman had gotten deep in his head and under his skin. It had to be more than just that she didn't seem to want to give him the time of day. Sure, he'd had more than his share of women who'd been eager to jump his bones, but there'd been a number whose heads hadn't even turned, just like any guy. He'd always considered it part of the game and moved on.

Until Persephone.

Now, while he dug into his lo mein and sipped at his beer without noticing much of the flavor, Kane started searching again. A friend of his who'd gone into private detective work had taught him some tricks about finding evidence of people who didn't seem to have left any tracks, and he put them into play now. Finally, just before he meant to give up and turn on a movie instead, something popped up.

The article was brief, the mention that had been linked to his searching no more than a sentence or two. It was the photo that caught his attention. A group shot of a bunch of children dressed identically, boys and girls with the same haircuts, all long hair past their shoulders, so it made it difficult to tell them apart. Most of them were smiling—at least there was that, considering the accompanying text told a horrific story about the cult at Collins Creek.

Kane hadn't heard about this group before, but that meant nothing. Cults were far from his area of expertise. Collins Creek turned out to be a fairly obscure cult as well, more mythical than anything according to the article. It said that rumors of the atrocities at Collins Creek were widespread and pervasive but had not been substantiated.

At Collins Creek, it had been all about the children. Pregnant women had purposefully exposed themselves to chemicals, drugs, sleep deprivation, while the men had also undergone voluntary exposure to environmental and mental stressors designed to not only affect the unborn babies but change them at conception. What the leaders

had been trying to do was the subject of some contro-
versy, but it seemed as though they'd been attempting
to force mutations. To create psychic powers. The suc-
cess rate was unknown, although there were plenty of
rumors about that, too. Mostly, though, the only truth
anyone could corroborate was that at some point about
twenty years ago, a private group had invaded Collins
Creek and taken away as many of the children as they'd
been able to. At least the ones that had survived. And
after that? All signs of the place had disappeared. Like
Area 51, Collins Creek existed, but nobody would admit
it or talk about what had gone on there.

Kane did not believe in aliens. He understood
conspiracy theories only as the workings of people who
had too much time on their hands and big imaginations.
Looking at this article, he would usually have scoffed
at the idea that there'd been a large farm full of psychi-
cally enhanced children running around it only a few
hours' drive away. But looking at the photograph, seeing
the smiling faces of all those children, something like a
chill skittered up and down his spine. He recognized the
smiles on the faces of not one of those children, but two,
and there in the fine-print caption below the picture, he
saw the list of names.

One of them was Persephone.

Chapter 6

Meeting a horny businessman for cocktails and domination was not exactly the worst way to spend the afternoon, Persephone thought. The hotel was upscale, the food was good and he was paying for it.

He'd ordered room service, as she'd told him to do in advance, along with a bottle of very nice champagne that she hadn't requested. She eyed it as she took a seat on the desk chair. "Celebrating?"

"Every date with you is reason for celebration," he said.

Persephone paused to look at him. "Are you falling in love with me, Werner?"

Werner looked uncomfortable for a second before nodding. "Yes. I think so."

"Don't." She raised a finger when he made to speak. "We talked about this right up front. What did I say?"

"You said that it would never be emotional, that it was

purely business. It's what I said…" He coughed, cutting his gaze from hers. "I said that was what I wanted."

"Which is why I agreed to it." She frowned, running a finger along the champagne bottle. For Werner, she wore her body older, taller, strong. Dark pageboy hair streaked with silver. She turned to him, still frowning. "You know this is only business, Werner."

"I know. But it's so difficult…" Incredibly, his voice hitched. He closed his eyes. Everything about him turned inward, away from her.

Persephone had seen Werner behave as though he was ashamed many times. It was part of his kink. One thing she had never seen him do was be genuinely distraught by anything they'd ever done. She took a step toward him in concern.

"Hey."

His fists clenched. "It's hard to find someone. Someone who gets it. Who…likes it. Well, who at least doesn't make me feel like some kind of creep for liking what I like. Do you know how hard it is, Chelsea? To find someone who doesn't make you feel like a freak?"

She sat next to him on the bed, aware that he was completely naked but not bothered by it. He'd been naked so many times in front of her, after all. Never quite like this. Nude skin, yes. This was different.

She took his hand. "Yes. I understand how hard it must be to find someone."

Hell, it was hard enough to find someone just to go out with on a date, much less who didn't mind making you beg for orgasms. Men like Werner could pay for sex, but the companionship also came with a price, and he'd always known it. She understood how it could finally have started to pale.

His shoulders hitched, and he still turned away from

her. "I'm sorry. I know this wasn't the agreement. You can leave. The money's on the table by the door."

"I'm not going to take your money, Werner." Persephone stood, for one moment taking his chin in her hand the way she'd done many times before. This time not to chastise, scold or humiliate him. This time she held his face still when she brushed her lips over his cheek. "You take care of yourself. Okay?"

He'd closed his eyes at her kiss. She felt him straining toward her, but she didn't kiss him again. He didn't open his eyes. She stepped backward, for an instant catching a glimpse of herself in the wall mirror. Her own self, not the one she'd presented to him over the months of their acquaintance. If he looked at her now, he would still see Chelsea, but that was how it should be.

Without saying goodbye, Persephone ducked out of the hotel door. She paused to shuck the heels and replaced them with a pair of flats she had in her bag. She didn't take the time to do anything with the tight, cleavage-baring dress that hit her midthigh, but she did shrug into a long loose-fitting cardigan.

She'd made it all the way through the hotel lobby and to the sidewalk beyond without so much as turning a head before a male voice stopped her short. She turned, certain she must not have heard him say her name. Surely it would have to be a stranger calling out to someone else.

Certainly, she thought with a sinking stomach as she faced him, certainly it could not be Kane.

"I thought that was you," he said cheerfully enough. He'd been leaning against the hotel near the smoking area, though to her knowledge he didn't smoke.

"Yep, it's me." She rocked a little on her heels and jerked a thumb toward her chest. Heat flooded her throat and painted her face scarlet. She coughed and pasted on a smile.

"What's up?" He glanced at the hotel entrance, then gave her a long, slow going-over that did nothing to relieve her rising blush.

"What's up with you?" she asked boldly. The best way to get out of a sticky situation was by confronting it head-on. She'd learned that long ago. Something told her, though, that Kane was not going to fall for it.

He grinned. "Just hanging out. Meeting a friend."

"Have fun." It was code for a stakeout or something— she knew that by the sly way his mouth twisted. She'd never talked with Kane about his work, but of course she knew exactly what he did.

"Hey, hey," he said as he stepped toward her. "Maybe I meant you?"

The moment he said it, he seemed to regret it. The expression was so comical that Persephone almost laughed. If ever a man wished he could take back what he'd just blurted out, that man was Kane just then.

"You're not waiting for me," she said crisply.

"No. We're not friends. Right?"

She eyed him, then gave a begrudging smile. "Nope."

"Not buddies, not pals, not chums."

"No, no and definitely not." She took a few steps backward before turning to walk away with a little wiggle of her fingertips over her shoulder.

Maybe being bold was going to pay off, she thought. God knew she'd played the same game with security officers at the mall with a bag full of lifted merch. Confidence and walking away without looking back had saved her ass a hundred times.

Not this time. Kane caught up to her in three or four

long strides, falling into pace beside her. She could feel him looking at her.

"It's a free country," she said at last without so much as a glance his way. "I'm allowed out of the building, you know. I'm allowed to do whatever things I want to do during the day, and I don't need to explain myself to you, either."

"Was I asking for an explanation?" Kane paused, allowing her to move a few steps ahead before he jogged to catch up.

"What were *you* doing hanging around outside a fancy hotel at two in the afternoon?" Persephone whirled to walk backward for a few steps. "Loitering!"

Kane laughed. "Yep, loitering."

"Hmm." She faced forward again, walking, although not quite as fast as before.

Kane fell into step beside her again, this time not poking her with words. Just walking. She hadn't intended to walk all the way home, but somehow hailing a cab now felt awkward, like he might try to jump in the car with her. Without saying anything, she turned into the park entrance to cut across it. Kane did, too.

It was a nice enough day for walking, at least. Sun bright but not too hot. Clear blue and cloudless sky. Walking the curving path through patches of flowers, Persephone let herself for briefest of moments imagine what it might be like if Kane took her hand.

Sappy, she scolded herself with a sideways glance at him. Even if she did want to risk getting involved with him beyond the anonymous sex, they would never be the sort of couple to skip through fields of flowers holding hands. Well, she wasn't, for sure. Too late, he'd caught her looking.

"What?" Kane said.

"Nothing," Persephone answered.

He smiled as though he knew she was full of it. "Uh-huh."

With a sniff, she went back to ignoring him. Fifteen minutes later they were back at their building, the neighborhood very different from the one where they'd met up earlier. She was definitely overdressed, but that wasn't what made her suddenly anxious.

It was the sight of Vadim sitting on the front steps, waiting for her.

Chapter 7

Kane knew at once something was wrong. Not so much by the look on Persephone's face—she would definitely be a winner at the poker table. It was something subtler than that. A shift in her posture. The soft hiss of a drawn-in breath. Without thinking twice, he stepped between her and the man now standing on the concrete steps to the apartment building.

"Persephone," the guy said in a deep, rich voice with a hint of an accent. "So good to see you again. I've been waiting for you."

"Clearly," she said. "Well, I guess you'd better come on inside."

"Kane Dennis," he said, stepping forward with a hand out for a shake. He kept his voice light. Easy. Non-threatening, even as he mentally ran through a checklist of what he'd do if the guy showed one second's thought toward harming Persephone.

"Nice to meet you," the guy said without offering a name. He smiled, but it was obvious he was not going to give Kane a damned thing. His attention turned back to Persephone. "That would be most appreciated. Thank you."

Kane touched her shoulder. "Everything okay?"

For a moment it looked as though she meant to say no. Her mouth pursed, her brow furrowed. He couldn't tell if she was annoyed with him for asking or if she was trying to tell him that no, she was not all right.

"Sure. Fine," she said. No shake in her voice. She met his gaze without hesitation. A faint smile, maybe the nicest she'd ever given him, tipped the corners of her mouth. "Thanks, Kane, but I'm fine."

Kane gave the nameless guy a narrow-eyed stare but didn't pursue it. No matter how much he wanted to go all caveman and leap to Persephone's defense, it was clear she didn't want him to. Instead, he nodded and stepped back. He gave the guy another steady stare that didn't seem to affect the other man very much at all.

Persephone didn't look over her shoulder as she went inside and down the stairs to the basement. Kane waited until the door closed behind them, then another few minutes before he went down after them. Persephone's apartment was down the hall from the storage space, and he conveniently needed to look for something that he'd packed away.

Fifteen minutes later, her door opened. The murmur of voices didn't sound alarming, but Kane listened, anyway. When the sound of a single pair of footsteps moved away and her door closed, he came out of the storage space. Quickly and quietly, he followed the man up the stairs and through the lobby, but stopped short at the sight of Persephone's mysterious visitor waiting for him on the sidewalk.

The other man grinned. "She has a good friend in you, I see."

"According to her, we aren't friends."

"You shouldn't let that deter you." The man shrugged. "Miss Persephone is a wary soul, and I would say she has a right for caution."

Kane studied the guy, assessing. "How well do you know her?"

"I don't know her very well at all. I am not a rival for her affections, if that's what worries you." The man's expression was smooth. Neutral. "I am not her friend, either. She'd be the first to tell you that. But I assure you, neither am I her enemy. I want only what's best for Miss Persephone."

"She's in trouble," Kane said flatly. "What kind?"

"I would think such a question might be best asked of her, not me. As for me, I must say goodbye. I have other appointments." With that, the guy turned on his heel and stalked away down the sidewalk, looking neither left nor right and definitely not behind.

After that meeting, Kane had done more searching, but he wasn't surprised to find nothing about Persephone's mystery guest. Still, he couldn't shake the feeling something was very wrong about the whole situation, even though he believed the guy when he said he wasn't interested in Persephone romantically and also that he wasn't her enemy.

He had done more digging into the Collins Creek situation. All of it rumor or urban legend. Nothing concrete. He'd found no more photos of Persephone, but he had dug up a couple reports about the children who'd survived the raid. Some of them had allegedly been put into research facilities. A few others were reported to have grown up on the streets.

It made sense now. The sense of wariness she had about her. Her sharp wit. The way she could either stand out from everyone else around her or blend in so completely you'd never know she was there.

As for the rest of it, the allegations that the children of Collins Creek were all somehow like that chick from the Stephen King flick, the one where she offed everyone at the prom—none of that seemed believable, though he could absolutely believe the cult leaders had thought it was possible.

He had no intention of mentioning any of this to her, of course, except that he did want to tell her that he would be there for her if that guy who'd been waiting for her was indeed going to bring her some kind of harm, even if it was just the painful kind of being reminded of things she'd rather not think about. She'd laugh or mock him; she might even get a little put out by what Kane knew was going to come off as patronizing. He didn't care. He wanted her to know that he would be there to protect her, if she needed it.

As it turned out, he was too late.

Chapter 8

Since Vadim had shown up on her doorstep, Persephone had been lying low. She ventured out of her apartment only to take care of repairs, but beyond that she'd been holed up doing nothing but binge watching television shows. She'd even sprung the extra few bucks for grocery delivery so she wouldn't have to go out.

Vadim had offered her a job. The first time around he'd found her and Phoenix at age sixteen, living on the streets. He'd offered them shelter and training then. This time he'd simply asked her if she'd like to work for him. She could keep her life here if she wanted. She didn't have to give up her other activities, as he'd called them, but for the first time in a long time, Persephone thought she might like to. The grifting was getting old. The petty thievery less profitable. And the sex work…she thought again of Werner, and how even though their arrangement had been meant to be only business, in the end she'd hurt him, anyway.

Also, there was Kane.

It wouldn't be long before he figured out she didn't make her living in any honest way, if he hadn't already. Once he did, even if he didn't arrest her, there'd be no way for her to keep living here. Not seeing him every day and knowing that he thought she was a criminal...well, she totally was a criminal, Persephone reminded herself as she gave Interflix the go-ahead to keep playing episodes of a '90s sitcom she'd never seen the first time around.

Thinking of Kane now made her shift and squirm a little on the couch. It had been over a week since she'd tried to seduce him and been summarily turned away without so much as an inch of him inside her. She hadn't been able to stop thinking about his mouth on her, though. How his tongue had lapped, slow and steady, pushing her closer and closer to the edge.

Damn, she needed him. She wanted him, anyway, and for Persephone that had to count as the same thing. Didn't it? Leaning back against the couch, the mindless TV show blaring in the background, she closed her eyes. Her hands drifted over her body. Her fingers slipped beneath the waistband of her jeans, the fit tight and not giving her much room to maneuver. She was already slick and hot, and she let out a small sigh of pleasure as she found her clit.

Kane is above her, his gaze intense. He moves his hands over her body, finding all the places that make her respond. When he dips his mouth to taste her flesh, Persephone arches into the embrace. His lips find her nipples, one and then the other, tugging each until they stand up in tight points that ache to be caressed further.

Lower, lower, he moves, tongue tracing wet patterns on her skin as he pauses for a moment to nibble her hip.

She laughs at the tickle and his hot breath puffs out on skin dampened by his mouth. When he moves between her legs, she lets out a long, low moan of pleasure that he echoes, and his hum against her pushes her higher.

Higher.

With a gasp, Persephone paused in her self-love, listening for the sound of the knock she was sure she'd just heard. Shit, it was someone at the door. Quickly she pulled her hand out of her jeans and got off the couch, running her fingers through her hair and trying to shake off the swell of arousal still surging through her. She absolutely did not want to answer the door to find Mrs. Cohen in 3B needed her toilet unclogged while she looked like she'd been happily getting herself off to fantasies of Kane.

Mrs. Cohen was not on the other side of the door.

It was Phoenix.

"You're being an asshole," Persephone said through gritted teeth even as she kept walking.

Her brother laughed, which only made her angrier. "Keep moving."

"You didn't even let me pack a bag!" Or grab her book full of cash, and that was the real shame. But every time she thought about stopping, she took another step.

That was Phoenix's talent. Persephone could make other people see what she wanted them to see, but her brother could make them do things he wanted them to do. As with her talent, it was limited. He couldn't command an army, for example, but then, he didn't really have to. Not when he could focus his will on one person who was helpless not to resist.

"You're being—"

"An asshole. You said so. Come on. I have a car."

Persephone chortled. "Oh, yeah? Where did you get a car?"

"I made a woman give it to me," her brother said with a cat-eating-the-cream grin that Persephone refused to admit she'd missed. Once in the passenger seat, she made sure to buckle up. Phoenix was a terrible driver. They both were. No parents to teach them. She didn't even have her license. He probably didn't, either, but he wouldn't care. There wasn't much to worry about if you got pulled over when you could tell the cop to simply walk away and let you go.

"Where are we going?" Persephone asked. "If you tell me to rob a bank, I'm going to punch you in the junk."

"I'll stop you."

"I'll do it so fast you won't have time," she countered. "And I notice you didn't say we weren't going to rob a bank."

Phoenix shot her an amused look as he put the car in gear and pulled out of the parking spot without bothering to look. "We're not going to rob a bank. We're going to save Leila."

Persephone groaned. "Phoenix, no. Why? What on earth do you want to do that for?"

"Because she's our friend, and I think she's in danger!"

For a moment she considered not telling him that Vadim had approached her about taking a job. She wasn't in the habit of keeping secrets from her brother, not exactly, even though there'd been plenty of times when she hadn't told him the entire truth. He always sensed it, though, and all he had to do was tell her to give up the story, and she would.

"Vadim came to see me. He said he had a job for me."

Phoenix didn't look surprised. "Yeah. Me too."

"Then why are we doing some kind of, what, secret

mission? Leila said she was fine. Vadim approached both of us... Holy shit, Phoenix! Look out!" Persephone screamed hoarsely as her brother nearly got in a head-on collision with a delivery truck because their car was lumbering down the wrong side of a one-way street.

With a laugh just short of maniacal, Phoenix swerved to avoid the truck, which let out a long, angry bleat of its horn. He took the corner too fast. Persephone closed her eyes.

"This is not how I want to die, Phoenix!"

Another laugh. "Oh, come on. It's going to fine."

She risked a peek, relieved to see that he was at least going down the street the right way now. They drove in relative silence for the next half an hour, with Phoenix changing the radio station every few minutes and singing along, badly, with all the songs. No conversation beyond that. Frankly, Persephone didn't have anything to say.

When they pulled up in front of a truly disgusting-looking roadside motel that looked like something out of a horror movie, she finally found her voice. "No. Oh my god, I'm getting hives just thinking about the bed-bug bites."

"We're not living here. We're just staying here to meet someone on the inside."

"The inside of what?" Persephone twisted in her seat. "Damn it, Phoenix, since when did you turn into, what, an international spy? What the hell is going on? Who are we meeting here?"

"Her name is Samantha. She's got information I want about the Crew."

"And how did you figure this out?"

"Met her on Connex," he said easily with a wave of his hand before he turned off the ignition and gave her a smug grin. "She tries to beat me at WordPals, but she hasn't yet."

"What makes you think she's going to give you some kind of secret information about the Crew so that you can bust in and 'save'—" Persephone used air quotes "—Leila?"

"I didn't tell her that's what I wanted." Without waiting for her, Phoenix got out of the car.

Of course, Persephone followed, because he was manipulating her like a marionette. It showed when she stumbled on the cracked piece of concrete that kept cars from driving straight through the window of the craptastic motel. She didn't fall, but she did let out a muttered curse that had him laughing at her as she managed to keep her feet. He was already holding open the door to the room, ushering her inside, then shutting and locking the door behind them.

It wasn't any better in there than it looked from the outside. Sagging double beds covered in plaid bedspreads that didn't quite match. Faded watercolors on the stucco walls. Through an open door she could see a white-tiled bathroom from which the faintest stink of air freshener wafted.

"Does she think she's meeting you here to fuck?" Persephone asked, since her brother hadn't answered.

He gave her a glance over his shoulder as he went to the window on the far side of the room to twitch the curtains and peek out. "I don't think so. It's not like that."

"So why, then, would she come and help you?"

Phoenix shrugged. "She thinks I can help her find someone who's missing."

"Why on earth would she think that?" Persephone put her hands on her hips. "That's not your skill."

"No, but I can connect with you. And with the rest of them, if I try," he said.

The rest of them. The other kids from Collins Creek. Persephone knew her brother could sense her general location, even when they were far apart, but this was the first she'd heard that he could do that with anyone else.

"He's our brother," Phoenix said at her look.

Persephone's mouth opened, gaping. Her eyebrows rose. "But we don't have—"

"He was younger. He'd just been tested when they raided. But same mother, same father."

"That doesn't make him our brother," Persephone said after a moment.

Phoenix shrugged, expression neutral. She studied him. In childhood, it had been the two of them. For so long after that, they'd been everything to each other, the only other person they could trust. She loved her brother more than anything in the world, but she didn't always like him.

"When is Samantha getting here?"

"I said I'd call when I got here. You hungry?" He leaned to pull a sheaf of what looked like takeout menus from the drawer in the nightstand. "You got the app on your phone that lets you call for delivery?"

"Yeah." She was hungry as well as disgruntled, and she knew that a well-fed Phoenix would be easier to deal with. "What are you in the mood for?"

"Chinese." He settled further onto the pillows with his own phone, tapping out some messages.

Persephone took care of the food order and checked out the bathroom, grimacing at the condition of it. She'd rather be dirty. She washed her hands, though. Catching sight of herself in the mirror, she took a few minutes to swipe away the smears of mascara that had crept down her cheeks. Her hair needed a trim. With a sigh, she leaned on the sink and closed her eyes, wondering what the hell Phoenix had gotten them both into.

"You want to hate me," her brother said quietly from the doorway. "But I know you can't. I know you want to help Leila."

"If you see her and she tells you to your face that she's all right, will you lay off this ridiculous idea that she's been kidnapped or something?" She looked at him in the mirror, then turned to face him. "Will you?"

Phoenix shrugged. "If it feels like she's telling the truth, yes. If I ask her to be honest and she tells me that she's really happy there with them, yes. I'll lay off."

There was more to this than his concern for Leila. Persephone knew it, because she knew the way her brother operated. She also knew she wasn't going to be able to figure it out right away.

The food arrived and Phoenix made the guy leave it without being paid, something that annoyed Persephone even though she'd done her share of cheating people out of food before. Still, they both fell on the fried rice and lo mein with the same appetite and polished off the order within minutes. Then they turned on the television, and despite her disgust with the room and the situation over-all, Persephone found herself drifting to sleep.

"Who is he?" Phoenix's voice curled out of the darkness toward her, across the space between the beds.

Persephone yawned. "Who is who?"

"There's someone. I can feel him in there. He's taking up space in your head."

She didn't answer right away. He could make her tell him the way he'd made her give him the bank account information, the way he'd made her get in the car. For a second she thought about forcing him to make her, but then, what difference did it make? No matter how annoying he was or how angry she got at him, Phoenix would always be her brother. The only family she really had.

"His name's Kane."

Phoenix snorted soft laughter. "What the hell kind of name is Kane?"

"What kind of name is Phoenix?" she asked flatly. "Or Persephone?"

"The man and woman who genetically produced us were messed-up people," her brother said.

The description of the people who had indeed created them but had never been parents made her laugh. "Maybe his parents were messed up, too."

"Is he a mess?"

"No," she said quietly after a few seconds had passed in silence. "I don't think he is. I mean, everyone has their damage, right, but no. I don't think Kane's messed up the way we are."

"Nobody's messed up the way we are," Phoenix told her. "Not in this whole world."

Chapter 9

Kane had found Persephone's apartment empty, which wouldn't have been alarming except that her door had swung open at his knock. Unlocked. A chair had been knocked over at the kitchen table. Her laptop was open, the screen dark but coming to life when he tapped the keypad. Aside from that, nothing else seemed out of place, but that was more than enough for him.

Someone had taken her. He knew it in his gut, and he knew it was somehow related to the stranger. With a quick call to the department and his partner to tell them he'd be working on following up some leads and wouldn't be in, Kane started figuring out how to find Persephone.

First, the obvious choice. Her laptop screen had gone dark again, but a quick tap of the keys brought up her screen. She did not have it lock protected, something that was going to make his job so much easier, even though it surprised him. It shouldn't have. In his experience more people didn't password protect their laptops than did. He gave her files a quick glance, not bothering to read any of them, not even the ones with super bland and therefore intriguing titles, like Accounting Receipts.

He found what he was looking for after a minute or so. The Find My Phone app was, as he'd hoped, connected to her phone, and also not password protected. All it took was a quick few taps of the keys to bring it up and he was looking at a map with her phone's location pinpointed with a small blue peg. She wasn't moving, there was that, but what she was doing in the Sentinel Motel was going to be his next task to figure out.

It was possible she was meeting someone, he thought. A lover? A client, more likely, Kane thought with a grim press of his lips together, thinking of how he'd seen her coming out of that downtown hotel dressed for something more than a midafternoon business meeting.

Grabbing her laptop, he slipped it into the soft fabric case patterned in skulls and roses that she'd left on the table. He'd need to get on the internet to access her location again, but that wouldn't be a problem. It would take him over an hour and forty minutes to get to the Sentinel, and if he found after assessing the situation that she didn't need his help, he'd discreetly leave without her ever knowing he'd turned into a creeper. But if she did need help, he thought grimly, whoever was hurting her better hope they knew how to run, because he was going hunt them down and make sure they paid for bringing her harm.

Slowly, slowly, he runs his fingertips up her arms. Then down. Tickling touches across the slope of her belly between her hip bones. Over her thighs. Pausing, he touches the backs of her knees as he pushes her legs up, opening her to his view. She is caught in his gaze, muscles tight and trembling, waiting for his touch.

He teases her.

Long minutes pass beneath this exquisite torment while she writhes and moans; his name on her lips is like candy. Sweetness. Magic.

The softness of his hot breath on her slick flesh makes her wriggle and cry out again. Body straining. She wants to thread her fingers through his hair and push him against her but satisfies herself with twisting her grip into the crisp white sheets.

That first touch of his tongue against her is so good, so fucking good, that all she can do is whimper. Arch. Roll her hips up to get more of him, get herself against him harder, get his tongue to press on her clit and lick and lick and lick...

Pleasure controls her. No words. Nothing but this aching and brilliant desire flooding every inch while she shudders and says his name over and over and over again.

"Kane." Persephone woke with a start, her body flooding with embarrassed heat when she sat up and saw Phoenix giving her a bemused look.

Her brother gestured with the TV remote. "You didn't tell me you had a boyfriend."

"He's not my boyfriend. He lives in my building. That's all." She got out of bed and went to the bathroom. She desperately wanted a glass of cold water, but the tap gave her only lukewarm and she wasn't sure she trusted drinking it, anyway. She settled for wetting a cleanish-looking washcloth and putting it on the back of her neck as she studied her face in the mirror. Through the door, she called out, "How long was I asleep?"

"Only about twenty minutes. You weren't snoring."

"I wasn't worried about snoring." She rolled her eyes. She was more worried she'd been moaning or something really embarrassing.

A knock at the door had her turning. She was expecting the mysterious Samantha, but when her brother opened the door, she saw a familiar face. Framed in the doorway, Kane looked taller and broader than she remembered him being, or perhaps that was because he looked so menacing. His head swung back and forth, gaze sweeping the room and taking in Phoenix, the pair of rumpled beds.

She should've been surprised to see him, perhaps even angry at this interference in her life, but instead relief swept over her in a wave so strong she had to put her hand on the bathroom door frame to keep herself from hurtling forward, across the room and into Kane's arms.

"Kane," she said.

Phoenix's head went up at once, his eyes narrowed. He took a step back as Kane moved forward, not trying to keep the other man from entering the room. He didn't have to do that physically. All he had to do was take control. He could only handle one person at a time, though.

"Persephone," Kane said without giving her brother so much as a second glance, clearly dismissing the threat. "Are you all right?"

She was all right, at least so far as she wasn't being harmed. But was she okay? Not really. Phoenix had forced her to come with him on this trip, and although he hadn't continued to control her every move, she wasn't here by choice.

"Tell him you're all right, sister mine."

"I'm all right," she said at once. No matter what she

might have wanted to answer, her brother's words came out of her mouth.

"She's fine. You can leave now, whoever you are." Phoenix didn't say it as a command, which meant he was still bent on controlling Persephone.

Kane ignored Phoenix. "I went to your apartment. I was worried."

A flicker of heat lit inside her, low in her belly but growing upward beneath her heart. She'd known this man for a little over a year. She'd spent hours with him naked, but for all of them she'd been wearing the faces of other women. She'd cold-shouldered him with her own face, but here he was.

He'd come to save her.

Then she was stepping forward, one hand out, her mouth open. What she meant to say, she wasn't sure. She wanted to thank him, maybe. To be grateful that even though she wasn't in any true danger, he'd been worried enough to come after her and find her.

"Sister mine, it seems strange to me that this guy would have figured out where you were. You should ask him how he found you."

"How did you find me?"

Phoenix had not said aloud that she ought to stop moving toward Kane, but he didn't have to speak in order to control her. Her feet wanted to move but would not. She wanted to struggle, actually. To call her brother out and tell Kane what was really going on—but what stopped her from doing that was nothing her brother was doing. She didn't want to tell Kane that her brother could manipulate other people with his mind. He might think she was crazy.

Worse, he might believe her.

She didn't want to tell Kane that she and Phoenix

had been conceived by a pack of insane cultists. She wanted him to keep looking at her the way he was now, as though she was exactly the treasure he'd been hunting. He wouldn't, if he knew the truth. Not only about her or about Phoenix, but the other truth, that she'd been sleeping with him for months without letting him know it was her.

"I looked on your computer," Kane said with a twist of his lips as though he knew the admission should embarrass him, but he was owning it, anyway. "I tracked your phone."

Phoenix curled his lip. "That sounds a little creepy."

"Yes," Persephone said because the tickling tendrils of her brother's control were twitching in her brain. "Super creepy. What the hell? I told you, we're not friends."

I hate you, she thought at Phoenix. He couldn't read her thoughts exactly, but he would get the feeling of what she was trying to convey.

"We don't have to be friends for me to be concerned about you," Kane said.

"So you drove almost two hours to find her? My sister's fine," Phoenix said. "If you ask me, you going all alpha-male caveman on her isn't cool. Not at all."

Kane flicked a glance toward Phoenix, who was probably more angry that the other man had been ignoring him than by the fact he'd shown up in the first place. "I was concerned."

"You need to go," Persephone said. "I'm fine. I'm taking a road trip."

Kane fixed her with a look, then a stare around the room before fixing his gaze back on hers. "A road trip without your computer, without locking the door behind you? Without luggage?"

"We're free spirits. Damn you, Phoenix," she manage to bite out when her brother's mental puppet strings sagged for a split second. "We don't need to answer to anyone. I was tired of working in that building—damn it, Phoenix, why do you have to be such a…good…damn it…brother." *Asshole*, she thought vehemently even though her face betrayed no hint of her anger.

"That's fine," Kane said mildly. "I didn't mind the drive. I like road trips, too."

Another ripple of heat trickled through her. She knew Phoenix would feel it. He rolled his eyes at her. Truthfully, she felt a little exasperated with herself. After so long fending off even the barest hint of interest Kane directed at her—at Persephone, not when she was in another guise—she didn't want to start getting all gooey about him now. Hell, the man had not only been concerned that something had happened to her, he'd tracked her down to rescue her. It might've made a girl cry, if she'd allowed herself to give in to emotion that way.

It might've made a girl fall in love.

"You can go. I'm really okay," she told him without needing any prompting or mental coercion from Phoenix. Kane needed to get the hell out of here before she lost her shit. "I'm sorry if I worried you. My brother came and got me and I just booked out of there because I… I didn't have anything there I cared enough about to take along."

Including you was the unspoken addition to that sentence, and she could see that Kane understood it. His lips pressed together, hard, and he nodded. He took a step backward, putting himself in the doorway again. He did not look at Phoenix. He looked at Persephone. That steely glare, the one that took in everything, that noticed everything, swept her up and down.

"I wanted to make sure you were safe," Kane said

steadily. "I would do anything to make sure you hadn't come to harm."

Offer or threat, she wasn't sure and didn't care. The sentiment was enough to threaten to buckle her knees. The heat beneath her heart flashed upward to paint her cheeks. Her fingers curled, making fists at her sides. She swallowed hard, words fighting to break free but kept inside the prison of her mouth by her brother's insistence she remain silent.

"If you need me, all you have to do is call me," Kane said. "I'll be there."

Phoenix snorted. "How romantic. You can leave now."

The way Kane did immediately without so much as a single word more, even closing the door behind him, told Persephone her brother had something to do with it. Before she could move or say anything, though, Phoenix had the lock on her thoughts again. He didn't let her move.

"I'll hold you here until you convince me you're not going after him," he said calmly.

Persephone frowned. "I'm not going after him."

"I can smell it on you," her brother said. "You're way into him."

"I'm not," she protested.

The hold on her released. She did not go to the door or even the window next to it. She wanted to run after Kane and tell him to wait for her, but that wasn't going to do her any good. Besides, as angry as she might be about Phoenix forcing her to go with him, he wasn't wrong about everything. She did like road trips. She did like adventure. And there really wasn't anything to keep her in that apartment—except for Kane.

"Do you want to go after him, Persephone?" Phoenix sounded confused and a little upset. "Oh my God, you... You're in love with him!"

"Don't be stupid. I barely know him!"

Phoenix shook his head. "That's not how you feel about him."

"You know as well as I do that it doesn't matter," she retorted. "It's not going to happen. Anyway, he's a cop. A detective. What do you think he'd do if he knew about all the things I've done over the years?"

"It doesn't matter," Phoenix began, but there was no time for him to finish because the motel room door broke inward, splintering.

It was not Kane.

Chapter 10

Six of them, six against one. They weren't odds in Kane's favor, although that wouldn't have stopped him from trying. At least not if he'd had the chance, but he'd seen five of them heading toward him and had turned. Another had come up behind him and hit him over the back of the head while he stood in front of the motel room door wondering why the hell he'd immediately gone out, no protest, when Persephone's brother had told him to, and why it had felt like his brain was itching when he tried to resist.

He came to with more than an itch in his brain. His entire head felt like it was on fire, throbbing and aching. His fingers came away bloody when he felt the giant lump on the back of it.

"Shit." He spat, tasting copper. They'd rolled him, all right. Taken everything in his pockets. Smashed his phone on the concrete. His keys were gone.

It hadn't been a gang attack, though. Those guys were military or at least something close to it, both by the way they'd been dressed and how efficiently they'd dropped him. Feeling like an idiot, Kane got to one knee on the cracked asphalt of the parking lot behind the dumpster where they'd dragged him. His head swam, but he pushed away the nausea and the pain.

He rounded the dumpster and came up short at the sight of a woman with blond hair pulled into a tight bun just coming out of the room Persephone and her brother had been using. Kane was already drawing his weapon. The way the woman came at him, he might have killed her if they both hadn't backed off at the same time, each of them breathing hard and on the defensive.

"Where did they go?" he barked.

The woman backed up a few steps, hands raised to show him she wasn't going to make any wrong moves. "I don't know. I'm Samantha. I was going to meet with Phoenix."

"I came to find out to make sure Persephone was all right." Kane lowered the gun. "The next thing I know, I'm standing outside the door and those goons are coming at me, and one of them hit me."

"You couldn't have known." Samantha put her hands on her hips and shook her head.

Kane's lip curled. "I should have known. I should've done better, anyway. Did they take them?"

"Yes. They would have." Samantha hesitated, eyeing him. "You have no idea who 'they' are, do you?"

"Not a one. You gonna tell me?" He gave her a small grin. "I have no idea what the hell's going on, other than she's in some kind of trouble."

"You don't want to know. You should just walk away." Samantha gestured with a sigh, then frowned. "Damn it."

"I'm not walking away. I want to know who those guys were, why they took Persephone and her brother, where they took them, and how I can get her back."

Samantha eyed him. "Is she your girlfriend?"

"No."

"Huh." Her eyebrows lifted. "You have a savior complex?"

"No, not that. She was the super in my building and I…" Kane shrugged, meeting Samantha's gaze steadily but not returning her knowing grin. "We were friends. I wanted to be friends."

"You wanted to be more than friends," the woman told him with a shake of her head and a rueful chuckle that led him to believe she knew far more about the situation than she should have. "Take my advice. Get out of here and forget about Persephone. Definitely forget about her brother—he's even more trouble. Just get in your car and go far away. This isn't for you."

Irritated, Kane spat to the side. "No."

"Don't like being told what to do, huh? Can't say that I blame you. But this is a real true mess. Beyond your scope—"

"Try me," he said.

Samantha fixed him with a steady look, studying him. Whatever she saw must've convinced her, because she nodded. "I don't suppose you've ever heard of Wyrmwood?"

One of them had gone to his knees with his gun to his head before another had come up behind Phoenix and grabbed his arms. Persephone remembered that another had hit her brother on the head with the butt of a gun, knocking him out. It was the only reason why they'd been able to take him. She had been much easier to grab.

Persephone didn't know where they'd taken Phoenix,

but she didn't think it had been far. She knew he wasn't dead, at least. That would've left an absence inside her that would've been impossible not to feel.

She was in the back of a van. Bars on the door. Plain benches on the inside. Manacles attached to the metal wall, although fortunately they hadn't shackled her. She was a little insulted they hadn't felt the need.

They'd been driving for what felt like an hour or so, over bumpy roads. She had to pee, desperately. Her stomach was growling. She could smell her own stink, sour breath and armpit sweat.

Kane wouldn't want her so much now, she thought and was surprised at her ability to laugh aloud. The chuckle swiftly became a sigh, and then a half-strangled sob. Not grief, exactly. Not sadness. A combination of both, for the opportunities lost to her. She was never going to see him again; she knew that as surely as she knew the set of armed brutes that had grabbed them were taking her someplace where the only reason there wouldn't be any bars on the windows would be because there weren't going to be any windows.

They were the same men who'd broken down the doors and come through the windows in the dining room where she and Phoenix and a dozen other of the Collins Creek kids had been eating their daily dose of porridge laced with hallucinogens and other drugs. They'd come from the same place, anyway, even if they weren't likely to be the same exact men.

The table overturns. People are screaming. Persephone freezes, spoon in her hand. Phoenix is beside her. He takes her hand. He pulls her, making her do what he wants her to without tickling her brain the way he usually does. He doesn't have to—she's willing to follow him.

Behind the table, a narrow space between it and the wall, they crouch and hide, quiet, so quiet.

The men have guns.

There is screaming and the stink of something like fire that burns her nose, makes her cough, makes her want to throw up. The table is shoved hard against them, trapping them. It bruises her ankle before she can pull it back. She's not crying, because Phoenix has her hand. As long as he's with her, Persephone isn't going to be afraid.

A man is there, wearing black. A mask. She's not scared of masks. The grown-ups here wear them all the time. She can wear one, too, whenever she likes. She's afraid of the gun in his hand, and the way he grabs at them both over the top edge of the overturned table.

"Go away!" Phoenix is pushing, pushing, he's not good enough yet, but he's afraid and this makes him stronger.

Persephone puts on another face. She is small but makes herself bigger, makes a beard and an old man face. The men with the guns want the kids, they're taking all the kids, so she makes herself something else. The man with the gun stumbles back.

"Get out of here, leave us alone, tell the others there's nobody back here!" Phoenix says in a voice so hard Persephone thinks it could break bricks.

The man leaves them. Somehow, they're all right. More screaming. Shooting. They find a way to run, to get out. There are cars with lights, there are men and women, there is lots of fighting, but they get out. They get away.

They run away.

Yet here she was now in the back of a van, being taken someplace that would make the very worst days on the street seem like a picnic. Persephone and Phoenix had heard stories over the years of what happened to the ones from Collins Creek who were taken away, and of those who were rounded up and also taken. Phoenix didn't trust Vadim or the Crew, but Wyrmwood would be so much worse.

With a shudder, she shifted on the hard bench as the van bounced. She had to grab one of the manacles to keep herself from falling off. Wherever they were taking her, they were doing it fast and without much care about avoiding the potholes.

She let herself think of Kane again. He'd promised he would come for her, but it was beyond stupid to think he'd be able to. He would have no clue she'd really been taken this time. No way to find her.

He would not be coming to save her, yet somehow Persephone clung to the hope that he would find a way.

Chapter 11

"They took my keys. We'll go in your car," Kane said, making it clear to Samantha that he had no intention of taking no for an answer.

She didn't argue, there was that, but she did insist on driving. "You have no idea where we're going—"

"Do you?"

"I know where they're taking her, and I can drive fast enough to cut them off. I think," she said grimly as she slid into the passenger seat of the black sedan nobody would ever have been able to remember seeing. "Buckle up."

Kane did, securing a heavy-duty three-point belt over his lap and across his chest. He gave her a look as she put the car in gear. "Racetrack?"

"No. But I do drive fast." She gave him a sideways look and a laugh. "This car is made to go off road. It doesn't look like it, but it's been tricked out for defensive driving. Pursuit."

"Can you talk and drive without running us off the road?"

She nodded, casting a sharp but quick glance at him. "Yes. You want to know about Wyrmwood."

"Talk," Kane said.

She talked. She told him about the hospital whose patients never got better and left only when they were dead. The security precautions. The studies, the tests.

"And Collins Creek?" Kane asked as Samantha maneuvered the car along the winding backcountry roads with impressive skill that still had his heart jumping into his throat. "That's all real?"

"It's totally real. Those kids are real, but they're not kids anymore," she added, shifting.

Faster.

Darkness whipped past the windows. The road curved and dipped; they didn't slow down and caught some air on a small hill, the car landing with a thud that rattled his teeth, but Samantha didn't waver, and the car handled as smoothly as if they were puttering along going thirty on a highway as wide and flat as paper.

"I was trying to get some information from Phoenix about a... About someone I care about. He was one of the Collins Creek kids. They took him during the raid and kept him in Wyrmwood for years. Testing him. Using him. They almost broke him," she spat, voice cracking. "I was assigned to get him out of there."

"Who assigned you?" Kane thought he already knew.

"Guy named Vadim. He runs an organization called the Crew."

"Bald guy? Older? Speaks with an accent?" Kane asked.

"Yes. That's him. They help people like Persephone and Phoenix. Like Jed."

"Your friend."

"Yes." She shot him another glance and took a turn, tires squealing. The road here was gravel, and rocks flew up hard enough that Kane was sure the glass was going to break.

"But you didn't get him out?"

"I did," she said. "But I lost track of him. I thought Phoenix would be able to help me because—"

Before she could answer, Kane caught sight of headlights in the distance. Three vehicles, what looked like two unmarked black vans and a third car, also nondescript. Running parallel with them, trees between them, all he could glimpse was the flash of the lights. Samantha stomped on the gas pedal, gaining on them. The road they were on curved again. No longer parallel, they were on a direct course to collide with the first van.

Samantha didn't slow down.

One minute Persephone was bouncing around in the back of the van. The next, the entire world shrieked and clattered, and Persephone went flying upside down to land in a sprawl of arms and legs. The van rolled. Glass shattered, though none of it fell inside. Safety glass. The metal walls shuddered but didn't bend or break. She ended up on her side, the bench above her head, a swinging metal cuff narrowly missing her face.

Another crash jolted her. The van skidded, no longer on its tires. It slid with a squeal of metal on asphalt. Another crash—something else hit them. She tumbled, ending up on her hands and knees with a ringing in her ears so loud she wasn't sure she'd ever be able to hear again.

The door opened. Light spilled in, hurting her eyes. She managed to put a hand up to block it, seeing only a silhouette. A man stood over her, and she swatted at him knowing it wasn't going to be enough.

"It's me, Persephone. I'm here."

"Kane?"

"Can you get up?" Big, strong hands shifted under her elbow to help her.

She was already pushing upward. "Yeah."

"How bad are you hurt?"

"Bumps, bruises. Nothing's broken." She let him help her toward the door. Outside, the long, low bleat of a car horn droned. "How can nothing be broken?"

"Those vans are so armored nothing much could bust them up. The only thing I could do was knock them into each other." A female voice turned Persephone's face toward the sound. "I took a chance that you'd be okay."

There seemed like there should be a smart-ass answer to that, but Persephone couldn't quite manage it at the moment. She let herself sag in Kane's grasp as he helped her out of the van. She didn't think she meant to kiss him, but that was what happened. Hard, almost an assault rather than an embrace, but on the mouth.

"Can you run?" he asked when he pulled away. "We have to run."

"Yes. I think so."

The three of them took off across the rural highway, but when they reached the edge of the woods, Persephone hung back. "Phoenix!"

"He's not in there," the woman said. "We checked. He wasn't in the car, either. And the gas I used on them won't last much longer. We have to run. I've already called for a pickup."

This had to be something out of a sci-fi movie, right? One of the cheesy ones about killer octopuses in hurricanes or something like that. The woman had just said she wrecked vans full of solider guys with guns and then gassed them, and someone was coming to pick them up?

"In a spaceship?" Persephone's words were suddenly slurred. She must've knocked her head harder than she thought.

"I got you" was the last thing she heard before it all went dark.

Kane caught Persephone before she could fall. Behind them, the noises of the wreckage were getting fainter, but there was no way they could keep up running this fast for much longer, especially when he had to carry Persephone. Samantha pointed to a small dirt trail in the woods ahead of them.

"There."

"You have to be kidding me." Kane shifted Persephone's slight weight, certain he was causing her some kind of permanent damage. No way had she come out of that crash without some serious injuries, maybe internal bleeding. Something.

Two black cars were waiting for them. Samantha got behind the wheel of the second one, waving him toward the backseat. He laid Persephone gently inside then followed, closing the door as Samantha pulled away. A man sat in the front seat, and he twisted to look behind them.

"Vadim," Kane said as he buckled Persephone into her seat, then focused on his own belt. "The Crew. Right? This is all insane."

"It is a methodical madness, I can assure you. Samantha, are you sure you can drive? You didn't get hurt in the crash?"

She shook her head. "Nothing too bad. That car was like a tank, and we hit that first van like a freight train. Thanks, Vadim. Everything worked like we'd planned."

"Wait, wait, what the hell? You planned this?" Kane was ready to reach across the front seat and throttle someone, but that would've meant one more wreck, and he wasn't so sure he'd make it through another.

"Not this whole thing, but the possibility of it. The eventuality of what might happen. We didn't plan for Persephone to be taken, nor her brother. So you can rethink threatening me." Vadim glanced into the backseat. "It's always been a possibility that Phoenix and his sister might be found. They both knew it. They're fortunate he'd already arranged a meeting with Samantha tonight, or else there would've been nobody to go after them."

"She had me," Kane said. He couldn't see if Persephone was bleeding anywhere, he didn't have enough light, but he had to hope that they were taking them somewhere to get medical help.

"Ah yes. She had you." Vadim's voice held a smile. "Lucky girl."

Kane leaned back into the seat. "I still don't know what the hell is going on. All of this."

"And you don't trust me. Nor should you, I suppose. I wouldn't if I were you. All I can tell you is the same thing I said the first time we met. I intend no harm to Persephone. You and I are on the same side. In fact, based on how you reacted during this entire situation, I think it might benefit us to offer you a position on our team."

"The Crew." Kane didn't want to close his eyes, but the pain was making him see double. Samantha had been right about the car she'd been driving; it had been enough like a tank that they were hardly affected by running straight into the side of a van. Still, it had been a long damned night and everything hurt, including his brain from trying to process all of this. "Whatever the hell that is."

"We'll tell you all about it when we get to a safe place."

"Isn't Wyrmwood or whatever the hell it is going to be after us? Shit," Kane said wearily. "Did you just piss off some kind of secret government facility? Am I on the run now, too?"

Vadim chuckled. "I daresay your name has indeed been put on a shit list of some kind. So the answer is yes. This is not to say that you can't return to your normal civilian life, of course. I supposed you could try it. See what happens."

"You're not worried about yourself?"

Another chuckle. "Oh… Wyrmwood has its methods, and it would not be impossible for them, certainly, to find us. Harm us. But to be honest, Mr. Dennis, the amount of bureaucracy and paperwork required to put together a group even as small as the one tonight is fairly enormous. There've been budget cuts. The economy isn't what it used to be. Wyrmwood is a privately run organization that answers to a board of directors."

"They're afraid of us," Samantha put in.

Kane opened his eyes. She still followed the other black car, but they were both driving on a regular highway at normal speed. He looked behind them, but nothing was back there except the night.

"I can see that," he said.

Vadim laughed. Their eyes met in the rearview mirror, and his gaze softened when he looked at Persephone. "She'll be all right. We'll take care of her."

Somehow, Kane believed him.

Chapter 12

Safety and comfort. The warmth of a body beside hers, not for a few hours but for the night. Waking up next to someone who would make sure she was all right.

It had to be a dream, Persephone thought without opening her eyes. Her entire body ached. She remembered the shitty motel. Men with guns. The van.

She remembered Kane.

It hurt to sit, but she did, noting that she wore the same dirty, torn-up clothes she'd had on the last time she remembered anything. The bed was big, soft, covered in a plain dark blue quilt. Kane was beside her, but he wore a pair of flannel pajama pants. No shirt.

His bare chest, she thought with something like wonder, her fingers uncurling to touch him before she stopped herself. How many times had she already run her hands over that skin? Those places that made him sigh? The scars, she remembered as she forced herself not to move in case she woke him up.

She felt the warmth of his gaze on her before she looked into his eyes. "Hey."

"Hey." Kane sat up with a wince. "How are you feeling?"

"Bumped up. But okay, other than that." She tested her arms and legs gently, but aside from a lot of achiness, nothing seemed too messed up. She drew her knees closer to her chest as she looked at him. "You?"

He yawned. Winced. Stretched. "I'm good, all things considered."

"You kept your word," Persephone said quietly.

Kane nodded. "I did."

"That has not been my previous experience with humans of the male persuasion," she said. Trying to be light about it. Funny, even. The fact that her voice cracked a bit on the words didn't help.

Kane reached to draw a fingertip along her arm, stopping at the back of her wrist before he took his touch away. "I'm sorry."

She closed her eyes. "Where's my brother?"

"We don't know. Vadim thinks he got away before Samantha ran into the side of the van."

She didn't look at him but nodded. "That could be true."

"He wasn't in the van with you when we got you out, or the other one, either." Kane shifted, dipping the mattress.

She opened her eyes then. "He got away, though."

"They're pretty sure he did. Yes."

"But he left me behind."

"I'm sorry," Kane said again, this time with a frown and a furrow of his brow. "But yeah. It looks like he did."

She could've been upset about it, if Phoenix had not in the past proven himself to be totally capable of ditch-ing her to save his own skin. She shrugged. "It wasn't the first time."

"Still." Kane looked as though he meant to touch her again, but didn't.

She wanted him to.

Suddenly it was all she could think about. She ran her tongue over her teeth, wincing at the sour taste. She glanced around the room, which was neat but sparsely furnished. It had no windows, but nothing about it felt oppressive. Through a half-open door she spotted a bathroom.

"I need a shower," she said.

"They left clothes for you." Kane gestured at the dresser in the corner. "Towels and everything are in there. They thought of everything."

"Are they keeping us here?" She could see another door, but it was closed. Could be locked, for all she knew.

"No. We don't have to stay. I did to make sure you were all right."

The question rose to her lips, but she kept herself from asking it. The shower was gloriously hot and the water pressure fantastic. She found an array of soaps and shampoos and spent the time scrubbing up quickly but thoroughly. She even shaved.

She thought he might be gone when she came out of the bathroom, but Kane had lain back down on the pillow, his eyes closed. Persephone wore only a towel when she went around the bed to his side. She waited for him to look at her.

When he did, she let the towel fall to her feet. She lifted her chin, meeting his gaze straight on, even when his dropped from her eyes to her body. Hers, not some illusion or mirage. The desire to change herself to be thinner, have bigger boobs, be prettier…she fought it. She kept herself as she was.

Kane reached for her, and she let him. He pulled her onto the bed and rolled them both so he was on top of her, bare skin to skin above, the thin flannel of his pajama pants a teasing barrier below. He rocked against her, already getting hard.

He kissed her, and Persephone breathed a small cry into his mouth. His tongue stroked hers. Their teeth bumped, and she laughed. He kissed her again, softer this time. His big hand came up to brush through her still-wet hair. The other cupped her breast, flicking her nipple expertly until she moaned. At the sound of it, Kane buried his face against the side of her neck and shifted to get his hand between them.

It should've been too fast. She should've needed something more than this, but she was already cresting when he slid his fingers against her. Then inside her, dipping into her ready wetness and pulling out to use them on her clit.

Persephone muttered a curse. Then his name. Without thinking, she put a hand on his head, desperate and eager for his mouth between her legs. With only the briefest hesitation, Kane slid lower.

She was wordless at the stroke of his tongue against her. Inarticulate, groaning, Persephone lifted her hips to press herself harder to the tantalizing pressure of his lips and tongue. She arched, giving herself up to this pleasure.

He hummed against her, then stopped. She looked down at him, her vision a little blurry with lust, but not so hazy that she couldn't see his look of surprise. He bent again to sample her, again with an appreciative hum. Kane slid both hands under her ass to pull her closer. He feasted, licking and nibbling and sucking until she couldn't stop herself, couldn't hold back. Desire consumed her. Kane waited for the aftershocks to fade, his mouth still covering her, then slid up her body to kiss her mouth.

Somewhere along the way he'd shed his pajama bottoms and now pressed against her. Heat and hardness. The head of his cock brushed her inner thigh, and Persephone shifted to open for him. She looked up to see him looking down at her. She had never been the sort to cuddle after coming. Never the girl to tenderly touch her lover's face. She was now.

"What?" she whispered.

"I don't have anything."

He meant condoms. Of course. Why would he, here? And she knew him well enough to remember that he never, ever went without one.

She reached between them to take his cock in her fist. "Let me use my mouth."

He shuddered when she said it. Closed his eyes. His lips parted on a moan. "Oh, fuck, yes...please."

She was more than happy to slide down his body, turning them both so that she was on top. Gently, she took his length inside her. The head of his cock nudged the back of her throat before she released him as slowly as she'd taken him in. She savored him. Pleasured him. At the touch of his hand on the back of her head, not pushing but encouraging her, she took him deep again. Her own desire grew again, an ache spreading throughout her body. With one hand on his shaft as she sucked him, Persephone slipped her other hand between her legs.

She was so wet her fingers slid without friction over her clit, which was still swollen and sensitive. She wasn't intent on getting herself off, because she wanted to concentrate on him, but still, it felt so good that she found herself rocking her hips as she circled her clit.

It took Kane only moments to reach the edge. His cock throbbed hard in her mouth as she eased off. She meant to make it last, but at his desperate groan, Persephone smiled and bent back to him. He began thrusting into her mouth. The sweet-salty flavor of his honey urged her own moan as she tasted how close he was. It pushed her closer to her own climax. They moved together. Pleasure overtook her. She couldn't do anything but ride it, the sweeping waves of orgasm shuddering through her and the tense pulsing of his cock into her mouth. She swallowed, and again, craving every single drop of his desire.

His hand fell away from her hair. Spent, Persephone rolled onto her back to stare up at the ceiling. She wiped her lips with her fingertips, her other hand still feeling the aftershocks of her orgasm.

Silence.

Kane rolled toward her, tugging on her shoulder until she moved up the bed to face him. She thought he might say something, but instead he studied her face with a small frown. Persephone waited, content to watch him looking her over as though it was the first time he'd seen her. Maybe, in a way, it was. It sure felt like she was looking at him with new eyes.

"Are we friends now?" he asked finally.

She smiled. "Yeah. We're friends."

Chapter 13

There hadn't been much for Kane to leave behind, which said a lot about his life. There were people who would miss him, but Vadim had assured him someone from the Crew was working on explanations for everyone. It wasn't like going into the witness protection program or anything. He wouldn't have to miss going to his mother's house for Christmas.

He did need to decide if he was going to stay on and work for this group, though. It seemed like a no-brainer, based on the salary Vadim had offered. The benefits. The work itself didn't seem much different than what he'd been doing before. Researching cases. Putting pieces together. Proving or disproving things. It was just that now, instead of figuring out who done it, Kane would be tasked with figuring out *what* done it.

He'd never been a man to believe in aliens or were-wolves, but that didn't mean he hadn't ever thought about the possibilities. If anything, he was more likely to accept the existence of what he'd always thought of as monsters and Vadim had called cryptozoological creatures. Chupacabra, Kane thought with a small laugh. Sasquatch.

Still, he hadn't yet confirmed he was going to sign on. He wasn't scared of the danger. He wasn't worried about not being able to talk about his real work, or living with secrets. No, the only thing holding him back was her.

Persephone.

He was so far from understanding all of her, but at least he'd gotten a good look at the background. Vadim had given him access to all the files they had on Collins Creek. The rumors and stories Kane had found on the internet had been only half-true. What had gone on there had been horrifying, from the active use of psychedelic drugs and other tortures in order to create what they thought would be superchildren... It had turned his stomach, but it explained so much about the woman who'd so intrigued him for the past year.

Kane didn't like thinking that Persephone had gone to bed with him out of some misguided sense of gratitude, but he knew it was the most likely explanation. She'd been a little distant since then, and because she'd been cleared by the staff doctor in this Crew facility, there had been no real need for him to continue sharing her room when he'd been given his own. He might not know her entirely, but he did know her well enough not to push the offer of his protection.

He wanted her to want him. He wanted her to need him. He did not want her to feel obligated to him.

Phoenix had disappeared, no trace, but Persephone didn't seem worried. She said she could sense that he was still alive, at least. Vadim had said they were tracking him down, trying to find out if he'd been taken to Wyrmwood or had indeed managed to get away.

There was one set of files Kane had not yet read, and they belonged to Persephone, personally. There were a few dozen documents labeled with her name, but although Vadim had given him permission to view them, it hadn't felt right. He wanted to ask her if it was okay.

He didn't find her in the cafeteria or the rec room, and she didn't answer her door when he knocked. He went to the library next, a vast room lined with floor-to-ceiling shelves and more books than anyone could ever read in a lifetime. She was curled up in an overstuffed leather chair with a hardbound volume on her lap, her brow furrowed in concentration and the pink tip of her tongue peeking occasionally from between her lips. She was so beautiful it made his heart hurt.

"Hey," he said.

She looked up, her gaze at first wary and then softening when she saw him. "Hey."

"Can we talk?"

She frowned, probably thinking he was going to try to have some big-deal discussion about "them" or something, he thought and almost laughed. Having been on the receiving end of a number of those talks, he understood her trepidation. She put her book aside, though, and sat up.

"Sure," she said hesitantly. "Here?"

"Here's fine. I just wanted to know if it would be all right with you if I read the files Vadim has on you."

Persephone's strawberry blond brows rose to meet the edges of her hairline. "I guess so?"

"You knew he had them, right?" Kane lowered his voice out of deference to being in the library.

"I figured, but I just thought you'd have already looked

at them." Persephone's lips pursed and her eyes narrowed for a moment before she blinked rapidly and looked away from. Her shoulders lifted and fell, and she cleared her throat before looking back at him with glistening eyes. "I assumed you would have already looked."

"I didn't want to do it without your permission. All of this has been weird. I didn't want to make it any stranger," Kane said.

She got to her feet then, the book forgotten. She had to stand on her tiptoes to get to his mouth, but the soft kiss she brushed over his lips made him smile. She smiled, too. She touched his cheek for a second or so, her gaze searching his, but what she saw inside it didn't seem to reassure her.

"Sure. Read the files," she said. "I'll be in my room when you're done."

She kissed him again, a little harder this time, and on the corner of his mouth. She pushed past him, her book in hand, and left him in the library. He watched her walk away without looking back. Then he went to one of the computer kiosks and typed in the credentials Vadim had provided for him. In seconds, Persephone's files were on the screen. He started to read.

The criminal activities didn't surprise him. Neither did the sex work. It didn't bother him, even if it should have because his job had been arresting people who broke the law. None of that seemed to matter now, and besides, with a history like hers, he was surprised she hadn't turned to worse vices.

When he learned what she could do, however, he sat back in his seat with a thick feeling of unease in his throat. He'd felt firsthand what it had been like when Phoenix had used his talents to send him out of the motel room, so he could believe everything he'd read in the files was true. He didn't want to believe it of her, but he knew Persephone had also used her talents on him.

The knock at her door had her heart leaping into her throat, and Persephone considered pretending she hadn't heard it. That wouldn't make him go away, though. She opened her door to let Kane step through it, then closed it behind him.

"It was you—all of them were you," he said in a low voice. Not looking at her. "For how long?"

She didn't try to lie about it. "Almost a year. The first time was at a dance club. I'd gone out with my friend Leila and saw you there. And I…"

"You what?" His voice deepened, hard. So did his gaze, turning intense and cold, spearing her. "You thought I'd be another mark? You targeted me? Were you disappointed when you found out I don't have any money or anything to steal?"

"It wasn't for that reason," she told him. "I hadn't been to bed with anyone for a while and I was… I liked you. I liked the way you look."

Kane's lip curled a little bit. "But why trick me? Then and every time after? It was a dozen times, wasn't it? My God, was it you every single time?"

"I have no idea," Persephone snapped, knowing she had no real right to be irritable with him but feeling defensive, anyway. "I didn't keep track of all the women you brought home. I'm sure there were more than just me."

"Maybe. But at least none of them lied to me."

She snorted derision. "They *all* probably lied to you, Kane."

"Not the way you did." He said the words as though he meant them to sound angry, but they came out rich with disappointment.

That was worse. Fury she could deflect. Looking into his eyes and knowing that she'd hurt him was a much heavier burden to bear. Persephone swallowed the lump of emotion trying to strangle her.

"How did you know?"

"It was the way you tasted. Here, in your bed. You were the brunette that last time. I remembered."

"The one you kicked out," she said, remembering how his mouth between her thighs had made her lose herself so hard she'd let the mirage waver. So he *had* seen it. "Why?"

"Because I wanted her to be you," Kane said. "Damn it, Persephone, from the first time I saw you, I wanted it to be you."

"It was me!" she cried. "No matter what face or body I was showing you, Kane, they were all me."

"But why trick me? Why lie? Why not just…you knew I wanted you. And you just kept shoving me away!"

She backed away from him to pace. "I couldn't trust you. I don't expect you to forgive me, but I hope you can understand why."

"Damn it," he said and trailed off.

She looked at him. "I'm so sorry, Kane. That first time was on a whim. I was lonely and horny and you looked so good to me. Every time I saw you, I wanted to see more of you."

"Do you still feel that way?"

She drew in a breath, one after another, until she could answer him without her voice breaking. "Yes."

"Do you trust me now?"

Her laugh glittered with sobs. "Yes. Of course I do now. You know everything about me. I wouldn't blame you if you didn't want to have anything to do with me."

"That's just it. I want to have everything to do with

you. All of it. I should be angry with you," Kane said. "I should feel like you played me for a fool. I should walk away from you and never bother with you again."

"You should," she agreed, risking a step closer. "I wouldn't blame you if you did."

With a low growl, Kane reached for her. She let him grab her, gladly. She let him kiss her. When he scooped her up and took her to the bed, she let him do that, too. They were naked in minutes.

"I have condoms in the drawer," she gasped when his hand moved between her legs.

"Not just yet," Kane said with a wicked grin. "I'm going to taste you first."

She groaned, arching beneath his touch. "So you can be sure it's me?"

"I always knew, somehow," he said against her skin, his lips teasing. Tongue tasting. "I'm not sure how I knew, but I think I must have always known it was you, every time."

Persephone arched, writhing in his embrace. Her fingers threaded through his thick dark hair, tugging his head until he looked up at her. She pulled him up to kiss her mouth. "I can be whoever you want, Kane, you know that? Any time you want. It will still always be me."

"Good," he said as his fingers continued to work the magic his mouth had begun. "Because you're the only one I want."

* * * * *

UNEXPECTED PASSION

Chapter 1

Willa Ambrose was absolutely not in the mood for crap from anyone. She'd spent the first twelve hours of her day on her feet at the library and the last forty minutes trying to get home through terrible traffic, construction and the sheer stupidity of people who couldn't figure out how to drive in bad weather. By the time she got to the grocery store, she'd had it up to her eyebrows with humanity. Therefore, of course, she'd bumped into— literally—someone guaranteed to set her teeth on edge.

Babs Miller. Perfectly coiffed, exquisitely attired, particularly bitchy. She stood blocking the cereal aisle while she scrolled on her phone. Babs needed to move her sculpted butt cheeks out of the way or Willa was going to have to throw down in the middle of Pappy's Market, and it was not going to be pretty.

"Excuse me," Willa said.

Babs didn't notice. She laughed at something on her

phone and took her sweet time typing out a reply, all the while still with her cart completely blocking the way for anyone who needed to get to the Captain's Cocoa Bits. Typical Babs, who probably wouldn't have been caught dead eating sugary cereal, Willa thought as she eyed the contents of the other woman's cart. Bunch of pricey grains and flavored coffee creamers in there, but not much that looked like it would taste very good.

"Excuse me," Willa said again, louder this time.

Babe glanced up. "Just a sec."

"No more secs," Willa said. "I need to get past you!"

Babs looked up then, gracing Willa with a glare that showed she was clearly disgruntled at being asked to consider the needs of someone else. Willa braced herself for the cutting comment the other woman looked ready to deliver. Before Babs uttered a word, she let out a small, surprised *oof.*

She moved the cart.

"I'm so sorry, so sorry," she said in a strained voice not at all like her usual tone. "I'll get out of your way right now. And here, I have this gift card in my purse, why don't you take it. It should cover the cost of your order, plus some extra. You're not buying that much. Let me give it to you as an apology for being so inconsiderate."

Willa was stunned into silence as Babs did indeed reach into her bag to pull out a small plastic card emblazoned with the Pappy's Market logo. "You don't have to—"

"I do, I certainly do, I've been blocking the aisle here for the past twenty minutes while I answered messages on this dating app," Babs said. "Not that it's working. The only guys who message me are losers. I'm going to die alone, with nothing but a dozen cats and a collection of vibrators that do strange things to my ass."

With that, Babs stepped aside to give Willa room to pass. There seemed to be something Willa ought to say to all of that truth tea Babs had just spilled all over the place, but words escaped her. She gave the other woman a firm nod and pushed her cart toward the bins of bagged cereal. She gave a glance over her shoulder as Babs pushed her cart away, muttering. With a shake of her head, Willa plucked out a bulk bag of Captain's Cocoa Bits to toss into her cart.

When she looked up, a tall, lean man with a mass of red-gold hair tied at the nape of his neck was smiling at her. He looked into her cart. Then at her.

"It's the last one," Willa said. "But they have plenty of Snappy Crisps or Cinnamon Squares."

The man laughed. "I don't really need any cereal, thanks. I was just getting what's-her-face out of your way so you could get what you wanted."

"Uh-huh." Willa eyed him, ready to back up quickly if she had to. "You did that? Sure."

"I did," he said in a low voice, leaning a little closer. "You're welcome."

She laughed, strangely not put off by him even though she should've been. "How'd you manage to do that?"

"I have a way of getting people to do what I want them to." He looked into her cart again. "You could give me those Captain's Cocoa Bits, if you wanted to."

Her hand was on the package and lifting it before she stopped herself with a self-conscious laugh. "And if I don't want to?"

"Then you won't, obviously." The man smiled again, although this time it seemed more as though he were studying her. Like she'd done something interesting, and he was trying to figure her out.

The sensation was a little unsettling. She studied him

right back, noticing again the red-gold fall of hair, longer even than her own shoulder-length dark brown cut. He had greenish eyes with dark lashes and crinkles at the corners, and a slightly crooked front tooth. Broad shoulders. Lean build. He wore a pair of faded jeans and a long-sleeved thermal shirt. No coat. Lace-up leather work boots, battered. She hadn't seen him around town, and in a place the size of Penn's Grove, that meant he was from out of town. A stranger—unusual. Intriguing.

"You're one who pays attention," he said, catching her eye when she looked up at him.

Willa laughed. "Yeah. Sorry. You're not from here."

"Passing through, that's all. Stopped here at Pappy's to stock up on toaster pastries and granola bars. The usual food for bachelors." He shrugged and held out a hand. "I'm Phoenix."

"Willa." His fingers were strong, his grip firm. Despite the flirty way he'd been addressing her, there wasn't anything creepy about the way he shook her hand. "Phoenix is an unusual name."

"So is Willa," he said with a grin. "Aren't we a pair?"

She realized he was still holding her hand, and she took it gently away. "It was nice meeting you. Thanks for getting Babs out of the way."

"Sure. My pleasure." He took a couple steps back so she could move around him.

He was watching her as she got to the end of the aisle; she could feel it. Something made her turn before she rounded the corner. He was still there.

"Let's say you *could* make people do what you want them to do," she said lightly. "Why on earth would you have done that for me?"

"I heard you say 'no more sex,'" he said with a tilted

grin, "and I knew there was no way I could let that happen for you."

In a world of catcalls, lewd gestures and unsolicited dick pics, his words were still verging on the edge of unacceptable—and yet Willa laughed. Loud. Hard. A short, sharp burst of hilarity wiped away all the anger and annoyances she'd had that day, leaving her with a grin that almost but not quite matched his.

"Thanks for looking out for me," she told him, and with a tip of her chin, she headed off to the register to pay for her groceries.

Penn's Grove was not quite the armpit of America, but it was close. Phoenix had heard of one-stoplight towns before, but he'd never actually believed they existed. Penn's Grove was such a place, one traffic light in the center of Main Street. It had a grocery store. It had houses and farms and a school. It didn't have much else, but that's what made it a perfect place to hide.

He wasn't going to last here much longer, though. Not without losing a large portion of what remained of his mind, and there wasn't that much there to begin with. Not for the first time since running from the men who'd tried to kidnap him and his sister, Phoenix wondered if spending the rest of his life always looking over his shoulder was better than signing up with the Crew the way Persephone had.

Yeah, he knew she'd done it. They had a connection that went beyond the talents they'd each been born with. Maybe because they were twins. Whatever it was, he knew if she was in trouble, and although he'd had a few waves of emotional upheaval from her over the past few months, it had more to do with the fact she'd fallen head over heels in love with the cop from her apartment building, not because she was in any kind of personal danger. Phoenix could've tried to save her from a lot of things, but he couldn't save her from love.

He knew she worried about him. He'd risked contacting her, just the once, a couple months after leaving her behind. He knew she'd forgive him for it—she'd had the cop with her, and Persephone had never hated the idea of joining the Crew as much as Phoenix had. She was all right. He was going to be all right, too, he told himself as he looked out the window at the falling snow covering the narrow alley behind the house he'd been renting.

The woman he'd met in the market earlier tonight was struggling with her trash can. Willa, he remembered. She'd been having a rough day. That irritating woman Babs had been in her way. He'd nudged Babs to move. Okay, so he'd done more than nudge. He'd mentally shoved her hard enough to leave her numb for a few hours, but damn, she'd been so absorbed in herself that he'd had to push that hard. He'd added the urge to spill her guts just so she'd embarrass herself. It was far from the worst thing he'd ever had someone do, and besides, Phoenix had always thought people that irritating deserved to be manipulated into doing stuff that made them look dumb.

He'd already known Willa, of course, even though he was a stranger to her. He'd seen her from this window every single day, morning and night, for the past four months. She'd never spotted him because he'd barely come out of the house. Bumping into her in the market couldn't even be considered a coincidence, since Pappy's was the only place in town to buy groceries, so seeing her there was no shock.

What had surprised him was the way she'd been able to resist him when he'd nudged her to give him the cereal.

He hadn't wanted it, not really. He'd done it as a test to see what he could poke her into doing for him.

Willa had resisted.

It wasn't the words he used that turned people into puppets, it was something different, something deep inside his mind that Phoenix had never and probably would never understand. Like flexing a muscle—you didn't think consciously about it. You just did it.

However, Willa had not done as he'd nudged her to do. She'd been about to, her hand on the cereal bag and her intention to follow his desire obvious. Yet at the last moment, she hadn't done it. Nobody had ever resisted him before. He supposed it was possible there were lots of people in the world who'd be able to, but Willa was the first person who ever had.

He watched her now, struggling with the metal trash pail she was trying to empty into the dumpster. She wore a pair of fleecy pajama bottoms beneath a heavy parka, her feet shoved into oversize winter boots that nevertheless were slipping in the mess of slushy ice. Before he'd quite decided to do it, he was ducking out the back door and down the alley. She looked up, startled and wary at the sight of him. He couldn't blame her. If she knew who he was and the things he'd done, she'd have run screaming.

"Sorry," he said smoothly, with a jerk of his thumb toward the house. "I live next door. Saw you might need a hand."

"I'm fine."

He watched her struggle with the pail again, her boots slipping in the muck. There was no way she was going to get the leverage to lift it into the dumpster. "I'm happy to help you, Willa."

She looked at him, eyes narrowed. Mouth thin, nothing like the smile she'd given him earlier in the market. "I said I'm fine."

"You should really let me help you," Phoenix said with a nudge.

Willa tensed visibly. Her frown deepened. "Look, I said I was fine. I don't need you to—"

With an easy reach, he snagged the can from her and lifted it, using his other hand to flip open the dumpster lid. He emptied her pail into it and handed it back as he closed the lid. Grinning, he waited for her to thank him. Ladies almost always did when he pulled that he-man trick. They went all fluttery lashes and heaving bosoms and usually invited him back to their boudoirs to show their gratitude. Not that he was going to go to bed with her, he thought, since they were neighbors and he was in Penn's Grove to hide out—not to get involved with someone he couldn't leave behind the next morning.

Willa didn't. "Wow."

"Wow?" Phoenix hesitated. He hadn't thrown on a coat before running out here, and he was starting to get cold. The hems of his jeans were soaked. And she was looking at him like he'd handed her a package of dog poop.

"I don't need a knight in shining armor." Willa looked him up and down, but instead of her eyes glowing with desire, she was barely concealing a sneer of disdain. Strike that. She was absolutely not concealing it—she was full-on sneering.

Phoenix, stung, tossed up his hands. "I was being nice!"

"You're being…weird!" Willa said with a glance over his shoulder toward his house, which was connected to hers. "I've never seen you here before."

"I haven't lived here very long."

"I've never seen you anywhere before tonight at Pappy's. Penn's Grove is a very small town." She took a step backward, keeping the pail between them.

"Hey, I'm sorry." He backed up a few steps, making himself less of a threat. "Really, I was only trying to help."

"Were you spying on me?"

"No, I was just looking out my window and I saw you, I thought you could use a hand. That's all. Truly." Contrite, uncertain what had made her react so strongly, he consciously made himself smaller and less of a threat. Without thinking, he nudged her again, trying to get her to trust that he meant no harm.

The nudge had the opposite effect. Willa winced again, her expression darkening further. "I didn't. I don't. I'm fine."

"Okay. You're fine." Phoenix didn't try to argue with her any further. He turned and walked away, hopping up the steps of his rented house with a backward glance at her. She'd already gone inside.

He'd really screwed that up, he thought, not sure how. Not sure why it mattered. Only that suddenly, it did.

Chapter 2

Willa had had the whole world to live in, but she'd chosen to stay here in Penn's Grove. She wasn't a fan of regretting life choices, but on days like this, she did allow herself to think about what her life might've been like if she'd gone away. She would be too far from her parents to help take care of them. Too far from her nieces and nephews to go to their school concerts and soccer games. She wouldn't run into her old elementary and high school acquaintances who'd grown up and had families of their own.

She wouldn't run into *him*.

She could have run away from Penn's Grove, but she'd stayed, and that had been braver choice. It didn't even bother her that much anymore when Brady Singer came into the library with his kids, or that his gaze skated over her behind the checkout desk without so much as a flicker of recognition. It was better than the times when he paid attention to her.

Today, with the snow falling thick outside, she hadn't expected a lot of patrons in the library. The early dismissal for the kids had brought a number of people to grab books and movies to keep them entertained, but that had been before the storm really began. She'd been looking out the window of her office, noticing the darkening sky and considering closing early, when the familiar SUV pulled into the parking lot and Brady got out with the three mini versions of himself. The kids had spent the past twenty minutes searching the stacks for books while their father waited impatiently at one of the computer desks, drumming his fingers.

Kathy hadn't made it in to work today, and Willa had already sent Tom home in advance of the bad weather, so it was up to her to check out their books. She waited in her office for them to come to the desk, greeting each of the boys with a smile and a comment on their choices. It wasn't their fault their father was an asshole.

"Come on," Brady said from behind the youngest boy, Tyler. "Move it. I want to get home before the roads get any worse."

His pale blue eyes flicked in Willa's direction, but she made sure not to meet his gaze head-on. They'd long ago come to the unspoken but mutual agreement that neither would acknowledge the other unless it was absolutely necessary, and even then it had become like speaking to a stranger. She checked out what Curt, the oldest boy, had chosen and handed them back. When she got to the middle boy, Parker, however, she frowned.

"Sorry, there's an outstanding fine for you, kiddo. You can't check out any new books until this has been taken care of." She tilted the computer screen so he could see the book and the amount.

"Son of a bitch," Brady said. "Damn it, Parker. How much is it?"

She cleared her throat, showing him the screen even though he wasn't looking at it. "It's twenty-seven dollars. Is it possible you maybe lost the book?"

"Did you lose it?" Brady cuffed the back of Parker's head.

The kid winced away from the slap. "No, Dad. I turned it in."

Brady fixed Willa with a cold stare. "Kid says he turned it in. Take off the fine."

"I can't just…" She could, of course, just remove the fine from the system. That it had gotten so high in the first place was a surprise, but Brady and the boys hadn't been in to the library in months, so there wasn't any way she'd have seen it before today.

A shift of motion behind them caught her attention. The front doors had swung open, admitting that guy from the market. Her neighbor with the white knight complex and the unusual name. He looked as surprised to see her as she was to see him.

Brady snapped his fingers in her face. "Eyes on me, hello. I told you to take care of this fine so we can get out of here."

"I can't just take the fine off, I have to list the book as lost, and if the price of the book is more than the fine you'll have to make up the difference before he can check out more books," Willa said calmly. Under other circumstances, she might have agreed to help. The finger snapping had done it for her.

"Are you fucking kidding me?"

Phoenix had been standing quietly behind Brady, but now he tapped the other guy on the shoulder. "Hey. Watch the profanity. There are kids here."

"They're my kids, and I'll say whatever the fuck I want in front of them," Brady said. "Or you. Back off."

Before Willa could say a word, Phoenix let out a low chuckle and shook his head. Snow was still melting in the red-gold lengths of his hair, which today tumbled over his shoulders and halfway down his back. He sported a few days' growth on his cheeks and chin, too. Dressed in a plaid flannel shirt, jeans and work boots, and again no coat, he was rocking the lumberjack look.

To Willa, he said, "If they pay the fine, the kid gets to take out books again?"

"Yes. And if they find the book, they keep it."

"Just pay her and be done with it, man," Phoenix said to Brady. "Why give her a hard time about it?"

Because he could, she thought with a glance at the man who'd made her life hell. Brady was looking back at her, gaze steely. She waited for him to go off, but instead he pulled out his wallet and flipped a couple of twenties over the counter toward her. Willa took the money before it could fall.

"Keep the change," Brady said.

I can make people do what I want them to do.

Phoenix's words echoed in her head as she scanned the rest of the library books and watched Brady and his sons exit the library. That left her alone in here with Phoenix. He wasn't looking at her; he was watching Brady leave. When he did turn his gaze to hers, he smiled at what she was sure was not a welcoming expression.

"You're welcome," he said.

"The library is closing," Willa said.

Phoenix looked around the empty space. The Penn's Grove library was small, cozy, and on a day not overcast with storm clouds, it would've been full of light from the bank of large windows along one wall. The shelves had been set up to maximize the space and provide plenty of areas for patrons to sit and read or work at small wooden cubicles or in the computer center. With the storm predicted to last for the next day or so, he'd intended to grab a stack of reading material to keep him occupied.

"I'll be quick," he promised.

He could tell she was hesitant, but on the other hand, it was a public place and her job was to provide services. She nodded after a second or so. She looked as though she might say something, but didn't. Phoenix made good on his promise, choosing a pile of books at random from the new and recommended-reads shelves right there by the desk. He could feel her watching him from her office, where she'd retreated while he browsed. He was careful not to look back.

Phoenix was willing to bet that she had a history with the man who'd been hassling her and that it had a lot to do with why she'd reacted so strongly to him showing up unexpectedly. When he set his choices on the counter, Willa came out of her office to reach for the books. She looked at him.

"You don't have a library card," she said.

"I was going to get one now."

"Of course," she said with a nod. "You'll need a bill with your name and address on it."

Phoenix frowned. "I don't have one."

"Driver's license?"

He didn't have one of those, either. He had credit cards in other people's names that he used sparingly because these days it only took a time or two of unauthorized use before the cards were revoked. He had his charming smile. He had his talent. Neither of those was working on her.

"I walked out without anything. Can you give me a break?" He tried again to nudge her. Again noticed the soft flinch she probably didn't even realize she'd made, but he did. Intrigued, he tried again, gentle but persistent.

Willa shook her head. "I shouldn't. It's against library policy."

"It's a blizzard. I don't have anything to read. Give a guy a break, please?" Phoenix had wooed women with less effort than this for greater rewards than a to-be-read pile.

Willa's smile curved the tiniest bit, not reaching her eyes at all, but it was better than a frown. "How about I take the books out for you, and when you have what we need to get you set up with a card, you can come back and get one. But if you run off with the books, you'll regret it."

"Yeah?" He leaned on the counter with one hand.

"Yeah," she said and started checking out the books quickly and efficiently.

Phoenix waited for her to pause and look at him before he said, "I won't run off with the books. They're safe with me. You can trust me."

"Oh, I'm sure I can't trust you at all," she told him lightly, but with no doubt in her tone that she meant every word.

"But you're letting me take the books."

Her smile widened, more like the one she'd given him in the market and not the way she'd looked at him in the alley. "Like you said, it's a blizzard. What kind of horrible person would I be if I left you without books to read?"

By the time they got to the parking lot, the snow had fallen shin-deep on top of the layers of ice from earlier storms. It covered the two cars there. Hers, an impractical black-and-red Challenger that she'd bought used but loved and treated like a baby. His, a four-wheel-drive pickup truck that had seen better days, the best of them long ago.

"You're not going to get home in that. You should let me give you a ride." He pointed with the hand not holding the library tote she'd lent him to carry his books in.

Willa frowned. Her car was not the best in the snow. "It's only a few miles."

"Fine. Risk wrecking your baby. I'll be at home sipping bourbon and reading books in front of my space heater." Phoenix opened his car door and tossed the books inside. "Suit yourself, Madame Librarian."

"Wait." She shuffled in the snow, her feet already going numb although she'd stopped to change from her black pumps into her winter boots. "Fine."

Phoenix grinned but didn't push the issue. He gestured toward the passenger side door, and she got in, shifting on the bench seat to make room for the tote of books and her own bag, which she'd also filled with reading material meant to last the length of the storm. Phoenix started the truck, which came to life with a coughing roar that made Willa laugh, startled.

"It's not pretty and it's not fast, but it won't let us sit on the side of the road," Phoenix said. "It can go off road, cross-country or get out of a ditch, should we find ourselves in one."

"Let's hope that doesn't happen."

He shot her a look. "I'll be careful."

Pulling out of the lot, he was indeed careful, looking both ways up and down the street even though there weren't any other cars out. The plow had come through some time before, but enough snow had fallen since then that the truck slid a bit despite the heavy tires and four-wheel drive. Not enough to be scary or anything, since they were going only a few miles an hour, but enough that she had the chance to watch him handle the vehicle with skill.

She didn't want to distract him with talk while he navigated the few miles toward home, but it wasn't like they were barreling down the street, and the silence felt strained. "Thank you."

"My pleasure."

She chewed the inside of her cheek for a second at that. "I mean, for everything."

"Again, my pleasure." He shot her a look. "No ulterior motives, despite what you seem to think."

Willa's chin went up. "You don't know what I think."

"I know that you don't like to rely on someone," he said.

She frowned. "That's not true."

Phoenix didn't answer. In another minute or so he was pulling in front of the house next to hers. He turned off the truck and turned to her on the seat.

"If that guy bothers you again…"

"You don't know me, and you don't know him," she said crisply, cutting him off before he could say more.

"I don't need to know him to see he was a major asshole."

Again, her chin lifted. "Yeah, he is that. But I can handle him."

"I take it you've done it before?"

She hesitated. To deny it would be stupid, but there was no way she was going to start in on that story. "It's cold. I need to get inside. Thanks again for the ride."

He waited until she was on her front porch before he called her name. He was still standing on the sidewalk, the tote slung over his shoulder and his hands in his pockets. "Are you hungry?"

"It's only the middle of the afternoon."

"That's not what I asked you," Phoenix said with

a smile she imagined he'd used many times on many women.

"Are you offering to cook for me or something?" She fit her key into the lock and turned it, opened the door but didn't go inside.

"Cook? Me? Oh, no." He laughed and tipped his face up to the sky to let the fluffy white flakes catch in his eyelashes before he looked at her again. Melting snow glistened on his lips, and he licked it away. "I was thinking maybe you would cook for me."

There was a small desire there for her to invite him in, to make some pasta with the tomatoes and basil sitting on her counter. A little olive oil. She *was* hungry, Willa thought. But cook for him?

"You're crazy," she called down to him.

Phoenix grinned. "I've heard that a time or two."

There'd been a time when any man who'd approached her had been shut down immediately. Even fiercely. There'd been a time when she'd allowed fear and rage to consume her. To keep her a prisoner of her emotions. Time had muted that response, but it had not entirely gone away. She was cautious, not coy.

"I have no reason to invite you in," she told him. "Other than because you want me to."

His expression became serious. He nodded. "True."

"Thanks again for the ride." She kicked her boots on the door frame to clear them of snow but paused to look back at him before she went inside. "Maybe I'll make you dinner another time."

Phoenix took a hand from his pocket and pressed it to his heart as he made a little bow. "Another time."

Chapter 3

The storm they'd predicted to end within a few hours had continued through the night. The power had stayed on, at least. Phoenix didn't have a job to go to. He had a fully stocked fridge and thanks to the library trip the day before, plenty to keep him occupied for the next few days while Penn's Grove dug itself out. He also had a laptop and the internet and a curiosity about his prickly next-door neighbor.

When he searched Willa's name, dozens of entries came up at once. The benefit of having a unique name. If he'd searched his own name, there would also be plenty of hits under his various aliases, he was sure, but nothing that could be tied directly to him. Willa had several social media accounts, both her own and the ones for the library. Her posts avoided religion, politics and sex, and told him nothing about who she was. He dug deeper.

A yearbook photo. "Best Smile." Beside her in the pic-

ture was a younger but no less douchey-looking version
of the man from the library. Brady Singer, read the caption. His arm slung casually around her shoulders told
Phoenix a lot, though far from everything. Phoenix sat
back in the uncomfortable desk chair that had come with
the house the way all the furniture had. He typed again
after a moment or so, but he wasn't getting quite the results he wanted, so he picked up the phone and dialed a
familiar number. He hadn't called his sister in months,
but she answered the way he knew she would.

"So you're not dead."

Phoenix laughed. "Not yet."

"Neither am I, thanks very much for being worried
about me."

His laughter softened as he propped his feet on the
desk and closed his eyes. "I knew you were fine. How's
Officer Friendly?"

"Kane is fine. He's great. We're great together." She
sounded defensive, and he couldn't blame her. "Where
are you?"

"Somewhere safe. Somewhere nobody would think
to look for me."

Persephone sighed. "Come back to me, Phoenix. Come
work for the Crew. They're not the enemy."

"I don't want to work for anyone, not ever again."
The words bit out of him, harsh and bitter on his tongue.
"Maybe they wouldn't have me working the streets, but I
guarantee you, I'd end up getting fucked again."

"Oh, Phoenix." His sister sighed.

"I'm not calling to chitchat, sister mine. I have a favor
to ask." He opened his eyes, knowing his voice had gone
a little harsher, so he added, "Please."

"What do you want?"

He told her quickly, outlining the searches he needed

and spelling Willa's full name for her. Persephone's voice was muffled again. He heard the sound of typing.

"Who is she?" his sister asked after a minute or so. "What do you want with her?"

Phoenix thought before answering. "She's my neighbor. That's all. And I'm curious. I looked her up online, but I feel like there's more to her."

"Yeah. There's more."

"Like what?" He put his feet down with a thump and leaned to look at his laptop, as though magically whatever Persephone was finding would show up on the screen.

"I'm not going to tell you."

"Persephone," Phoenix said like a warning.

His sister, however, wasn't intimidated. "It's not any of your business. Why do you want to get into her secrets? Are you trying to get something out of her?"

"No. I just…"

"You have the hots for her," Persephone said flatly. "Well, maybe trying talking to her instead of creeping on her. I'm sure you could pull everything right out of her, whatever you want. Isn't that how you do it?"

Okay, so she was still pissed off about what he'd done to her before. "It doesn't work on her."

Persephone's scalding laugh burned his ear through the phone. "Oh, for sure. Right. You want me to believe that?"

"It doesn't," he repeated, "work on her. I don't know why. I tried to nudge her, but she won't do what I want her to do."

"Sounds to me like you're screwed, brother mine." Persephone's laughter cycled up, sounding less bitter and more delighted. "Get ready for it. You're about to fall in love."

"You shut your mouth," Phoenix shot back without a second's hesitation.

Persephone guffawed, then went quiet. "If you want to know about her, you really need to get to know her. You could make me tell you, of course. We both know that. But it won't be any good for you to know if she's not the one to share it."

"It's bad?"

"It's hers," Persephone said fiercely. Harsh. "You don't understand what it's like, Phoenix, when you nudge someone. How it can feel after. You ought to know, since—"

"Shut your mouth," he told her, already knowing what it was she meant to say. "Stop."

"Get out of there, wherever you are. Come home."

"I don't have a home," Phoenix said.

"Your home is wherever I am. That's all we need." She sounded as though she might be on the verge of tears.

Phoenix shook his head, even though she couldn't see him. "I am not all you need. Not anymore."

And she could not be all he needed, either. They weren't kids anymore. They were adults, and she was starting on her own, real life with Kane. She didn't have to say it for Phoenix to know it was true.

"Come here, anyway, to us. We have a place for you. You don't have to take the job—"

"I'm good where I am. Thanks." He held the phone away from his ear for a second or so before putting it back. "It all ended up okay, you know. For you."

She didn't answer him for a bit. "That doesn't make it okay."

"Nothing is ever okay," Phoenix said and disconnected the call before she could say something more.

Chapter 4

Willa had exhausted her patience for bingeing on streaming television shows, a feat she might have thought impossible if not for the past day and half of official road closings and a governor-mandated state of emergency that meant the library had remained closed. She'd run through everything she had an interest in watching alone, and without someone to watch with, she didn't feel like starting something else. That left books, of course, and the internet, but something about the steady, softly falling snow was making her restless.

It was because it made everything so quiet.

Snow made silence in the world. No cars passing outside. No voices from the sidewalk beneath her window. The occasional rumble of the passing plows was loud, but infrequent. The quiet was getting to her, making her pace and run her hands through her hair over and over again until it tangled around her fingers.

She needed...something. There was an aching in her

chest, an emptiness that echoed throughout her body. Lower. She could pace and stare at the walls and eat cookies until she thought she might explode, but none of that was going to help her. It had been a long time since she'd felt this urge, this desire, and back in the days when she had sought the comfort of a stranger's touch to help her get past everything that had been happening, she'd always made sure to go away. Out of town, at least two or three hours' distance. She didn't have that option now.

"Breathe through it," Willa said to herself, muttering although there wasn't anyone here to overhear her talking to herself like some kind of deranged lunatic.

They used to put people in asylums for this, she thought as she ran her hands over her arms, and then across her belly. One moving between her thighs even as she walked, cupping herself briefly. Sexual hysteria. Masturbation. They'd have tossed her in a cell and thrown away the key.

She didn't want to admit it was because of the man in the house next door. She didn't want to think about the waves of red-gold hair, the green eyes, the strong jaw with that delicious stubble. Not the jeans or the work boots or the way he went out in the cold without wearing a winter coat, not about his crooked smile or the fact he liked to read so much he'd checked out fifteen library books. Certainly not how he'd insisted, several times over, that he wanted to help her.

She didn't have his phone number, thank whoever looked out for horny women who really ought to know better. She did, however, share a wall with him. He was right next door. Which was exactly why she wasn't going to take a shower and shave everything that needed to be presentable, she told herself. He was within literal shouting distance, which was why she was absolutely not going to twist her hair into a tangled braid with sexy tendrils hanging down around her face. Why she wasn't going to dress in fresh, matching panties and bra, the kind that showed off her curves, why she wasn't going to line her eyes and mouth and dip a finger into her slick heat to tuck a bit of her own scent at each pulse point. Pheromones. No perfume had ever smelled as good on her as her own arousal.

Phoenix was a stranger, but not one she picked up in club or on the internet and met in a cheesy hotel hours away. He was her neighbor. Which was why she was not going to put this casserole in a thermal carrier along with a loaf of bread she'd baked in the machine while she blew through two dozen episodes of an obscure '90s teen comedy she barely remembered minutes after finishing.

He lived. Next. Door.

Which was why she had not added a bottle of red wine and some glasses, and why she was not knocking on his door.

"Hi," she said when he answered. "I thought you might be hungry."

It had been a while since Willa had done any kind of seduction. The men she'd gone with had been found on the internet, screened ahead of time, the parameters of their arrangement laid out well in advance of any meeting. Watching Phoenix look her up and down now, though, she thought how easy it could be to make a man want a woman.

"Thanks for dinner." He'd polished off two big plates of the casserole she'd brought over, along with half the loaf of bread and most of the bottle of wine.

She'd limited herself to one glass, craving the warmth

of being tipsy but not drunk. "You're welcome. I thought it was the least I could do."

"Neighborly," Phoenix said with a smile.

She smiled, too. "Yes. Neighborly."

"So," he said, "you're not going home."

"No."

Phoenix stood and held out a hand. She took it, although he hung back when she headed for the stairs so she could lead the way. This house was the mirror of her own, and she found her way without problem to the biggest bedroom, the one she assumed he'd taken as his. The rest of the house had been decorated in a style she could only figure was early American rental home, but here in the bedroom, at least, Phoenix had asserted his own taste.

"Wow," Willa said. "This is...amazing."

Phoenix closed the door behind them and locked it, something she noticed at once was strange, since they were likely to be the only ones in the house. Strange and yet oddly comforting, to her surprise, because she also locked her own bedroom door as a matter of habit. She watched him look around the room as though trying to determine what, exactly, she'd found so amazing.

"You like?"

She nodded. "It's not what I expected."

"You put some thought into what you might find in my bedroom, Willa?" Phoenix laughed, low, and came up behind her to put his hands lightly on her hips. His breath tickled the exposed nape of her neck, making her shiver.

She didn't answer that, but stepped out of the embrace to move toward the king-size bed. Covered in white sheets with a solid black comforter and black-and-white-striped pillowcases, it was also draped with a skein of netting that could be drawn around it to curtain the entire thing. No headboard, but the wall behind it had been painted with briars and roses. Small white lights were strung around the ceiling.

"Did you paint that?"

Phoenix didn't reply at first, not until she glanced at him. "Yes."

"You're very talented."

"I have good hands," he said. "Good with my fingers."

It was a totally cheesy line, but it made her laugh. "Uh-huh."

She turned slowly and found a seat on the edge of the bed. She didn't beckon him closer. She waited, each breath rising and falling and her heart starting to thump a little faster in her chest when he stood and stared.

She wasn't expecting him to tug his shirt off over his head and toss it to the floor, or to open his belt buckle and push his jeans down over his hips, to step out of them and leave him entirely naked. Willa's breath caught at the sight of him, long legs and lean muscle. Around one hip curved a lick of red and orange and gold, a ribbon of flames. She gestured, a crook of her fingers.

"Come here."

He did, standing in front of her. She studied the tattoo, very aware of his nakedness. She drew a fingertip over the inked skin, over his hip and around to his back.

"Turn."

He did that, too, without protest. A scar feathered out from the edges of the flames, pale against his golden skin. Fine golden hairs glistened. He shivered when she touched him on the scar, then on the twin dimples at the base of his spine. He shifted, moving his feet apart so she could glimpse a hint of his sac between his thighs.

"What happened?"

"Someone cut me," Phoenix said without turning.

Willa ran her hands up the backs of his strong thighs,

covered in more of that same red-gold hair. She traced the curves of his ass, hearing his low, soft groan. He shifted again, widening his stance even further. Granting her access to his body. Heat rushed through her as she slipped a hand between his thighs to run her thumb along the seam below his balls. She cupped them for a second.

"Turn around," she whispered.

He was already hard when he did, and she drank in the sight of his erection. Greedy for him, she put her hands on his hips and pulled him closer so that she could drag her tongue along his length. He shuddered. How gratifying to have such a reaction, she thought as the tip of her tongue teased the small divot beneath the head of his cock. She didn't take him inside her mouth, but she licked him again as her hand cupped him.

"Who?" She breathed the question against his inner thigh as she nuzzled him.

"It doesn't...matter..."

She licked the soft skin there, bare of fuzz. When she nipped, his hips jutted forward. She pressed her face to his skin, her eyes closed as she drank in his scent.

"Someone you trusted," she whispered.

The muscles beneath her lips jumped and tensed. "...yes."

She looked up at him as she took his shaft in her fist and brought the head of his cock to her mouth. "I'm sorry."

"We all have scars."

Willa took him inside her mouth then. His moan encouraged her to take him deeper, as deep as she could. His cock nudged the back of her throat before she released him, adding a brief extra bit of suction on the head. He was already slippery with sweet precome.

When she pressed her teeth to his sensitive flesh, Phoenix cried out, but not in protest. He fucked against the scrape of her teeth. One hand went to her hair to urge her on. Gripping his shaft hard, Willa looked up at him. Warning without words. He understood her at once, taking away his hand. Holding them at his sides, muscles bunched and taut with the strain he was obviously feeling in not touching her.

Again, she pressed him inside her mouth and gave him the edge of her teeth. Her hands ran up the insides of his thighs, finding heat and the sweet spots she knew just how and where to pinch. Lightly, enough to make him jump but not to leave a mark. She let his cock slide free of her mouth, slick with her saliva.

"You should tell me to stop," she said.

Phoenix looked down at her with glazed eyes. "I don't want you to stop."

An electric jolt sparked through her. Every nerve. Every muscle. Right to the center of her. Her cunt clenched, clit throbbing. Her head fell back a little, lips parting on a sigh.

"Get on the bed," she said. He did obediently, on his back. She watched him for a second, then tapped his foot. "Wider."

He spread himself for her, showing her everything. The small red spot from where she'd pinched him sent another thrill through her. She stood, shedding her clothes swiftly, not a striptease even though he watched her as though she were putting on the sexiest of shows. Naked, she moved up the bed between his legs, running her hands up and over him to rest on his hip bones.

She had been with men who proclaimed they wanted to obey, and a lot of them meant it, at least as long as she was asking them to do what they wanted to do. She'd been with men who'd said they wanted her to hurt them, but only so long as she did it in the way they wanted her to. Most of the time it didn't matter. She met with them for a night, never more than two, and she did what she wanted to them and got what she needed, and never much cared if she'd left them unsatisfied.

There was something different about this man. The way he responded to the simple commands and to the small but precise pains she'd deliberately inflicted. It made her want to hurt him, but it also made her want to please him.

When she climbed over him to straddle his face, Phoenix was already waiting with his mouth open, tongue out. His hands cupped her ass, bringing her closer. She cried out from that first slow, exploratory lick and put her hands on the wall. Fingers curling. She rocked her hips into his kiss.

For long minutes, the only sounds were the softness of his tongue on her and Willa's murmured instructions to him of exactly where she needed it. Phoenix's rising hum of arousal. The room had not been warm when they entered it but she was hot now, straining and tense with desire that rose and teased and softened under his expert caresses. Sweat slicked beneath her thighs on his chest, and sometimes she could not stop herself from squeezing her thighs against his head, from grinding on his mouth before she relaxed and allowed him to keep working her flesh.

There were many times when she took this sort of pleasure hard and fast, fierce. When she'd used a man's mouth and tongue to get off by orchestrating every motion, fingers in his hair to tug his head where she wanted and needed it. Now, although it was taking her a very long time to reach the pinnacle, she felt no desperation to get there. No lingering feeling that she needed to finish soon or he would be bored or give up on making her come, or that she needed to finish quickly so they could get to his part of the pleasure.

Willa rode him leisurely, making it clear when she wanted or needed something different but also when he was doing it exactly right. She let him set the pace. Slow, slow, then speeding up with flickering strokes of his tongue. Dipping lower to slide in her folds and sample her sweetness, something that made her cry out and press her forehead to the wall as her body jumped under the sudden sensations.

Then, finally, there it was. No going back. Nothing stopping this rising crash of pleasure that overtook her and made her shake. A wordless stream of sounds slipped from her mouth. Her eyes had been closed while she concentrated, but now she looked down between her thighs to watch him bring her to orgasm.

He looked at her in that last moment when even though her eyes were open, she was not quite seeing the real world. She lost herself in his gaze, her hand going gently to his bright hair but not to tug or yank or move him. Her touch was reverent, recognizing this moment between them even as she lost the ability to focus on anything else.

Ecstasy burst inside her. She cried out again, something more like his name this time. Shuddering, she let the climax rocket through her. Phoenix pressed his lips against her, feeling the ripples of aftershocks. After another moment or so, Willa rolled off him and onto the pillow beside him. She felt light-headed and drained, empty, almost aching in the aftermath of the explosion of desire.

Now he would roll on top of her, she thought, knowing she would allow it. She wanted it, even, to feel the thickness of his cock inside her still-throbbing cunt. It would be a different kind of pleasure, one she was willing to grant him since he'd been so, so fucking good with his mouth.

Phoenix did not roll on top of her. He turned his face to look at her. She looked at him. They studied each other in silence, until she propped herself on her elbow to look into his eyes.

"What do you want?" she asked quietly.

Phoenix closed his eyes. "I want you to hurt me."

She was like something out of a dream…or one of those movies he looked up on the internet when the night was late and his cock was hard without anyone around to help him relieve it.

Phoenix could not ever recall being the target of such a seduction. Women liked him. Men, too. He'd never had any trouble getting laid, and he'd never had to nudge anyone toward it.

"Please," he added when she made no move toward him. He could still taste her and swept his lower lip with his tongue to get every drop of her flavor. His cock was still so hard it cast a shadow. A silver string of precome had left a puddle on his belly.

Willa sat up. "That's what you want? Really?"

"Yes." He wanted to touch himself. He could come within a minute or so, the way he felt right now, but he wanted something more than an orgasm at the moment.

She straddled his hips in a second. The flash of her hand cracked across his face, rocking his head. Fuck, yes, that was it. The bright flare of pain sent an answering shock of pleasure straight to the base of his cock. Something deep inside him pulsed and throbbed. She smacked him again, then grabbed his chin to force him to look at her.

"You want that?"

"Yes. Please."

Her gaze never leaving his, her lips pressed together, Willa dug her knuckles into his sides. Harder. Harder. She ground them between his ribs until he bucked and writhed and gasped out a plea; it was not for her stop, but she did. He hadn't realized he'd closed his eyes, but now he opened them.

She was looking at him with something like wonder.

"This," she breathed, raking her nails over his belly and his thighs so that her fingers slipped between his legs and she dug her nails into the soft skin there.

He arched, groaning. "Yes, yes, yes..."

She began to work him, then. Pinching fingers. Scratching nails. When she bent to take a mouthful of his flesh between her teeth and bite him, just above the hip on the opposite side of the flames, his cock leaped. The throb of orgasm swelled inside him, but he didn't spill. He muttered her name.

"Oh my god," she breathed over the marks of her teeth. Her voice shook. She licked the pain, then kissed it. "Oh my god, Phoenix..."

Gripping his cock in her fist, she spit on it to wet him. Again, he almost came, but the clutch of her fingers was too tight. She smiled when she stroked him, and he lost himself in the wickedness of her glee.

She worked his cock, up and down, sometimes twisting around the head while he bucked. She shifted, kneeling at his side so that she could keep stroking him as she used the other hand to dig her nails again into all the places she was discovering made him leap.

"You want to come?" she asked him.

It was hard to find the words, but he managed. "Yes."

"Please?"

"Yes, please...fuck!"

Without letting up the steady stroking, she also slapped his face again. Again. The crack of her hand on him was bright and shining—the truth was that she was not actually hitting him hard enough to do more than sting. He could take so much more, and yet something in the deliberate way she held back from using full force was as erotic as anything had ever been.

She bent to kiss him—the first time her mouth had been on his. Her hand kept up the steady pace. He was thrusting, aching, writhing. Her other hand went to the back of his neck to dig her nails into him there. He gave her his tongue, and she bit it.

It sent him over the edge. He jetted into her fist, incredibly feeling every spurt. His orgasm boiled out of him, wrenching every drop from his balls and spilling into her hand. Onto his belly. She had not let go of his tongue with her teeth, and the pain sent wave after wave of pleasure shuddering through him until, at last, he was spent and she sat back with his softening cock in her fist.

"So pretty," she said, and Phoenix thought if love were a thing he might ever have found it possible to feel, he'd have fallen into it right then.

Chapter 5

The orgasm he'd given her had left her sated and weak, but what had just happened had coiled her up inside again, tight. Not so much that she needed another climax, Willa thought, although she would not have refused one. It was something else, a feeling that pricked her like the painted thorns on the wall behind the bed would have if they'd been real.

She'd gone to the bathroom and brought back a warm damp cloth for him, pleased and amused that he'd allowed it without protest. She thought it was more that he hadn't managed to rouse himself enough to get up rather than any expectation on his part, but it satisfied her to take care of him that way, after what he'd allowed her to do.

She thought he would sleep and she would leave, but Phoenix had not yet closed his eyes. They weren't cuddling, but she sat with one hand on his chest, feeling the slowing beat of his heart. She caressed him, touching the scarlet marks her nails had left.

"You'll bruise here," she said quietly, touching him in one spot. Lower, to the place where she'd bitten him. "There, too."

"That's all right."

She ran her hands over him some more, not trying to arouse him. Exploring. Marveling. At the light touch of her hand on his side, Phoenix shuddered. Willa stroked his tattoo. She generally had no opinion one way or another about ink, but it was obvious whoever had done this piece was a true artist. The design was simple but elegant, not cartoonish. The shading magnificent. It looked like real fire.

At this angle, she couldn't see the scar, but she let her fingers drift around his back to touch the edge of it. "Was this…?"

He closed his eyes, remembering. "It wasn't meant to cut so deep. She didn't want to. I thought I knew what I was doing. It was bad. There was a lot of blood."

"Look at me."

He did with obvious reluctance but responded to the quiet command in her voice. He sat up when she gestured and put his back against the wall while she knelt between his legs. Willa studied him. She'd come next door in the hopes of getting laid, because over time she'd learned that satisfying her body could sometimes—although not always—lead to quiet in her mind. The scene with Brady in the library had left her restless and out of sorts, so she'd sought the comfort of a seduction.

"Tell me about what happened," she said.

At first Phoenix shook his head. She would have let it go. After all, it wasn't like she owned him. He was not required to obey her, not that Willa had any idea of what it would've been like if any of those untruths had been fact. She'd had lots of sex with men who got off on pain, because she'd learned she got off on giving it. She'd never actually been in a relationship with one. It had been a long, long time since she'd been in a relationship at all. She was just about to get up and start getting dressed when he spoke.

"I didn't love her," he said. "Maybe that's why it went wrong."

Curious, Willa leaned a little closer. "Did she love you?"

"She said she did. I didn't believe her. I should have." He shrugged, looking away. "She said she would do anything for me. She meant more than just fucking me, I'm sure, but that was all I had for her. She said it would be enough."

"It's not usually enough," Willa said.

Phoenix gave a low laugh. "Not for most people."

"So, she said she wanted you enough to settle for sex. And then what?"

"I told her what I wanted. What I needed. At first she thought I was joking. I mean, who would think—"

"That a guy like you would want a woman to hurt him? That he'd get off on it?" Willa shook her head.

Phoenix nodded with a smile and leaned his head back against the wall. He lifted one hand over his head to touch the painted wall behind him, tracing a line of briars with his fingers even though he couldn't possibly see them to know where they were. "Yet there are so many people who get off on hurting others."

She wondered for a moment if he was digging at her, but decided he was not. In the short time she'd known him, he'd proven to be rough yet charming, and roguish. Something of a storyteller. She thought of his proclamations about being able to get people to do what he wanted. She hadn't seen him be deliberately nasty without provocation.

"So…she did it?"

"Yes. Not very well," he said, again without sounding mean. "She didn't like it. She didn't really, in her heart, want to hurt me. Because she loved me."

"Sometimes," Willa said in a low voice, "you hurt someone specifically because you do love them."

Phoenix didn't answer for a moment. His pale eyes narrowed as he looked at her. Something passed between them, a tension, something dark that didn't linger but left a stain behind.

"I was frustrated by her, and I was cruel. I put the knife in her hand. I told her to use it on me. She didn't want to, but I made her. I made her," he repeated with a curl of his lip. "I pushed her too hard, and she cut too deep."

Willa again traced the line of the tattoo covering the scar. "How bad was it?"

"I nearly died."

"Oh." She frowned and let her fingers curl around the back. "Why didn't you cover the whole thing?"

"I left a small piece of it to remind me what would happen if I pushed someone too hard who loved me too much again. What I would have to live with."

She nodded at that. It made sense. "Scars are memories. Reminders of what we've lived through."

"Something tells me you have scars, Willa, even if they're not anywhere I can see them."

Now it was her turn to leave without saying anything. She owed him no more of herself than she'd already given, but Phoenix had told her his story. She supposed there wasn't anything so bad about sharing hers.

"Brady and I were a couple in high school," she said. "On and off. He was possessive. Obsessive. I went away to school, and he followed me there. We broke up again. He wouldn't let it go."

Phoenix frowned. "He hurt you?"

"Nothing that left marks. Nothing that showed, especially if you weren't inclined to believe a good boy from a nice family could ever possibly be a nasty son of a bitch who thought taking what he wanted was always okay. I was working at a bar in the next town to help pay off college, before I got the librarian job. He'd show up. Wait in his car to be sure I wasn't going home with someone else. He said he loved me," Willa said. "He said he would do anything to be with me."

"Did you ask him to let you hurt him?" The question might've been snotty or patronizing, but Phoenix only sounded curious.

"No. I didn't know, then, that I liked it. That came after." Willa closed her eyes for a moment or so, thinking about the paths that had led her to this place. This room, this man. This life. "He got out of hand."

"And you didn't tell anyone?"

"There was nobody to tell, really. Everyone in this town had known us both forever. As a couple. Even when we broke it off, there were people who were just waiting for us to get back together. And he wasn't doing anything I could report," Willa said. "He wasn't hitting me. He wasn't threatening my life. He was just making me miserable. Finally, he said he would kill himself if I didn't get back with him."

"Shit."

"I did not get back with him," Willa said. "He tried to hang himself, but didn't manage it. Everyone knew why he did it. The sympathy was mostly for him."

"Fuck." Phoenix waved a hand. "Why stay? Why

didn't you move away from here? Get away from that asshole forever."

"My parents were here. My sister. And I carried a huge burden of guilt for a long time," Willa said. "Thinking it was somehow my fault."

"You know that you can't be responsible for someone else's mental health issues," Phoenix said. "God knows, I have my share of baggage—"

Willa cut in, "Like everyone else in the world."

"—but you can't unpack someone else's bags for them," Phoenix finished.

She knew that, of course. She had for a long time. Yet somehow here she was, this was the life she'd chosen, and for the most part it wasn't a bad one.

"So…what about…this." Phoenix touched the bruise she'd left. "When did you figure that out?"

"It wasn't easy getting a date in a town this size when everyone thought I was the big bad wolf who'd done her best to blow Brady's house down. Even when he got married, which he did almost exactly a year later, people didn't forget what had happened. So, I tried online dating. I met someone. We went on a date or two. Things went well. I agreed to meet him the next town over in a hotel. He asked me to slap him when I came."

Phoenix quirked a brow.

"I couldn't come," Willa admitted. "Too much pressure. Too soon. I wasn't used to casual sex, despite all the accusations Brady had thrown my way. I didn't see that guy again after that, but I thought about him, and that, a lot. I started to seek it out. Men who were into pain. It's both easier and more difficult than you might expect to find someone."

"I believe it." Phoenix shook his head. He leaned forward, offering his mouth, which she kissed briefly before sitting back again. "But I have to ask you. About me. How...how did you know?"

Willa's brow furrowed as she thought how best to answer that. "I didn't."

"So I guess that makes us lucky, then," Phoenix said.

He looked as though he meant to say something else, but from downstairs came the shatter of glass and the thud of the front door breaking open.

Chapter 6

It could've been anything—a strong gust of wind from
the storm. A home invasion. The landlord forgetting his
keys. Phoenix was up and out of bed in seconds all the
same. Moving. Grabbing his clothes and throwing them
on as fast as possible while he shoved the heavy dresser
in front of the door.

"Get dressed," he shot at Willa without looking to see
if she was going to.

Whoever was coming for him would have no interest in her, unless she had some hidden talents she hadn't
shown off, and not the ones of the bedroom sort. That
didn't mean she wasn't going to get hurt when whoever
was thudding up the stairs burst through this door and
tried to take him. Dressed, shoving his bare feet into
boots, Phoenix backed her up toward the window.

"You're going to have to go out there," he said. "Drop
to the roof of the back porch. From there you can climb
the trellis to the street."

"What the hell is going on?"

Already the thunder of feet in the narrow hallway was trying to drown out her words. There wasn't time for her to argue with him. He needed her to get out the window, and now. He nudged.

"Out."

Willa moved toward the window, tearing wide the curtains and pulling up the sash, but she did not do as he'd told her. She looked outside. "They're out there, too, whoever they are."

"Go out, anyway," he said. "They're going to come through that door in a minute and they probably have guns."

She ignored him, moving into the long, narrow closet that he barely used. "No. This way. Come on."

He nudged her harder. She stumbled as though he'd pushed her, a hand to her head, but she did not go to the window the way he was trying force her to. Phoenix pulled back, not wanting to hurt her, his attention torn between Willa and the bedroom door shaking as someone tried to get in. The glass in the window shattered inward after that.

"Up here." She'd pulled down the set of folding stairs into an attic he hadn't known existed. Already halfway up, she turned to gesture at him. "Our two houses share an attic. I can get us into mine. From there we can get out."

He didn't argue but followed. They took the time to pull up the stairs after them, and without a second's hesitation she grabbed an extension cord coiled next to some boxes. She looped it through the folding stairs' metal hinges, securing it from being pulled down, at least easily.

"I read a lot of books," she said when he looked at her. "I learned things."

With an easy, loping step, she navigated the attic's center line where the beams were high enough to let her pass without ducking. At the door in the center, she pushed hard, and after a moment it opened. The attic on her side was brighter, cleaner, with boxes and discarded furniture and racks of out-of-season clothes neatly placed in rows along the side. She had identical folding stairs. In moments they were in her bedroom.

"Will they have surrounded this house, too? Will they be trying to get in here? Quick," she cried, snapping her fingers in his face until he answered.

"I don't know. I don't think so. They try not to engage civilians."

It was the wrong word, because he was a civilian as well. Words were failing him, though not because of the sudden attack on his house. It had been only a matter of time before Wyrmwood caught up to him, he'd thought, but he was left stunned and reeling by how swiftly and with such prowess Willa was reacting.

"Your truck's parked in the alley. If we can get to that, we can get out of here."

"You don't need to get anywhere," he put in. "You can stay here in your house. They're interested in me, and if you're over here—"

Willa cut him off as she grabbed a winter coat hanging from a coatrack. She found a pair of boots and slipped them on as she answered. "You really think they won't come over here asking for me? We left two plates on the table. Two glasses of wine. The thermal bag has my name on it and my address. If they don't figure out we were together just now, at the very least I think they'll come over to ask me some questions."

She was right, although it still knocked him for a loop that she'd reacted so quickly. So smart. He nodded, feel-

ing in his jeans pocket for his keys. Thanking all the gods
and goddesses or whoever watched over those who'd roy-
ally fucked up their lives that they were in there.

"Let's go," Willa told him as she slung a bag over
one shoulder.

Years ago, Willa had gotten into the habit of keeping
a go bag near the back door. In case she needed to run
away. In case there was a natural disaster that required
evacuation. Just in case. She grabbed it now and slung
it over her shoulder with a look at Phoenix. There'd be
time for him to tell her what the hell was going on, but
it didn't seem to be now.

She was doing this. Running out of her house with
a man she barely knew, as strangers with guns pursued
them. Why? Because he'd let her hurt him? Because she
was afraid of what might happen if she stayed? Because
it was a chance to get out, she thought as she let Phoenix go out the door ahead of her, onto her slightly sloping back porch and down the rickety stairs she always
meant to get repaired but never had.

Screw those stairs, she thought as he took them two at
a time, landing on the snowy sidewalk with a grace she
admired even in this hyped-up state of fight or flight.
There was a man in a black uniform, wearing a mask,
holding a gun, but he was looking the other way. He
turned as Willa also leaped the stairs of the porch. She
slipped on the ice, going to one knee as the gun swung
up. She didn't see what happened next, but the soldier
or whatever the hell he was fell to his hands and knees
in the piled snow.

Eating it?

Chowing down on it like a dog with a bowl of meat
and gravy. Tossing his head from side to side. He got
right down to pavement while she watched.

Phoenix yanked her arm. "C'mon."

"What the—"

She took another look over her shoulder as Phoenix pulled her toward the truck parked in one of the shoveled-out spots in the alley. From upstairs in his house, lights flashed in the windows. Shadows moved behind the glass. They were quiet, whoever they were. No shouting. No gunfire, thank god.

Another of them stepped out of the shadows as they approached the truck.

A minute after that he, too, was on his hands and knees gobbling at the snow and ice. Willa looked a few feet down the sidewalk to the first guy, who was now getting to his feet and trying to find his gun from where he must've tossed it into a snowbank when he decided to make a meal out of the slush.

"Get in." Phoenix sounded grim, but there was a glee in his eyes, and his mouth had stretched into a tight, wide grin. He opened the driver's side door so she could slide across the bench seat. He followed.

Keys in ignition. Truck in gear. Lights off. He could do nothing about the roar of the engine, but the truck's wide tires took the curb and jumped it without effort. Willa put her seat belt on.

Men came out of both houses. She had a moment to think about how much of a mess they must have made, how much it would cost to fix the door they'd broken on the way out. How much she didn't give one good goddamn, she thought as Phoenix put the pedal to the metal and flew down the alley, over the snowbanks and piles of ice that had built up because of the storm.

There was a bad few seconds at the end when the wheels were spinning, but with a shift of gears he put the truck into four-wheel drive and they got over the barrier.

Incredibly, Phoenix was laughing. Even more astoundingly, so was she.

"Are we going to die?" Willa cried out, hanging on to the roof handle as the truck got air from a pile of snow and came down hard enough to rattle her teeth. "Are they going to chase us down?"

"They've been chasing me down for years, and I haven't died yet." Phoenix shot a glance into the rearview mirror, still grinning, as he guided the truck onto Elm Street and kept going, taking turn after turn until somehow they ended up on the main highway out of town.

The roads had been closed for the past day or so, and although plows and salt trucks had come through, more icy snow had fallen and the road was not even close to clear. The truck, battered as it was, took the road without trouble, sliding now and then but recovering under Phoenix's guidance. Willa wisely kept her mouth shut to allow him to concentrate. She kept her eyes on the rearview, but so far, nothing seemed to be following them.

The body can only sustain tension for so long, and she found herself nodding off. Every time she felt her head droop forward she managed to wake herself back up, but soon enough it was a losing battle. She piled a sweatshirt from the bag between them on the seat against the window and let herself drift off. She woke when the truck stopped.

"I need to eat. And sleep," Phoenix said, peering through the windshield at the flickering neon sign of the roadside motel. "This place looks okay."

Dubious but figuring they didn't have many options, Willa also looked. "I have cash in my bag. I don't know how much, but I figure you won't want to use your credit card? I don't have mine, anyway. I left my purse at home. Shit."

"I don't have my wallet." He shifted on the seat to look at her. "Tell you what, you stay here and keep warm, I'll go get us a room. Unless you need your own."

"Safety in numbers," she said, thinking how ridiculous it would be to balk at sharing a bathroom with a man she'd already had an orgasm with. "Right?"

Phoenix laughed. The light from the neon highlighted his red-gold hair and cast shadows on his face. "Be right back."

"Wait, the money."

"I won't need it."

Before she could ask him why not, he was out of the truck and striding across the lot toward the motel office. Inside she could see a gray-haired woman wearing a sweater festooned with Christmas presents, although it was the middle of January. *Well, fa-la-la-la-la,* Willa thought and burst into a scattered flurry of semihysterical giggles. She hadn't quite managed to calm herself by the time Phoenix came out of the office, holding up a key— an actual metal one—hanging from a red plastic key ring.

"I got a room with two beds," he said. "But there's a fridge and a microwave, and the guy at the front desk said there's free coffee in the lobby all day long."

The room turned out to be cleaner than she expected, and if the furniture was worn and the decor outdated, the bathroom had a brand-new shower and the pillows were fluffy. The radiator ticked and tocked as she checked everything out, tossing her bag onto the bed closest to the bathroom.

"I'm hungry," Phoenix said. "There's a diner across the street. Let me go get some food and bring it back."

The last thing Willa expected to want was food, but at the idea of it her stomach rumbled. She put a hand over it. "I'll go with you."

"I can bring it back," he said.

"And leave me here all by myself?" She tilted her head to study him. "Or maybe you're planning to ditch me here."

The startled look on his face told her she'd been spot-on. Frowning, she put her hands on her hips. Phoenix shrugged.

"It would be safer for you if I weren't with you," he said.

"I'm not convinced of that. I don't think I want to take that chance. Do you want me to?"

He shook his head. "No. I guess I don't."

"Good." She paused. "Look, it's not like I expect you to marry me now or anything like that."

He burst into a choking laugh. "Oh…fuck, no. Sorry, but…no."

"No?" She laughed, too. "Never thought about getting hitched?"

"Let's talk about that with our mouths full."

"I can think of something I want in your mouth," Willa said, "and it's not eggs and toast."

His reaction was immediate. Intense. He shivered, visibly. His fingers curled into fists.

Oh, she thought. Oh, so it was going to be like this.

Oh, yes.

Yes.

Chapter 7

Phoenix could not stop himself from devouring the sight of her as quickly as Willa was consuming the platter of food in front of her. The diner across the street was the sort open twenty-four hours, breakfast all day, and she'd ordered the hunter's special. He hadn't thought she'd be able to finish it all, but damn if the girl wasn't putting it away like a trucker.

"I need to keep up my strength," she said now, noticing his stare. Deliberately, she ran her fingertip over the corner of her mouth to catch a drop of syrup that had lingered. She licked it.

He got hard.

There was no way she could see that, not with the table between them, but something in the way she looked at him told him she knew. He'd finished off his meat-laden omelet already and now sat back with a mug of coffee, casually, as though nothing in the world was making him think about how sweet she'd tasted. How hard she'd made him come.

This was not the time to be thinking about this. Not with Wyrmwood probably still on their trail. Still, the gleam in her eyes was as intoxicating as if he were drinking a fine whiskey, straight up without stopping to breathe.

"So," she said as she dug into hash browns drizzled with hot sauce, "what's the story? What is all this? Can you even talk about it here?"

He looked around the diner, deserted at this time of night aside from them, the bored waitress tapping away on her phone and whoever was in the back. "I suppose it's possible this place is just a front for a pseudo-government organization and we're about to be hauled away in the back of a black SUV to an undisclosed location where they will definitely perform experiments on us. But it's probably just a diner. So yeah, I can talk about it here."

"Is that what's going on?" As if defeated by the amount of food, Willa pushed back from the table and lifted her coffee cup to sip.

Phoenix saw no point in lying. She was going to believe him or she was not, and it shouldn't much matter to him either way. It did, somehow. But there was nothing he could do but tell the truth.

"Yes," he said. "They've been after me for years."

"Why?"

"Because I can make people do things." It was not the first time he'd said it to her. It was not, in fact, the first time he'd said it to anyone—most of the time he opened with it as truth, because hardly anyone ever believed it was true until he showed them. He only did that when it mattered.

"You've said that." Her eyes narrowed. She shook her

head. Laughed a little, looking away, then back at him. "What does that mean?"

Here was the part of the story that he didn't usually tell. At nearing three in the morning, adrenaline fading, stomach overfull from too much food, it was not a story he wanted to start unless he could finish it. He drank coffee instead, draining the mug and setting it down with a *thunk*.

"You realize it's a hard thing to believe," she said. "Without any kind of explanation."

"You're a librarian," he said. "Isn't it your job to have faith in all sorts of stories?"

She laughed. "Sure. Fictional ones. If you're trying to convince me this is nonfiction, though, you're going to have to be a little more forthcoming."

"I was born to a woman who'd had seven previous pregnancies. So far as I know, the only children to survive were me, my sister and a younger brother I've never met that I can recall."

"I'm sorry," Willa said.

Phoenix shook his head. "It's nothing to be sorry about. She allowed herself to get pregnant by a series of men, all of whom were engaged in the use of various drugs and other things that she also took. There were other things, too. Everything was meant to affect the unborn children. Make monsters."

"I don't understand."

"Collins Creek was a ranch owned by a guy named Harrison Collins, who believed the next step in evolution was the ability of the human brain to do...things."

"Telekinesis? Stuff like that?"

"Yes," Phoenix said, and watched her expression of incredulity. "He and all the people in his cult did their best to create offspring with talents. Mine is the ability to influence people to do things against their will."

Willa's brows rose for a second before her eyes narrowed. "The lady in the grocery store. Brady."

"Yes."

She looked uncertain. "Me? Oh my god. Did you... did we because you...?"

"No," he said. "Not you."

Willa shook her head. "How can I believe that? If what you say is true, how would I even know? I mean, not that I can believe you—it's just crazy."

Without saying a word, with no more than a glance in her direction—and only that to show off to Willa what he was doing, since he didn't need to see the person in order to nudge them, he just needed to be aware of their presence near him—Phoenix had the waitress come to their table.

"I hate my job," she said. "I would like to pour this coffee all over the register and walk out. Can I get you something else?"

"Just the check," Phoenix said at Willa's startled expression. "Which you will have comped. Then you'll forget us both, and if anyone asks, you never saw either one of us."

The waitress grinned. "Sure thing, no problem. Here you go, you have a nice night."

Phoenix waited until she'd wandered back to the counter, where she pulled out her phone and started tapping away again without so much as a glance toward them. Then he looked at Willa. "Ready to go?"

She'd seen it happen, but that didn't mean anything. Did it? Willa didn't even look at him as they crossed the highway to get back to the motel.

In the Penn's Grove library, there was an entire section on the occult and paranormal. Willa had acquired titles and shelved them in that section for years and had never once picked one up. She didn't watch horror movies or read scary books. She didn't hold on to superstitions. Yet she'd seen the waitress respond to something, and it had clearly not been free will.

In the room, she excused herself to use the bathroom. A long, hot shower. Tooth brushing. She put on a pair of soft sweatpants and a T-shirt from the go bag since she hadn't packed pajamas. She swiped away the steam from the mirror to take a long, hard look at her reflection.

"So who were those men?" she said without preamble when she came out to find Phoenix with his head propped on a pillow and watching something on the TV with the sound turned so low he couldn't possibly hear the dialogue.

"They come from a place called Wyrmwood," he said without pause. He sat, back pressed against the headboard. "It is exactly what I said it was in the diner. They found out about Collins Creek years ago and raided it. They took some of the children."

"You?"

"No. My sister and I got away. We ran. We lived on the streets for years."

Willa sat on the edge of the second bed, facing him. "How old were you?"

"Ten. On the farm, all the children lived in the nursery until they turned five, and then we were tested to see if we had any talents. If we did, we got to move into the dorms."

Willa frowned. "If you didn't?"

"You went away. I don't know what happened," Phoenix said, voice free of inflection. No hint of emotion on his face. He might've been talking about the TV show still playing.

"So you and your sister, at age ten, were on the streets and on the run, after years of mental and physical trauma?"

Phoenix said nothing. His steady stare didn't waver. He looked at her, but that was it.

Without thinking of why, without holding back, Willa got up and knelt on the bed in front of him. She pulled him close, his face pressed to her neck. She stroked the length of his hair. When he tried to resist her by pulling away, she tightened her grip, and he sent still. He sighed against her.

"I'm so sorry," she whispered into his ear. She held him tight, not understanding what had pushed her to this offer of comfort. She was not the sort to hug, and while she'd never thought of herself as being unkind, she wasn't totally a warm and fuzzy personality, either.

This time when he made to pull away, she let him. He didn't meet her gaze. Her fingertips rested on his shoulders, no longer holding him, but the connection was still there.

"It was a long time ago. Decades. And I made it through. I'm fine."

Willa had gone through her own hell, but she was sure not one bit of it compared to whatever Phoenix had endured as a child. Being on the streets had to have been awful, too.

"How did Wyrmwood find you this time?"

"I called my sister. She's been…" He paused, then shook his head. "There's another group, kind of the opposite of Wyrmwood. Run by a dude named Vadim. Group of people, some of them with abilities like mine, most just able to do other stuff like computer hacking or whatever. It's called the Crew. They research stuff like this, or they're paid to prove or disprove the existence of this sort of thing. When someone sees a chupacabra, they end up going after it."

"A chupa… I don't even know what that is." Her fingers curled a bit more on his shoulders until he looked at her face.

"So why would calling your sister bring down Wyrmwood on you?" she asked, mind whirling, trying hard to put the pieces together.

Phoenix shrugged. "It's the only thing I can think of. The Crew uses encryption and all that shit, I'm sure. But I was on a phone that might've been monitored. I don't know."

"All of this is crazy," she said.

He smiled and touched a strand of her hair that had curled, damp from the shower. "Totally bat shit."

"I don't like thinking you made me do something," she said bluntly. "How do I know you haven't? How do I know that I'm not here right now because of something you forced me into?"

Phoenix closed his eyes. Said nothing. Beneath her hands, his muscles shifted and bunched, tensing, before he relaxed.

"I tried with you," he said. "It doesn't work."

She sat back then, putting distance between them. "What?"

"It doesn't work with you," he repeated, opening his eyes. The pupils had gone wide and dark. "I've never met someone I couldn't nudge, but you just won't be nudged. I don't know why."

Something twisted inside her at those words. That look. A slow and spiraling heat began low in her belly, spreading upward.

"You expect me to believe that out of all the people in your life you've ever met, I'm different, somehow?"

Phoenix let his tongue slip out to dent his bottom lip for a second. "Yes."

"I don't think I can believe that," Willa said.

"I can't prove it," he said finally. "You'll always wonder if I'm making you do something. You'll never be able to fully trust me, because you won't be able to trust yourself."

It sounded like he'd been down that road before, but she wasn't going to go there right now. Now she was tired, her stomach full, and at least for the moment it seemed as though they were safe. She stifled a yawn.

"I need sleep," she said.

Phoenix nodded and used the remote to turn off the TV. "Sure. That's a good idea. I'd like to get out of here first thing in the morning."

"It's already first thing in the morning," Willa said.

He smiled. "We don't have to leave at dawn or anything. You can sleep for a few hours."

"What about you?"

"I'll be fine. You sleep," he said, and whether it was because he'd told her to or she could no longer fight the exhaustion, Willa crawled into bed and was asleep almost as soon as her head hit the pillow.

Chapter 8

They'd been driving for an hour before Willa said more than a few grunted words. Apparently she was not a morning person. Phoenix didn't blame her. He didn't love mornings himself.

"So…where are we going?"

He glanced at her. "I'm taking you to meet my sister."

"What?" Startled, she did a double take. "Where is she?"

Phoenix focused again on the road. "Not sure. But I know how to find her, or how to let her find me, anyway."

"You're taking me to the Crew?"

He nodded. "Yes. They'll be able to keep you safe."

"So you do think I'm in danger."

"Because you were with me," he said. "Yes. They wouldn't keep you, I don't think. But the things they'd do so that you didn't remember them or your time there wouldn't be good."

Willa made a face and looked back out the passenger

side window. Without turning back to him, she said, "I don't have anything to go back to, really."

"Your family," Phoenix told her at once.

She nodded, still looking out the window. "Will they be all right?"

"I don't know."

She turned. "Could the Crew protect them?"

"Yes. I think so," he said. "To be honest, though, I doubt Wyrmwood would go after them. I heard they have money problems."

She laughed. Hard. "Are you kidding me?"

He hadn't realized how much he'd been hoping to see her smile until she did. "Nope. Everything takes a budget. Do you know how much it costs to get all those black uniforms?"

She was giggling then, rolling her eyes. It lifted something in him that had felt very heavy for a long time. She waved a hand at him.

"Imagine the dry-cleaning bills," she said.

Then both of them were guffawing, the cab of the truck filling with their laughter. He couldn't recall ever losing himself to humor the way he was in this moment. Maybe once or twice, but not for a long time.

Willa looked at him with shining eyes. "This all feels so surreal, you know?"

"I know. I'm...sorry." He was not used to apologies, but one felt necessary now.

Willa shook her head, her smile softening but not disappearing. "What are you sorry about?"

"Everything." Carefully he navigated the truck off the rural road they'd been following since this morning and onto a smaller road that had not been plowed. There wasn't as much snow here as there'd been in Penn's Grove, but it was enough to make driving difficult.

"Oh," she said.

He glanced at her. "You wouldn't be in this mess if not for me. You'd be at home now, safe."

"Don't be sorry about everything," she said after a second or so. "I'm not."

Again, her look. Her voice. His cock thickened, pressing the front of his jeans. He wanted to answer her but had no words. He wasn't used to that. It made him a little angry but did nothing to release the pressure in his crotch. If anything, it got his cock even harder.

She didn't say much after that, and neither did he. They drove for another half an hour, slow going on the dirt road even with the four-wheel drive. The snow and ice had not been plowed, and it required almost all of his concentration to keep the vehicle on the road. By the time they got to the clearing in the trees and the small wooden cabin there, his fingers had cramped a bit from clutching the steering wheel. He pulled up through the snow to park in front of the cabin and turned to her.

"We're here."

She'd told him in the truck that all of this felt surreal, and that hadn't changed. If anything, several times Willa had stopped herself to make sure she was indeed living this adventure and not dreaming it. Even so, she kept waiting to wake up.

Phoenix had brought them to what he said was a safe house for the Crew. A hunting cabin deep in the Pennsylvania mountains. Fully stocked with food, beverages, with heat provided by a wood-burning stove. Comfortably furnished with everything a hunter might need…or a pair of people on the run from what she was still not certain was a real thing.

"How'd you know about this place?" she asked, watching as Phoenix moved from the stove to the counter and back again. He was cooking something for her from things he'd pulled from the pantry. She wasn't going to argue about it. She liked watching him move.

Phoenix glanced at her as he sliced some onions and set them sizzling in a pan. "Vadim brought me and my sister here a long time ago. He said if we ever needed anything, we should find a way to get here and someone would be along to get us shortly."

"Is that what we want?" Willa frowned at the thought of this. "I get the idea you don't like the Crew."

"I don't want to ever be beholden to anyone," Phoenix said sharply. "I don't want to ever be put in a place I can't get out of. I don't want anyone to tell me what I should do with my abilities. I don't want to be controlled."

She could understand that, for sure, although she couldn't help thinking about the night in his house. "You let me tell you what to do."

He'd been turned toward the stove when she said that, and his back straightened. He half turned. "That was different."

"I'd like to know why," Willa asked quietly.

He didn't answer her. She didn't push. He kept cooking, a simple dish of pasta with sauce made from canned tomatoes, onions and garlic. He put it on the table in front of her and didn't take a seat.

She looked up at him. "Thank you."

"I didn't let you tell me what to do," he said after a second. "I let you do things to me. That was different. I chose it."

"Fair enough." She didn't push. Instead, she picked up the fork he'd given her and twirled it full of pasta. She tucked the bite into her mouth, murmuring with pleasure at the flavors. She chewed. Swallowed.

He watched her, waiting until she'd finished the bite and looked up at him before he put his own plate on the table and took a seat. They ate in silence. She didn't stare at him, although she felt him looking at her a lot. When they'd finished, she cleared the table and started washing the dishes, waving him away when he tried to help.

"I got this," she said. "You made dinner. I'll clean up."

"How domestic," Phoenix said.

She glanced at him as she rinsed a plate and put it in the drainer next to the sink. "How long until someone comes?"

"I don't know. Could be hours. Could be a few days."

"How do they know we're here?" She asked.

Phoenix shrugged. "I don't know."

"Well," Willa said as she finished the last dish and turned to face him. "I guess we'd better make the most of the time we have, huh?"

She'd been testing him, not entirely sure how he was going to react. But there it was again, that fine shiver, the brief flutter of his lashes as his eyes closed and he forced them open immediately. The slick pink point of his tongue on his lower lip before it disappeared.

"Go upstairs," she said, her breath catching and her heart beginning to pound even though she was doing her best not to show it. "Take off your clothes and wait for me."

He didn't move at first, and she thought he was going to refuse. Or make a comment, a joke, maybe even a cheesy retort. There was a second when a hard light flared in his gaze when she thought he might flat-out tell her to fuck off.

He didn't.

He got up from the table with a scrape of the chair on the faded linoleum. Silently, he left the kitchen. She heard the tread of his footsteps on the narrow set of stairs leading up to what she'd already seen was a gabled attic room lined with several beds.

She finished with the dishes, not because she had any sort of cleaning fetish but so she could make him wait. The creak of the floorboards above her had ceased after the first minute or so. She imagined him waiting for her, and her breath slipped out of her on a small hissing sigh as she fought to keep herself from shaking. Desire and need made her fingers tremble so much that she dropped the pot in which he'd cooked the pasta. It hit the sink with a clatter so loud she was sure he'd be down the stairs in an instant, but there was only silence.

Willa gave a breathless laugh at her foolishness and got herself together. They were doing this, she thought with something like wonder, and that idea—that she would climb those stairs and find him waiting for her—was as surreal as anything else had been for the past couple of days. She let the water from the faucet run cold for a half a minute so she could dab it at her throat and over her forehead.

Then she went upstairs.

"Oh," she said at the sight of him. "Oh my god."

He had done as she'd told him. Naked. Stretched out on a sagging double bed. His cock was hard. His eyes were closed, lips slightly parted as she moved to stand over the bed. He let out a small sigh when she ran a hand up one muscled thigh and over his hip to rest on his belly, close to but not touching his erection.

Swiftly, Willa undressed. The cabin was warm downstairs, but up here it was chilly enough that she could see her breath. Her nipples peaked at once. So much for heat rising, she thought, and nearly let out another burst of those semihysterical giggles that so plagued her when she was faced with a situation she couldn't quite believe was happening.

She didn't want to think of this as a dream or a fantasy, though. She wanted it to be real. This man and the things he'd allowed her to do were all too real. Too precious, too sexy, too delicious…too rare, she thought as she dug her fingernails into the taut skin of his stomach and watched him arch beneath her rough touch.

"Open your eyes."

He did.

"Tell me," Willa said in a voice so low and rasping she wasn't sure he'd heard her.

"Hurt me," Phoenix said.

She dug deeper. She would leave marks. She would bring blood. He didn't protest; in fact, his cock swelled, thicker and harder and going a sweet, dusky shade of red that pushed a soft moan from her throat. He groaned when she softened her touch and bent to press a kiss to the gouges.

She let her mouth drift over his hip, where she bit him. Slowly at first. Then harder. He cried out, something between a prayer and a curse, and she laughed as she let go and sat up to look at him.

"We could be interrupted," she murmured.

Phoenix's gaze had already gone a little starry, but he smiled. "Yeah. At any moment."

"What might they think, whoever shows up? Seeing us naked. Fucking." She dipped her head again, this time to fasten her teeth to the tender inside of his thigh. She took the tiniest bit of flesh between her teeth, knowing it would hurt worse than a larger bite. She nipped, hard.

He strained upward, not bucking. "Oh…damn… I don't care what they think."

"No?" She licked the spot she'd bitten. "Me neither."

In truth, she wasn't one to crave an audience, but the thought that someone might find them this way did strangely excite her. Someone seeing her with this power over him. Of him giving in to her.

Of watching her bring him to the edge.

She stroked his cock, watching his face as he lifted his hips to her touch. "There are so many pretty ways to hurt you, Phoenix. I hardly know where to start."

"Please start," he said.

She laughed, but it turned into a half-sobbing sound at the sight of him pushing himself into her fist. None of the men she'd been with had moved her the way Phoenix did. She didn't want to think about why. She didn't want to consider what he'd said in the diner, that she was different to him than anyone else had ever been. She could not let herself even contemplate that perhaps he was different to her than anyone else, too.

There weren't any toys or tool to use, but she had her teeth and pinching fingers; she had her hands. She worked him all over, watching the glorious way his skin went pink and then red beneath her touch. His cock, too. Slick, sweet precome leaked from the head of it, and she used that to circle a fingertip on his cock head while he gasped and groaned.

"Sometimes," Willa said, "pleasure can hurt, too."

She began to tease him. She took his cock into her mouth and sucked, stroking his balls. Her other hand on the shaft. He was pumping inside her mouth in a minute or so. She withdrew, laughing at his groan of frustration.

When she straddled him and took him into her, he put his hands on her hips at once. His cock felt so good, deep inside her, that she almost let herself ride him hard but stopped herself to go slow, achingly slow. Up. Down. Grinding her hips. Any time he started to act as though he were getting close, she stopped to feel the pulse and throb of him inside her. She dug her nails into his chest, leaving a pattern of half-moon marks that filled in with crimson.

She didn't think she was going to get off this way. She needed more pressure on her clit. Still, it aroused her to watch the way his eyes went glazed, his mouth lax. How he groaned each time her touch cut into him. When she raked him with her nails, leaving a long swath of marks, she thought she'd tipped him over.

"No," Willa said and gripped his chin to force him to look at her. "Don't you come."

Phoenix breathed out. Grinned. "No."

Again she began to move, letting her clit rub along the ridges of his belly muscles and the crinkling hair there. The pressure wasn't quite enough. She tantalized herself. Then she lost herself in the slowly building pleasure. Her head fell back. She rocked on him.

"Oh, yes, fuck, yes," she breathed. Her knees pressed his hips. As her desire mounted, again and again she dug her nails into his skin.

She opened her eyes to see him watching her, his gaze sharp now. Focused. He'd begun lifting his hips in time to the grinding of hers. The motion pressed her clit just right, and although she hadn't expected it, she was getting closer and closer. *This, this, this*, she thought, incapable of saying it aloud. Wordless noises slipped out of her. They worked together.

"Don't," she managed to say.

"No," Phoenix murmured.

She stopped worrying that he was going to get there before her. She let herself move. Minutes passed, desire building in breathtaking increments. She eased to the edge of orgasm and didn't go over; she could have touched her clit or ordered him to, but this was too delicious to stop. Tension coiled inside her. Her thighs began to shake. She became aware that she was saying his name under her breath, her voice almost pleading, but for what she couldn't be sure. Everything was going tight inside her. Her clit was swollen, hard, brushing him every time she moved. Her ass clenched. When he cried out, she realized she'd again drawn blood from the smooth skin right over his hips.

Willa's eyes wanted to close so she could give herself up to this pleasure, but she forced herself to look at him. Everything else in the room had faded away, a nimbus of light surrounding them. The headboard creaked in a steady pattern that sounded like music.

She moved faster. Harder. She no longer thought about needing an extra touch on her clit—the throb of his cock inside her was enough. Oh, it was so much better than enough. Her hands pressed his chest, feeling the tight muscles of his pecs. She pinched his nipples, hard, twisting them, and at his hoarse shout she almost went over.

She had to kiss him. His mouth on hers, tongues stroking, the clash of their teeth. She bit his lower lip, and he fucked upward so hard and deep inside her that she cried out in pain, not caring even though it was the giving and not receiving of it that got her off. This was sweet agony, a counterpoint to the rising, throbbing tide of ecstasy inside her.

She could think of nothing else.

She could do nothing but ride him.

Closer and closer, she spun, until there was nothing that could keep her from this. She pushed upward on his chest so she could look into his eyes. His mouth was open and she could not stop herself from spitting into it, then kissing him; she could not stop from biting his tongue the way she had two nights ago. His muffled shout was another push toward the edge. Kissing, kissing, kissing hard enough to bruise, she rocked on him so hard the entire bed moved along the floor.

She came so hard she could not draw breath. She tried, shaking, but could only cry out, long and low and guttural. Her orgasm went on and on, waves of it rushing over her only to crash back.

"Come for me," Willa demanded without the breath even to speak.

Somehow, despite that, Phoenix heard her. She actually felt him swell and throb inside her. Felt the flood of him jetting inside her. Heat and slickness kept her moving, writhing on him to get her clit pressed harder on his stomach and sending another wave of contractions through her. She couldn't tell if she were coming again or if her first climax simply had not ended. All she knew was in this moment there was only pleasure.

Only Phoenix, only him.

Chapter 9

Phoenix was so hard he wasn't sure he was even going to come until her breathless command pushed him over. Then he wasn't sure he was ever going to stop.

Shaking, he let himself go. Blinded, deafened, the sound of blood whooshing in his ears, he was sure he would pass out from the rush. His tongue ached from her teeth; it was too much and not enough. He could never get enough. Not of this, not of pain. Not of her.

Then he could think of nothing but this. When he could focus and breathe, he became aware that Willa had fallen forward to press her face against his neck. Her knees pressed his sides, making him notice the sting from the places she'd scoured with her nails. It sent another throb through his cock, which had not quite softened yet.

"Oh my god," she said into his ear. "I can't move."

"Don't." He put his arms around her, holding her tight against him.

She chuckled, perhaps at the syrupy, drunken tone of his voice that should have embarrassed him. Maybe at the echo of the command she'd given him not to come. Either way, her laughter tightened her internal muscles around him in a way that had him shifting a little to push up inside her again.

"Mmm," she said.

After another minute or so, she sat up and disentangled herself from his grip. Sticky, slippery, she slid off him to lie on her back in the lumpy bed. One leg crossed over his so her toes tapped his foot. She turned her face to press a kiss to his shoulder.

He hadn't been cold during, but now the chill in the attic was apparent. He twisted to tug up the comforter over both of them. Willa let out a sleepy murmur as he did, and he lifted his head to look down at her. She was smiling, her eyes closed, her breath puffing out of her lips. Falling asleep.

He was not much of a cuddler, especially not after sex, but right now he couldn't make himself move. He tucked the comforter around her shoulder and shifted her a little bit so that she would have more of the pillow. His arm was going to fall asleep, he thought as he stared up at the ceiling. He should get up and clean off. There were plenty of other beds to use here—he could use one of them. There was no need for him to sleep with her, not even for a few minutes. Certainly not for the night.

Yet somehow, without knowing quite why or how, that was exactly what he found himself doing.

Willa woke to the sound of a woman's voice. It took her half a minute to struggle up from dreams before she was conscious enough to realize where she was. She still didn't know who was speaking, not at first, but the woman standing with her hands on her hips at the foot of the bed could only be Phoenix's sister.

"What is wrong with you?" she cried, gesturing at Phoenix. To Willa, she said, "Hey. Sorry about the interruption."

Phoenix got out of bed, apparently not caring if he scandalized his sister, who turned with a roll of her eyes. He grabbed his clothes from the floor and started getting dressed. "How'd you know it was me?"

"I wasn't sure, I was just assigned to come here and get whoever it was," she said. "Maybe Vadim knew."

Phoenix's lip curled.

The woman ignored him and looked at Willa. "He probably did. I'm Persephone, by the way."

"Willa."

Willa had clutched the blanket to her chest and now took advantage of the semiprivacy to pull her own clothes on. She'd fallen asleep in a weird position, and her neck creaked. She'd also fallen asleep sated and sticky, she remembered with a glance over her shoulder, but now was cold.

"A shower would be nice," Phoenix said. "Don't guess we have time for one."

Persephone snorted. "Sure. Let me just wait while you take your time, brother mine."

"I'm sure Willa wouldn't mind one, either," Phoenix said mildly.

Persephone looked startled and cast Willa a curious glance. "Right...you're right. Of course. Do you need some time?"

Both of them must have reeked of sex, but Willa shook her head after a second's look toward Phoenix. He had no expression at all. "I can be ready to go. Where are we going?"

"I'm supposed to take you someplace safe," Persephone said. "I mean, safer than this. Phoenix, shit. You're
coming with me? Really?"

His sister had crossed to him now that he was dressed.
She didn't hug him, but she took him by the front of the
shirt until he looked at her. Phoenix shrugged.

Persephone looked at Willa. "Who are you?"

"She's a librarian," Phoenix said in a slightly mocking
tone. "She's just along for the ride. She got caught up in
it without knowing what she was in for."

Willa paused before answering. "Right… I got caught
up in this, that's all it is."

If Persephone wondered what was going on between
them, she didn't show it. Probably, Willa thought, Phoenix's sister was used to stumbling across him in bed
with women she didn't know, who meant nothing to him,
who'd merely been caught up in whatever tragedies he
was going through at the time.

"I'm so glad to see you," Persephone said to him.

Phoenix waved a hand. "You don't have to get all
gooey about it."

"I'm not…" Persephone stopped herself and gave
Willa a look. "What's been going on? He won't tell me.
He'll be a smart-ass about it."

"Wyrmwood," Willa said.

"Oh, shit." Persephone gave her brother a startled look.
"You called me on an unsecured line?"

Phoenix said nothing but pushed past her and went
down the stairs, leaving the women alone in the attic.
Willa finished pulling on her sweatshirt. Persephone gave
an awkward laugh.

"Wow," she said.

"It's been an interesting few days," Willa answered.

"I bet. So…listen, you're welcome to come with us,

of course. Vadim will take care of you, make sure you're okay. I'm sorry you got caught up in this… How did you get caught up in it, anyway?"

"He was my neighbor," Willa said. "I just brought him dinner."

There'd been so much more to it than that, she thought, although apparently it hadn't meant so much to him. It shouldn't mean anything to her, actually, this fuckery her life had now become because she'd allowed the aching in her soul to lead her next door with a casserole and a bottle of wine. She'd screwed up in the past, for sure, but this had turned out to be an epic mistake.

"If he…" Again, Persephone trailed off, clearing her throat. "Look, if you think that you've been coerced or anything, in any way…"

"No," Willa said sharply. "Definitely not. Anything I've done has been totally my choice."

Persephone didn't look convinced. "Because my brother can—"

"I know what he can do." She had not been so sure she believed it, really, not even with all the proof he'd shown her. She wasn't sure, to be honest, that he had not in fact influenced her. He was right about what he'd said. She would never trust him.

"Did he tell you?"

"We should go," she said, which wasn't the answer to Persephone's question but the only one she gave.

Being in this room was like being tossed into a pit full of fire ants. Phoenix continually felt the sting of them crawling on his skin. The prick and tingle of constant anxiety.

"Stop pacing," Persephone snapped. "God, brother,

it's like you think someone's going to do something awful to you."

He swiveled on one foot to look at her. "Like they won't?"

"They won't. I promise you. What will it take until you can believe me?" She looked so sad it ought to have made him feel sad, too, that he'd caused her distress.

He didn't. He felt on edge. Ready to roar. He wanted out of here. So why, then, had he not simply walked away, the way Vadim had sworn he would be able to? Why had he suffered the somewhat invasive medical exam that he knew had been meant to catalog everything about him so they could use it to their own purposes? The Crew might not be as nefarious as Wyrmwood, but that didn't mean he would ever trust them.

Why was he still here?

"Look," he said stiffly. "I can see you're happy here. With what's-his-name."

"Kane," Persephone said. "And you knew that."

Again, he should have felt like the asshole he knew he was being. "Whatever. You're happy here. You like playing gofer for that guy, good for you."

"It doesn't have to be like that. There's so much else you'd be good at."

Phoenix frowned and went to the small counter of the kitchenette. He couldn't complain about the accommodations, that was for sure. The food wasn't as good as the dinner Willa had cooked for him, but it was all right.

"Willa's thinking about it," Persephone told him. "Vadim said he could use help with the library system."

Phoenix turned. "And she said yes?"

"She said she'd think about it, I guess. She's not completely convinced about a lot of the stuff she'd be cataloging, but she said she was still able to put it in order, keep the collection organized. Vadim said it was okay if she's skeptical. He said we need some people who still need to be convinced, now and then."

"I don't need to be convinced. I just don't want to hang around here. I'm going to get back on the road soon." He said it without conviction. The thought of leaving here, hitting the streets, finding a new place to live, dealing with more people he'd have to influence and manipulate…suddenly he felt too tired to deal with it. "Soon."

"You haven't even listened to Vadim. He would absolutely set you up in something that works for you. I don't know why you're so against it."

"You don't have to understand," he told her. "You just need to accept it. Accept *me*, sister mine. We are not the same person. Never were, never will be."

He'd stung her, he saw that. Persephone frowned and shrugged. She got off the chair and went to the door.

"Please don't leave without saying goodbye, that's all. And at least let us set you up with encrypted phones so you can call me every so often. Okay? Can you at least do that for me? I miss you, brother mine, when you're not around. I worry about you."

He looked up at that. "You know I can take care of myself."

"I know you can. But that doesn't mean I don't want to know where you are or what you're doing."

"Fine," he said. "I'll try."

She closed the door behind her with a soft click, and he opened the fridge to dig around inside and see what might make a decent meal. Most people staying in the Crew's Pennsylvania location ate communal meals in the cafeteria, but you could order limited groceries to be delivered from the commissary if you preferred to eat in your room. Phoenix didn't want to go out and deal with the hassle of talking to other people, but this room, as nicely furnished and full of amenities as it was, still felt too much like a prison cell.

He used his new, encrypted phone to thumb a text to Willa but erased it before he could send it. She knew where to find him just as much as he knew where she was. If she'd wanted him, she should have reached out. Instead she was making friends and getting herself settled in here with a new job and all of that business.

He made his way to the cafeteria, which featured a buffet line more suited to a Vegas casino than a business facility. He loaded his tray with small tastes of whatever he thought looked good, then took the plates to sit at one of the heavy wooden tables lined with comfortable chairs.

"Mind if I join you?"

Phoenix looked up at the unfamiliar male voice. The guy in front of him wore a pair of faded blue jeans and a white T-shirt with the sleeves rolled up. His reddish hair had been cut in a vintage style, adding to the '50s *Happy Days* look.

"There are plenty of other places to sit. Why don't you go find one of them?" Phoenix dug his fork into a slippery pile of chicken potpie.

The guy didn't leave. He set his tray down across from Phoenix. "Look, it's time we met, anyway. I'll move if you want me to, but I was hoping we'd have the chance to talk. Get to know each other a little bit. I'm Jed. Collins."

Phoenix paused with his mouth full of soft noodles slippery with chicken gravy. He chewed. Swallowed. He took another slow, careful bite, giving Jed no indication that the introduction meant anything to him at all.

"I'm your brother," Jed said.

"We shared the same parents. That doesn't make you my brother."

Jed nodded. "Fair enough. Does it have to be such a big deal, though? It's not like I'm trying to get good old Mom and Dad to take my side over yours about who gets to pick which television show we watch. We share DNA, Phoenix. And experiences. There has to be something to that."

"Why?" Phoenix gestured around the cafeteria. "Betcha half a dozen people in here have had similar experiences, if not directly at Collins Creek, at least someplace like it."

"Not related to each other." Jed smiled and tilted his head.

Phoenix felt a small, tickling nudge he was quickly able to ignore, although he did sit back in his chair to stare at the younger man. "What's your thing? Can you make yourself look like someone else, the way Persephone does? Or do you influence people to do things, the way I can?"

"I might be able to do a little bit of both, but mostly I affect things. Not people." Jed began peeling the paper off a blueberry muffin encrusted with sugar. "Persephone said you weren't staying around."

"I don't plan on it. No." Phoenix eyed the other guy.

Jed glanced up. "Yeah, I don't stick around here for more than a week or two at a time, then I'm off in the field working. I spent the first twenty years of my life locked up in a tiny room. I get antsy if I have to stay here for very long."

"...Locked up?"

"Wyrmwood," Jed said. "You've heard of it."

"Hell, yeah, I've heard of it. Bastards have been after me for a long damned time. I don't intend to let them get me, and I don't intend to get stuck here just to avoid having them catch me, either." Phoenix stabbed his fork into a pile of noodles again but didn't bring a bite to his mouth. "You were in there?"

"Yes. They took me from the farm and put me in there until Vadim and the Crew came to break me out."

Phoenix put the fork down without eating. His entire life for the past twenty years had been spent running from Wyrmwood. Every decision he'd ever made, it seemed, had been to keep himself out of there.

"It was bad?" he asked.

Jed didn't answer at first. Then he nodded. He took a bite of salad, crunching it before speaking. "It was very bad."

"And you don't feel like the Crew is just more of the same, maybe the cells are bigger, maybe your walls aren't quite so high, so you can still see the sky, but don't you feel like it's still a prison?"

"No, not at all." Jed gave Phoenix another curious look. "There's nobody here telling me when or where I'm allowed to go, unless I'm on a job, and even then it's my choice to take it or not. I mostly take the jobs. If you don't work in some way, you don't get paid, but that's how it works anywhere, isn't it?"

Phoenix had never had a normal job, not really. "You said you can't stand to stay here longer than a week or so."

"True, but I get to travel all over. I spent years never getting out of a single room, except to be taken into another single room for testing. I want to see as much as I can. I want to stand on the edge of the Grand Canyon and smell the air. I want to swim in every lake and ocean I can. I want to live my life."

"And you're not afraid Wyrmwood will find you, grab you? Get you back?"

"Nope." Jed grinned. "Not anymore. Not with what I can do to keep myself out of their reach. The Crew's helped me with that. Helped me train, learn. With the kinds of resources we can access here, anything is possible."

"But you have to answer to Vadim."

Jed looked surprised. "Huh? No. I mean, sure, he's the boss, but again, you do a job, you get paid. He's the boss—he's in charge of that. But the rest of your life? No, man. He doesn't get involved with that stuff."

"Somehow, I can't believe that's true." Phoenix had lost his appetite, and he pushed away his tray.

"You don't have to, I guess." Jed shrugged and forked another bite of food. He chewed slowly, looking Phoenix in the eyes. "Speaking for myself, though, I spent a long time wishing I had a family, and now I do. You're a part of that, even if you don't want to be. We don't have to arm wrestle or anything. You don't have to teach me how to ride a bike. I just thought it would be great to have someone else around who understands what it was like where we were born, and what it's like to live with what they made us into."

"I want to forget all that," Phoenix answered sharply. "I don't want it following me around all over the place for the rest of my life."

Jed shrugged and took a long drink of water. "Seems to me that it is already following you around, and you can't get rid of it."

Phoenix was not going to give Jed the satisfaction of knowing how deeply he'd dug with those words, so although he wanted to get up immediately, he made a show of finishing his food and tossing the trash before leaving the cafeteria with a casual, deliberately neutral wave in Jed's direction. Once he left, there was no place to go but to follow the winding halls of the complex to find Willa's

room. He figured she wouldn't be inside. She was probably off in the library somewhere.

She answered. She wore her dark hair piled on top of
her head. A pair of steel-rimmed glasses dangled from
a chain around her neck. Her white blouse, formfitting
but unbuttoned to the throat, and the black skirt that hit
just above the knee were such a cliché that he laughed.
It came out of him on a stuttering sigh, not sounding
much like humor.

"Come in." Willa stood to the side to let him pass. "I
was just finishing a shift in the catalog room."

"Looking like that?"

She hesitated, glancing down at her clothes. "It's a professional outfit, Phoenix. Do you have a problem with it?"

"No. I love it. It makes me want to tear it off you."

He wanted more than that. He wanted to go to his
knees in front of her while she began to work her magic
on him the way she'd done every time they were together.
He wanted her to thread her fingers through his hair, tip
his head back and scour his throat with her teeth.

He did not want to tell her that.

"Really?" She smiled and gave him a considering
look. "I suppose that could be arranged."

Chapter 10

Willa hadn't seen much of Phoenix over the past week or so. She'd been busy learning as much as she could about the Crew and the facility here, about the library system and how she could be of use in running it. It was a dream job, no doubt about it. The only strings attached were that she needed to live on-site, but since room and board were included with a very generous salary, including full health benefits, there didn't seem much reason to turn down the offer. With the money they were going to pay her, she could afford to travel during her vacation time.

The only drawback she could think of was that it meant embracing a whole bunch of ideas she'd discounted for most of her life. Even that wasn't insurmountable, she thought as she stepped aside to allow Phoenix to move past her and into the tiny kitchenette she hadn't used much. He went straight to the cupboard to pull down the bottle of whiskey that had come with the place. Glasses. Ice from the freezer. He poured two drinks and handed her one. He downed his at once, grimacing, the set the glass on the counter so hard she thought he might have cracked it.

"Come here," he said.

She did at once, curious about his intentions. Heat already had begun its slow and sensual rise from her belly toward her throat. When she got within reach, Phoenix grabbed a double handful of her blouse. He tore it, buttons flying, and left the thin fabric in shreds. He'd yanked hard enough to rock her forward, and she put a hand on his chest to keep herself from falling.

"Oh," she said.

His mouth was on the slopes of her breasts, exposed over the lacy edge of her bra, before she could make a protest. Not that she had any to make. She wanted his mouth on her. His hands. His lips tugged the points of her nipples through the soft lace. She moaned. His hands moved on her back, unhooking the bra and exposing her bare skin to his teeth and tongue. When he fastened his mouth on one nipple, Willa cried out.

"Take off your skirt."

She reached behind to get at the button and zipper. The motion thrust her breasts harder against him. He bent to the other nipple, suckling and nipping at the soft flesh surrounding it. She let the skirt drop and stood before him in only the matching lace panties.

He touched her at once, his forefinger stroking along the seam between her legs and up, up to center on her clit. Seconds only of pressure before he was slipping his fingers beneath the waistband to dip low and find her slickness. He brought it up to coat her clit, making small but firm circles.

His other hand went to the back of her neck, fingers curling tight. His gaze dug into hers. His mouth thin, grim, his expression bordering on fierce. A challenge.

"I want you to suck my cock," Phoenix said. "On your knees."

She went at once, wincing only a second at the hardness of the floor. He'd unzipped his jeans, freeing his erection. Willa tipped her head back, staring up at him. She opened her mouth. Waited.

Phoenix grabbed his cock at the base and guided it between her lips. He sank deeper than she would've, had she been controlling this, but she took him in as best she could. He throbbed on her tongue. With a small groan, Willa moved to let his cock slide free of her mouth. Then back in, slicking him thoroughly with her spit until he moved easily in and out of the heated cavern of her mouth. It was easy for her to pleasure him in this position, especially when his fingers sank into the back of her hair and he used that grip to guide her.

With her hand in a fist between her thighs, it was also easy for her to rock herself against it, getting herself off. And oh, she was, turned on by the taste of him, by the way he spoke to her, hard and fierce, as though it made any difference at all in the matter of who, in fact, was truly in charge. He could think so, Willa knew that, but in the end she was still the one who decided whether or not she got on her knees.

She shook with her impending climax, but subtly. Quietly. She focused on taking him in deep and letting him out slowly, until he grunted and started urging her to go faster. She let him fuck her mouth, doing little more than keeping her lips wide and her tongue flat.

She thought he was going to climax then, and she was ready for it. On the edge herself, needing only a little more to tip her over. When he withdrew and took a few steps back, Willa needed a second or so to orient herself to the fact he'd moved away.

She didn't try to interpret his expression beyond that he looked distressed. She thought she knew why, but there wasn't time now to dissect anything. She simply got up and went to the bed, where she placed both hands on it and bent at the waist. Feet apart. Ass tipped. She made an offering of herself, at first uncertain if he meant to take it, but when he did she closed her eyes against a sudden rush of emotion she hadn't been expecting.

He pushed inside her, fast and deep. Pounded. His hands gripped her hips, moving her body in time to his pace and rhythm. He reached around once to stroke her clit with his fingertips, but after that he resumed his rhythm. She touched herself, instead. It was enough. Better than. She was on the edge in seconds, riding the waves of pleasure as he thrust into her from behind.

"You feel so fucking good," Phoenix said. "I feel so good inside you."

Willa had words in response but kept them to herself. She answered with only a moan, a sigh, the rolling of her hips to bring him in deeper. She urged him harder with the motion of her body. Her orgasm rushed over her, and she shook with it, knowing he would feel the pulse and clench of her body around him as he moved inside her.

"Oh, fuck, yes..." Phoenix thrust again, covering her back with his body and shuddering as he came.

They stayed like that for a half a minute or so. Breathing getting slower. The pounding of their hearts easing into a normal pace. He pulled out and backed away from her, and Willa turned to sit on the edge of the bed, very aware of the slippery heat of him on her thighs.

"When do you plan to leave?" she said when it became clear he had no intentions of speaking.

Phoenix frowned as he tucked himself back into his jeans and zipped them. "Was my sister talking to you?"

"She didn't have to. I could see it on your face when you walked in here, that you meant to tell me you were going. So go, then," Willa said. "You have no reason to stay here."

"No? You're not going to ask me to stay?"

Her heart hurt a little at the hard tone of his voice, but she refused to allow him to see that. "I can't make you do anything you don't want to, Phoenix, and I would never want to."

"Because you're not like me," he said. "That's what I do, isn't it? Force people to do things against their will, all for my own gain."

Willa lifted her chin to stare into his eyes, trying to make him understand what she wasn't sure she did herself. "You don't do that with me."

"I just did!" he cried, advancing on her so fast, with such ferocity, that she recoiled. He got up in her face. "I just fucking did it with you, Willa. I came in here, and I made you do all of that stuff you'd never have agreed to if I wasn't forcing it on you…"

"That's not true!"

He shook his head. "What we just did? That's not how we are. It's not who *you* are. I did it to prove to you that I was capable of it. That you should never, ever trust yourself with me, because you'll never be able to tell if what you are doing is because you want to."

"I am perfectly capable of knowing that I want you," Willa said and stood, not caring that she was naked and he was fully clothed. "Tell yourself whatever lies you have to, Phoenix, but you don't get to make me doubt my own mind or what I want to do. No, that's not who we are or what we do, but that doesn't mean I didn't allow it. Willingly. On purpose."

He sneered and scoffed. "And you're going to tell me that you want me?"

She crossed to him, hating the way he flinched from her touch. "Do you know how rare and precious it is that we found each other? That we bring each other such pleasure in such a unique way? That's not easy to find. I certainly haven't found it with anyone, not as good as this. And believe me, I've been looking for a long time."

He didn't look at her. "You say that, but good sex—"

"Phenomenal sex," Willa cut in.

"Sex," Phoenix repeated as he looked at her, finally, "is not the only thing that matters. Because, believe me, I've done more than my share of bed hopping over the years, and in the end it doesn't last. No matter how hard you come, someone always, always wants to leave."

"Right now that person is you." She stepped back, releasing the front of his shirt. "So go, then. Find your way out there in the world, doing whatever it is you think you need to do."

"And you'll just wait here for me?" Derision fairly dripped from his voice.

She shook her head. "No. I haven't decided yet if I'm going to be here. They offered to let me work remotely. I could go home, back to Penn's Grove, but with security measures in place in case Wyrmwood thought they needed to come back around for me. I'd be able to work for Vadim with almost all the same benefits. The money is fantastic. But no, I don't have to stay here."

Phoenix shook his head. "You'll still be answering to him."

"I have to answer to someone," she told him. "Unless

I become independently wealthy, I'll always need a job. This one seems to be pretty damned good."

She thought he'd turn on his heel and storm out then, and this would be over. She was ready for that if it happened. She would find a way to move on with her life.

"You're the only person I've ever met who I can't force to do what I want," he whispered.

Willa took a chance and moved forward. She put her hands flat on his chest. She pushed up onto her toes to kiss his mouth.

"I don't ever want to force you to do anything for me," she said. "Whatever happens with us, it's always got to be your choice. I don't want it if it's not good for you, too. I mean any of it, Phoenix, not just the stuff in bed."

"What happens if you ask me for something I don't want to give you?" he demanded in a low voice. When she tried to pull away, his hands on her hips kept her close.

"Then we talk about it like normal people," she said.

Phoenix laughed, low. "I'm not normal people, Willa. I'm so far from normal…"

"Shh," she said against his mouth. "For now, all we should both ask of the other is to listen. To try. Maybe to not walk away when something goes wrong. Beyond that, who knows? It could be nothing. It could be everything. We don't know unless we try."

"I've never had to try at anything. If I didn't get what I wanted, I made someone give it to me."

She smiled, undaunted. "So walk away."

"Damn it," Phoenix said. "I don't want to walk away from you!"

"So stay." She laughed a little bit through a haze of tears at the way he was fighting this. "Phoenix. Baby."

At the endearment, he looked at her in surprise. When she pulled him close and took his chin in her hands, holding him still in a grip tight enough to hurt, should he try to get away, she forced him to look into her eyes. She said nothing, waiting to feel at least some of the tension in him ease.

"You never know when you start something new if you're going to end up getting hurt," she said. "But I promise you, I'm going to hurt you as much as you want. As often as you want. For as long as we both want me to do it."

With a growl, he kissed her hard and lifted her, carrying her to the bed, where they both fell down in a tangle of sheets and pillows. There he leaned over her to stroke the hair out of her face. His expression was serious.

"Please," Phoenix said.

Willa smiled and kissed him again.

* * * * *